THE GIRL
WHO RAN

THE GIRL WHO RAN

NIKKI OWEN

BLACK STONE

PUBLISHING

Copyright © 2017 by Nikki Owen
Published in 2018 by Blackstone Publishing
Cover and book design by Kathryn Galloway English

Printed in the United States of America

ISBN 978-1-5047-8073-5
Fiction / Thrillers / Suspense

1 3 5 7 9 10 8 6 4 2

CIP data for this book is available
from the Library of Congress

Blackstone Publishing
31 Mistletoe Rd.
Ashland, OR 97520

www.BlackstonePublishing.com

To my two beautiful, clever girls, Abi and Hattie

CHAPTER 1

DEEP COVER PROJECT FACILITY

Present Day

The room is strange and yet familiar. I know where I am but it is all new, and when I arrive at a white door marked PROJECT CALLIDUS— CLEARANCE GRADE TWO, I know that this, finally, is the right place.

I know I am truly home.

I enter. I return the black security card into a zipped pocket and proceed. Everything is neat and ordered. The walls are white and gleaming, and the door three meters and eleven centimeters ahead of me is brown, neat and straight, a gloss to its surface reflecting the strip of muted, butter-yellow lights above me. There is barely any sound. My black boots brush in clipped, precise patterns on the cream polished tiles and, as they do, I count my steps, pausing at the now familiar notice that sits encased on the wall, a note repeated at careful, measured intervals throughout the clean, frosted walkways of each Project facility in the world.

ORDER AND ROUTINE ARE EVERYTHING.

THE PROJECT IS OUR ONLY FRIEND.

I read the words on the wall and a feeling passes over me: I am one of them, finally the rightful place for me in the world is here. For is that not what we are all searching for? Acceptance? I reach the far wall, stop and turn right. In every way now I know where I am going, but there are moments when I wonder who I truly am, when I think it's hard to find a place in the world when you don't know who you are supposed to be.

Striding seven more steps in the glow of the bulbs above, I reach a small gray monitor. Ahead, another subject number talks in hushed tones to a fellow colleague, and while we follow protocol and acknowledge the other's numerical existence, each one of us is careful to make no eye contact at all.

There is a quick crackle from the monitor. "State your name and subject number."

I clear my throat. "Dr. Maria Martinez. Subject number 375."

One second passes, two, until a mild buzzer sounds and, as per measured routine, I lean in to allow a soft pink light to scan my retina. The door ahead of me clicks, followed by a familiar whoosh of air and, striding seven more steps, I knock on another door. This one is thick, metal, and heavy with silver casing and deep, solid locks with a sensory entrance system designed to withstand the harshest attack.

"Enter," announces a familiar voice from inside.

In my nightmares and memories, the sound of him, of his accent, used to bother me. It would pull me into a downward spin of fear, but now my mind has learned to find the Scottish lilt comforting, helpful to me and a welcome element in my daily routine. Placing my hand on the steel of the door, the internal scanner tracing every groove of the unique lines on my skin, I walk in. There is a banging noise from somewhere, a mild moan, but my brain ignores it and my eyes remain facing forward.

"Subject 375," he says, inhaling through flared nostrils on a thin, pointed nose, "you are three seconds late."

His skeletal fingers drum on a white file that sits on a metal desk, eyes as dark as oil, two round patches of bitumen pressed into deep, bottomless sockets. As he breathes, his head tilts and his tissue paper skin shines translucent, stretched across bones so thin that the blue roots of his veins glisten, crisscrossing his face and neck and arms, down to where two spindled wrists hang on hooks from his triangular joints. He wears a white coat and a brown lamb's-wool sweater, his shirt cornflower blue, and on his legs that bend like twigs about to snap hang trousers scratched from polyester and cotton that stop at his ankles where the bones jut out.

I speak. When I do, I am careful to ensure my voice does not shake or flip or fold. "Forgive me, Dr. Carr."

He regards me. He taps a single finger on the metal table and looks to the right where a large, rectangular mirrored window rests. I catch my reflection. Hair back to black, cropped neat to the scalp and neck, my green contacts are now gone to reveal birth-brown eyes that match a tan skin which softens to honey in the glow of the light hitting the curve of my elbow. Since I was brought here and recommenced training, much of my body has changed. Where before I was lean, now I am strong, muscular, the definition of my biceps and triceps outlined under the soft cotton white T-shirt and the smooth black brush of my Project-issue combats. My stomach is taut and when, on instruction of Dr. Carr, my legs stride to the chair and sit, my quads tighten automatically, flexed, honed.

He installs a smile on his face, no eye creases, and clicks his pen. "Time for our daily chat."

A ripple of nerves passes through my spine down to the soles of my feet. I smell in the air, for the first time since entering, his familiar scent, a scent I have known for the almost three decades since the Project took me and began their conditioning program. Hot garlic, stale tobacco—the odor trail of his presence left long ago in my road map of memories. My immediate instinct is to run, to bang on the door with curled-up fists and yell for them to let me out, yet instead I find a way of breathing through it, of practicing mental yoga in my head and moving my mind in a gentle rhythmic flow of reassurance and calm. He has taught me to react this way. When pushed to its limits, the mind can achieve so much, he says. And so I inhale his aroma and ignore the bubble of worry that threatens to burst, and gratefully channel the emerging inner strength that the Project has helped me cultivate.

Dr. Carr crosses one leg over the other and opens a folder. From the mirrored window, the moan from earlier sounds again, low, but audible.

"Have you received your Typhernol injection today at the allotted time?"

"Yes."

"Any reactions, symptoms?"

"I had a headache at 0601 hours, followed by a short nosebleed that lasted forty-seven seconds."

He makes a note. "Now, Maria, as we always do in order to reinforce why we are all here, can you state for me your name, subject number, age, status, and reason for being at this Project Callidus facility."

I clock the four corners of the white room, note the laptop on the table and next to it one picture frame with a photograph of two people unknown to me, and yet somehow there is a flicker of familiarity at the sight of their faces, a grain of remembrance I cannot place. My eye switches to a second, smaller, clear window that throws a view onto a bank of subject numbers working silently on rows of computers beyond, each with their sight locked in front of them on their tasks. Satisfied all is in order, I begin.

"I am Dr. Maria Martinez. Subject number: 375. I am thirty-three years old—"

"Soon to be thirty-four," he smiles. "Soon."

I nod at this fact and continue as per routine. "I am a member of Project Callidus, conditioned with my Asperger's to assist in the Project's covert cyber- and field-operative missions. We protect the UK and global nations against terrorist attacks of all kinds, and, due to the NSA prism program investigation, we are black sited and no longer affiliated with MI5."

He sucks in air. "Good. Now—my name, the special one you reserve just for me, what is it, Maria?"

"Black Eyes," I say, delivering the response as per requirement. This is his favorite part of our talks, or so he says. "Your name, Dr. Carr, the one I have always given you since you trained me from a young child, is Black Eyes."

He nods and smiles, and I notice tiny crinkles fanning out by his eyes. "Thank you." He leans back a little in his chair, his stomach concave, and his sweater seems to sink into him.

"Now, since you arrived here, how do you think you are adjusting?"

"I have fully memorized the map of the facility and know all routines down to the last second."

"Do you recall yet the immediate events leading up to your arrival at this facility for your Project reinitiation?"

I hesitate. Images sometimes come at night, blurred events, faces, but nothing yet definable or real. "No."

"And so when you see this"—he slides the laptop to me and clicks to a page—"what do you think about?"

I read it fast, photographing the data to my memory banks within ten seconds. Facts. The file contains spool upon spool of facts about me. Dates, times, images all collected by my handlers over the years, undercover Project handlers at school, university, work who watched me grow up and who took me, with the help of my adoptive mother, Ines, to train me on missions, then drug me with Versed to make me forget what I had done. There are facts about my time in prison for a murder I did not commit, a murder I was set up for by the Project to get me out of the way while the NSA scandal blew up. Details on my adoptive family, how Ines killed my real father, Balthus, and shot my adoptive brother, Ramon, after pretending it was he who had given me to the Project. Facts about how I killed Ines at her Madrid apartment to protect my then-friends, Patricia and Chris, the whole scene covered up by the

Project, dressed up as a gangland drug killing. There are pictures of each person I have known, intelligence on them, and I resist the urge to reach out and touch the images of their nearly forgotten faces; at this black site facility we are taught that the Project is our only friend.

I look to Black Eyes. "When I look at this data I think about the killings."

"Done by you or by others?"

"Both."

"You have killed several people, Maria—how does that make you feel?"

I hesitate. Feelings, for me, are the hardest questions to answer.

"You see, Maria," Black Eyes says now, "you are vulnerable, or at least, you have been vulnerable to outside influences, and it affects you from time to time, as I suspect it's doing now. But that is why I am here. You must learn to lock it away, shut such trivialities from your mind, forget your past, forge your future. Ines gave you to us from Balthus and Isabella, your *real* mother, so you could be someone better."

"Ines gave me to you so she could have cancer drugs from the Project in return," I say, struggling to keep a worm of emotion from rising in me. "Ines lied to all of us and was working with the Project all along. Ines … Ines helped to kill my papa."

"He is not your papa," he suddenly snaps. "He is Alarico. He was your *adoptive* father."

My eyes flicker to Papa's image on the computer: warm smiles, creased eyes. "I … I miss him."

I drop my head, feeling an acute sense of failure. I have tried to forget my family, my friends; I have come a long way and it has been hard, too hard sometimes. I glance around the room, at the walls and the window, deeply sad yet resigned, my feet weary and heavy, and the thought arrives that this here now, with Black Eyes, with the Project, is the only option I have left. The only option now. I am on my own. Everyone has deserted me. Gone or dead, I don't know—it always varies, but one thing throughout it all has been consistent: the Project. It's all I have left. I have tried, in the past, to fight them, have actively railed against them, but for what? What good has it done? What good does it do to fight for what you believe in when all you are is a wounded soldier in a losing battle? Is it not better to lay down your arms and surrender? To try and at least see down the barrel from their point of view? Here, with the Project now, with Black Eyes every day, I can see that it offers me something of what I need: a routine. And maybe this is where I was meant to be all along, a place where a daily routine is standard, surrounded by people like me, working, perhaps, for a greater good. I can learn, maybe. I can attempt to understand what it is they are really trying to do and possibly then acceptance of it all will be easier. You can't control everything and sometimes there comes a moment when you must accept that this is the way your days are meant to be. This is, all along, who you were meant to be.

Black Eyes lets out a long sigh and shuts the laptop. He glances to the picture frame on the desk. "The past is hard to deal with sometimes." He lingers on the image for a second then looks back to me. "And, Maria, a lot has happened to you. But what you have to remember is that it's the future that truly shapes us, if only we let it."

I listen to him and as I do, the Project's phrase, the one bolted to the corridor walls, enters my head, clear and true. "*Order and routine are everything,*" I find myself chanting.

Then we say, together: "*The Project is our only friend.*"

A smile spreads on his face and reaches his eyes, then, clearing his throat, he flicks a page. "Now"—he taps a file with photographs—"to pressing matters. You know these two people, correct?"

He presents me with two images. I take a sharp breath.

"This," he says, pointing to one, "is Patricia O'Hanlon—your cellmate at Goldmouth Prison when you were incarcerated for the murder of the Catholic priest before your acquittal."

"Yes."

"And you were good friends, close, yes? Your first real friend, would you say?"

I swallow, nervous. Why is he asking me this? "Yes."

His finger traces Patricia's swan neck, her shaven head and blue saucer eyes, and as he does, I feel uncomfortable, concerned, but I don't know why. "And this," he says now, "is Chris Johnson. We have a lot of data on him. Convicted American hackers tend to pique our interest. I believe it was Balthus who originally put you two in touch?"

"Yes," I say, my throat oddly dry. "I met Chris at his villa in Montserrat, near Barcelona. I went there after MI5 found me at the Salamanca villa. Chris was in prison for hacking a US government database. Balthus was Chris' prison governor before he was in charge of Goldmouth."

Black Eyes moves the file nearer to me and my vision catches Chris' familiar deep brown eyes, his uncut hair flopping to sharp cheeks and stubbled chin, and somewhere inside me, I feel an indefinable pull toward him, and toward the faces on the pages, an urge to scoop them to my chest and hold them tight.

"Maria?"

I whip my head up in fright at his sudden voice. "Yes?"

"The *Project* is your only friend."

His eyes reduce to small slits, one second passing in the silence, two. He looks from the faces in the file to me, then back again in a seesaw pendulum of time. I shiver, not knowing what to do, worried, scared even at how strongly I felt just now when I saw the faces of my friends, yet shocked at how much I want to please Black Eyes, please the Project, do whatever I can for them, find a place where I belong, accept that this is where I am to live my life.

After ten seconds pass without a word, Black Eyes scrapes back his chair and, striding to the glass mirror on the far side, he turns and faces me.

"Maria, I have something to show you."

He steps back and presses a buzzer. I watch, a nervous swell inside me licking the shores of my brain as the mirror of the window begins to move and a gray blind behind starts to rise. It reaches the top, clicking to a halt but still I cannot see fully what is beyond, when another snap sounds and this time a light switches on from the other side. A brightness floods the room and I have to blink over and over as it assaults my eyes, my hand shielding them. I have to resist the strong compulsion to duck and curl as, slowly, I finally see who was causing the moaning earlier.

"Doc! Doc!" the familiar Irish lilt of a voice shouts out.

I manage to stand and step forward, as what emerges in front of me, limb by limb, bone by bone, is a beaten, bruised, and tied-up body.

When I find my voice, only one word comes out. "Patricia."

CHAPTER 2

MADRID BARAJAS AIRPORT, SPAIN

32 Hours to Project Reinitiation

Even the earbuds I wear can't cancel out the chaos and noise. People march back and forth, left and right, crisscrossing the glaring bright gloss of the polished airport walkways. Babies scream and toddlers yell, coffee cups clink and luggage carts screech, speakers above my head bark the next flight departure as in the near distance, wine glasses tinkle at a champagne bar and a group of people laugh at a joke I will never understand.

I stand and blink and watch it all as the airport scene crashes into my senses, body and mind temporarily paralyzed by everything. The noise, the smells. Tinny music from open shops. Coffee, beer, oil, sickly sugar, stale cigarette smoke, burger fat, perfume, leather, sweat, the faint soak of cinder block urine. The slurp of a straw. The bite of a sandwich. Every single scent, I smell. Every tiny pinprick of noise, I hear. It all smashes into my brain, colliding into my white and gray matter until I don't know which way to look.

"Doc?"

I slip out an earbud and look to my friend.

"They're not going to spot us," Patricia says, her voice low, calm. "We've got through security and I know airports are a nightmare for you, but look at us." She points to herself. "We're in business suits and wigs. Jesus …" She smiles. "I've never looked so smart. So it'll be all right. Okay?"

I nod and tap my finger.

Another smile. "Good. You're doing great. I'm right here with you."

She looks down at herself now and I watch her angled arms, her swan neck and her shaven head disguised by a long, mouse-brown wig that settles on suited shoulders. A cream silk blouse slipped under a black jacket sits against smart tailored trousers and neat, flat ballet pumps on the end of flamingo stalks for legs. My friend. My first true friend.

"It is too loud here," I say.

She takes my palm and presses her five fingertips into mine as she has always done. "I know, Doc. I know it's too much information flying into your head from the airport, but I'm here." A group of passengers shuffle nearby and Patricia forms a little bubble of space around us so no one brushes against me. I catch her familiar scent of talcum powder, fresh linen, bubble baths. It makes me breathe a little slower.

Chris wanders over. He fiddles with his suit and his newly dyed bottle-blond hair, and shakes his bright red Converses. "The security guards are hanging around a bit back there. We need to get moving toward boarding."

Patricia eyes his feet. "You couldn't have worn a pair of smart shoes, could you? We're supposed to be pretending to be professional business people."

He fidgets, pulling at his yellow tie, at the sleeves of his smart navy suit, shoulders twitching. "I feel like an idiot."

"You look like one."

Chris glares at Patricia. He scratches where a white shirt clings to a flat surfer stomach and pulls at his trouser band, muttering, "It's too fucking tight."

I observe my friends without any understanding of what their exchange means, the glances between them, the words. Funny or serious? Heartfelt or fickle? Ahead, a large bang slices the air as a café tray clatters to the floor, cups and plates and cutlery smashing into cold cream tiles, the sound of it hammering my head. I wince. It's exhausting. I need stability, something factually familiar for my mind to cling onto, a lifeboat of facts.

I turn to Chris. "The term 'idiot' means a person of low intelligence. You hacked into a CIA website, that takes intelligence to achieve. Therefore, the term idiot in describing you is wrong. On this occasion."

Chris pulls his tongue out at Patricia. "See." Then he turns to me. "Thanks, Google."

"I have informed you before—that is not my name."

He smiles, big and wide. "I know." Then he starts humming a song I have come to recognize from a singer he seems to greatly admire called Taylor Swift.

"That is the melody entitled …" I listen … "'Shake It Off.'"

He grins. "In one."

Patricia rolls her eyes. "We have to go. Doc?"

"Yes?"

"Stay by me."

We find a semiquiet patch in a coffee shop and sit. Immediately anxiety hits. The slurp of peoples' lips and tongues as they sip their drinks. The clink of cups. The steam from the milk machine and the mechanical grind of coffee beans. Teeth biting down into crunchy lettuce. Someone's lace undone, the thread hanging loose, dragging along the floor. It all collides inside me. I try to focus, count, look to Patricia who mouths to me, "How can I help?" except I don't know the answer, only know that here and now I need to keep any potential meltdown under control so no attention is drawn to me or to us. Three hours ago we were in Ines' apartment and I killed her with an iron nail to the neck, and watched Ramon and Balthus die. The last thing we need is a scene.

"Doc, deep breaths."

I nod, watching Chris closely as he walks to the counter, orders our drinks, but immediately, this tips me into a panic.

"I want a black coffee," I say. "What is he ordering for me? It can only be black."

"It's okay," Patricia says. "He asked me and I said black coffee. I told him for you." She smiles. Soft cheeks, lines opening wide at her eyes. "Okay?"

I nod, but inside I am panicking.

Chris is talking to the barista now, easy, light, making random conversation about the bustle of the airport. To give myself something to focus on, I examine his movements, his facial expressions. How easy it seems to come to him, how simple such dialogue appears for him. I try pressing some of it into my memory, the way in which he acts, remember it so I can perhaps use it, mimic it, to cover up me. It's hard to find a place in the world when you don't know who you're expected to be.

Done with that yet still anxious, I turn my focus to checking and rechecking the time of our flight to Zurich where Chris has secured us a safe house through his hacking contacts until we can get further away and out of sight. Finally, Chris returns and it's only then I can be assured that the right drink has been bought. I sip slowly. The liquid is hot, scalding my palate and tongue, but I like it, as if it polishes the tips of my mind so they are ready to be used. Now and then the multiple sights, sounds, smells of the airport hit me, make my body go rigid, but breathing and counting help, and so I do that, run through numbers in my mind, murmur the digits with the tips of my fingers pressed one after the other into my thumb, all the while glancing to my friends, grateful that they are here.

"Okay, so, I checked my email," Chris says, emptying two full sachets of sugar into a latte, "and my buddy in Zurich is all set for us to rock up there. All secure. Also, from what I can tell, it looks as if the Alexander woman has read the message we sent her."

Patricia looks up. "What? The home secretary?"

"Yep, Balthus' wife, Harriet Alexander herself." He draws out a computer tablet and taps the screen. "About twenty-seven minutes ago. No, wait … twenty-eight minutes ago she read the whole file that reveals the Project Callidus bombshell, from way back in 1973 up to right now." He starts listing things off with his fingers. "The thousands of Basque blood-type people they've been testing on, the cancer drugs for Ines, the Project taking Maria and drugging her, Maria being Balthus' kid, all of it, all of the stuff we hacked into in Hamburg." He grins at us and I wonder if his face has ever, in his life, been fixed into a frown; I resist the temptation to stick my finger into the dimple on his chin.

"Well," Patricia says, "hopefully that'll be it. That'll be enough for the government to kick-start an investigation into the whole Project bollocks and it'll finally all be over. No more running."

"Can your software connect to her server system?" I ask.

"Ah, you're thinking of hacking into her emails, tracking who she contacts about the subject of our little message. Yep, thought of that. There's something blocking me at the moment, don't know what it is yet, but I'm on it."

We finish our coffee. Chris taps on his computer the whole time and, ten minutes to go until our flight is boarding, he excuses himself to go to the lavatory. I use the spare time to carry out a reassuring check of the contents of my rucksack. One by one, I place them on the table in a neat line: three pay-as-you-go cell phones, two fake passports, money in several denominations, one wash bag, two packets of energy tablets, and the other essential items I require to be on the run and hide, all itemized on a list in my head. But it is the last three things that I unpack, that now amid the din and the cappuccino milk steam and the idle chatter around tea-stained tables, give me the most sense of calm and reassurance: my notebook and two old photographs.

I rest my hand on the worn notebook cover, flick a finger over the dog-eared pages, pages that have housed my thoughts and calculations and mathematical probabilities for years, each spare section crammed with drawings and codes scribbled feverishly after awaking from dreams and nightmares that would jolt some distant, drug-induced memory.

Patricia leans in, looks at a page filled with algorithms and coding. "I may as well be seeing spots as to understand what on earth all that means." She inhales. "It's been hard for you, hasn't it, Doc? Everything that's happened."

I touch the page with my fingertips, let them skim the curve of the equations before me, the lines, the sketches of penciled memories forgotten and only sometimes remembered. "Ines killed Balthus," I say, sticking to the facts, unable to express the sorrow I truly feel inside.

"Yes, Doc, she did." Her voice is a soft pillow, a floating feather.

I blink, turn my attention to the two photographs from my bag.

"Is that your dad with you when you were young? He has the same dark hair and eyes as your brother."

"Yes. Except they were never my biological father or brother."

"No," Patricia says. "No, I know. Balthus was your biological father, and that's hard—you watched him die when you'd only just found out who he really was."

I swallow. My eyes are a little blurred. "Yes."

Patricia touches the second photograph, this one more sepia-toned and worn. "You were a cute baby."

I take the second image between my fingers and stare. In it stands a woman, my biological mother, long hair falling in wisps around her face, two grainy, willowed hands on the ends of ribbon-thin arms cradling me, her new swaddled baby. I map the skirt that skims the ground where ten toes on bare feet rest on a bed of gravel surrounding a sprawling, stone hospital-cum-nunnery with a crucifix on the door. I blink at the photograph and battle with a feeling inside me, strange and unwelcome. Anger and sadness, a tumbleweed of sorrow that, try as I might, will not go, but instead rolls along the barren land of my heart and mind, leaving behind trails in the sand that vanish with one whip of the wind. *Isabella Bidarte—my real mother.* I try the phrase out in my head, wear it like a new pair of shoes, walk it up and down the corridors of my mind, but it feels odd, stiff, as if using it for too long would create a blister filled with pus that would burst and seep and hurt.

I turn the photograph in my hands. On the back is scribbled an address and the geolocation coordinates of a hospital—Weisshorn Psychiatric Hospital, the place Isabella was last kept in Geneva, and next to it the date of her death, all etched out by my papa and hidden from Ines before he died.

Patricia stares at it. "He knew she was kept there, didn't he, your dad? He'd found out about what Ines was doing—getting the cancer drugs to keep her alive in exchange for you."

Too sad to speak, I trace the address and date with my fingertips as, to the right of the café, a television repeats a news feed detailing the killings at Mama's apartment.

"A triple homicide was reported in Madrid, in what is being cited as a cartel crime. Spanish lawyer and member of parliament Ines Villanueva, her lawyer son Ramon Martinez, and a British prison chief, Balthus Ochoa—the husband of UK home secretary, Harriet Alexander—have all been implicated in what sources are saying is a decade-long fraud ring stretching into millions of dollars and which includes trafficking in illegal medical drugs. The bodies of the three were found at Villanueva's central Madrid house this afternoon. Villanueva, who was a likely pick to become the next leader of the right wing, and prime minister …"

Tilting her head so I can see her smile, Patricia nods to the television. "Same story they're telling like before, same bullshit."

"It is all lies. The deaths did not happen in that way."

She sighs as the television screen flashes across the faces of Ines, Balthus, and Ramon.

We finish our coffees. I carry out a final check of my belongings, secure the photographs in an inside pocket near my notebook and, acknowledging the presence of my passport one more time, in my head I begin to carry out a run-through of the airport journey when Chris runs up to the table, breathless.

"Jesus," Patricia says, "what's with you?"

He swallows, pointing behind him. "People ..." He gulps air, slaps two palms to the table and hauls in some oxygen. "C-coming ..."

"What d'you mean?" Patricia says, frowning. "You're not making any sense and we've got to—"

"Shush!"

Patricia opens her mouth on the verge of speaking when Chris raises a hand and finally spits out the words he wants to say.

"The Project—they've found us!"

CHAPTER 3

I turn, stand, focus. "Tell me."

He swallows. "So, I was just walking back and looking around duty-free, and they have the mirrors and stuff there and I'm sure there were two guys watching me."

"This is ridiculous," Patricia says.

"What? No. I was followed." He looks straight to me. "I'm telling you—they were different, these guys."

"How?"

"Just, well, I guess they were, like, rigid, you know. Kind of robotic and—"

"Christ," Patricia says, "this is the last thing we need, you freaking out on us like this."

"I'm not freaking out."

"You are, and you're going to upset—"

"No!" His voice is raised. I flinch. The people at the next table stop eating mid-sandwich bite and narrow their eyes.

Chris lowers his head. "No. Please," he whispers, "you have to listen to me. I know they have to be different because I recognize them, from when I was locked up, okay? One of the two guys who investigated me via the UK, well, they were MI5. The other one, I'm not sure …"

"You have to be sure," I say. "Now." My eyes scan ahead, quick-fire.

"I'm sorry. I recognize both of them, just can't place the second one."

"One of them is definitely MI5?"

"Yes."

The cogs in my head, as if tripped by a switch, begin to turn at such a rate that for a second I feel dizzy.

"Shit," Patricia says. "Doc, MI5 wanted you dead. If they're here, this is not good."

"Oh fuck." Chris rubs his head. "Oh fuck, oh fuck."

As my friends swear repeatedly, I scan the crowds.

"Maria," Chris says now, "I'm sorry. I sent that email. MI5 must have tracked it."

"Why would you be sorry?" I ask. "This is not your fault."

"It is," Patricia snaps.

I look between the two of them. "We cannot determine with any mathematical certainty why these men are here. We can only assume." I pause, my mind firing at such a rate now, the probabilities and conclusions whip out. "We can only assume a level of danger which requires some amount of action on our part."

Patricia blows out a breath. "Shit a brick."

Chris nods. "You said it."

I scan the busy foyer, the noise so loud, my body wincing at the near-physical hurt it causes me. Heads, hats, citrus perfume, detergent, the smell of ice cream and pancakes, a series of buckles and trailing laces.

"I can see them," Chris says.

"Where?"

He gestures to an area by a burger bar thirty meters away. "Right ... there."

I follow his line and spot two men, black jackets, casual clothing, no suitcases, no definable baggage, just coffee bean eyes and steady strides.

"Doc," Patricia says, "is it them? Could MI5 be back working with the Project now, you know, running it or something?"

"I do not know," I say, sight missile-locked on the two figures. Flickering fluorescent lights, the clatter of suitcase wheels, the hum of a fan somewhere in a nearby store, the oppressive stench of chip fat. It all collides in my head, making it harder to think straight, but even in the chaos, a cold calm descends and a phrase, one drummed into me by the Project, that, despite my resistance, enters my head as easily as walking through an open door. *Prepare, wait, engage.*

I turn to Chris. "You are certain it is them?"

He gulps. "Yes."

"Then we have to go."

He rubs his face. "Oh man, oh man, oh man."

Bags secured, Patricia moves backward, her feet stumbling a little, Chris following as the three of us slip behind a large silver pillar that houses neat billboards for expensive Parisian perfumes.

"Doc, what do we do now?"

I glance to the area ahead and watch the two men. They walk five steps then stop and as they do, my brain carries out a full and rapid assessment of the immediate threat. Each man is approximately 166 centimeters tall, the right man blond, the left brunette, no distinguishable facial features, no definable scars, and by quick track of their frames, each appears to be built to endure long-distance runs over twenty kilometers, yet still bulked-out enough to carry the weight of a full army training kit on their backs.

Patricia bites her lip. "They're not real travelers, are they? Oh God." There is a shake to her words. She chews on a nail. "You think they've seen us?"

Chris risks a glance. "Maybe ... Fuck." He slips out his phone, sets up a fast proxy, starts tapping on a screen I cannot see. "Let me ... Hang on."

"What are you doing?" I ask, but he shakes his head, taps his phone and does not reply.

I scan the shops to calculate the best route forward. By the entrance of a chain of toilets, a toddler is squirming in a ball on the floor, screaming while his mother flaps around him, coils of hair springing up, shored by sweat, the father nearby, scratching his head, tutting into a smart phone that's stitched into his hand. The noise of it all ricochets around my brain.

"Doc," Patricia whispers, "should we get out of the airport?"

"No." I take a breath, try to count the noise away. "We must board our flight and travel to Zurich as planned."

"You think that's wise? Won't they know where we are going?"

"Negative." I swallow. Someone make the toddler be quiet. "We look different. Our email tracks have a high probability of being invisible."

Chris, head up from his phone, points. "They're moving."

Patricia bites down harder on her fingernail. "Doc, I'm bloody shitting it."

"If you soil yourself, you could impede our escape."

She ceases eating her hands.

The billboard with the perfume advert on the pillar is a rolling one. I observe it. Every six seconds, there is a change of posters, promoting gilded watches, branded clothing, vintage bottled cognac, champagne and truffles, and each time a new poster flashes, the entire board moves from side to side creating one small yet significant space behind it, a scooped-out hole. A blind spot.

I turn to my friends. "There is a place to hide, there." I point. "It will provide us cover to plan the next move. When I say go, we all go. Do you understand?"

They nod.

"Does that mean you understand?"

Two frantic nods. "Yes."

"Good. I will count to three. On three, we will run to the billboard."

"We won't be seen?" Chris checks.

"No."

"Okay." His eyes flick ahead then back to me, a breath billowing from his chest. "Go for it."

"Okay. On my count: one …"

Patricia slaps a hair from her face, mutters for some reason what I believe is a slang word related to a man's genital area. The billboard begins to revolve to the side.

"Two …"

Chris taps his foot. He shields his phone screen with his hand as his eyes dart left and right in the glare and bustle of the concourse beyond.

"Three. Go!"

We run. Lights, sounds, sharp slaps of heat and noise. They all fly through my ears as we weave in and out of the crowds. The men do not immediately follow us and yet still there is something about the way they move, about the assurance of their steps.

We reach the billboard. "Which way?" Patricia whispers.

To our right is a concourse of cafés and shops, people spilling out of them in various states of speed and urgency. To our left is the open floor, shining, twinkling in a yellow-brick road that leads off to the departure gate announcing cities and flight numbers. My brain photographs it all. Istanbul, Melbourne, Washington, Paris, locations that span the world across data lines that lay hidden underground.

"They know we are here," Chris says. "I'm certain now."

I whip round. "What?"

He turns his phone to me and my heart starts to race at an alarming speed.

"I hacked into the Madrid police database," he says, "you know, to be on the safe side, get some firm intel. I found this."

"Oh, holy fuck," Patricia blurts. "It says *wanted*. It's us!"

There are pictures of all three of us. My mouth runs dry so fast that I have to lean against Chris to steady myself.

"Hey," he says, "you okay?"

"They have us in different wigs," Patricia says. "Shit—they'll know what we look like!"

"I have put you in danger."

"Huh? What? Oh, Doc, no. None of this is your fault. Doc, it's okay."

"Er, no," Chris cuts in. "It's not okay."

We both look to him, mouths open.

"Why?" I say.

Very slowly, he guides his eyes to the left. "Because they're looking right at us."

CHAPTER 4

MADRID BARAJAS AIRPORT, SPAIN

31 Hours and 13 Minutes to Project Reinitiation

"Oh, Jesus, they're—they're looking straight toward us," Patricia says, ducking behind me.

I stare now at our faces on the police alert in Chris' hand, and a feeling wells up inside me, one of guilt, of shame and confusion. By making friends, have I done the wrong thing? Is life not easier, better, safer when we are on our own?

"Doc? Doc, you all right? Should we go?"

My head snaps up, refocusing. "Negative. If we move now it will alert the men. They have images of us. We must wait. We must prepare."

Chris tips his head to the left toward a landslide of bodies approaching. "What about them?"

I direct my sight to where Chris points. A pack of students has entered the walkway, flooding the air with chatter in a melody of Italian and French, a river of language rushing forward amid a sea of brown limbs, all long and lean and clad in assorted patchwork pieces of denim and cotton and hooded drawstring sweats. Tinny music, the tap of phones, beeps, rings. The sounds send my brain into red alert, and I am about to move when two teenage students stop almost next to me and kiss. I find myself staring, unable to look away, and when I inhale I detect bubble gum, washing powder, body odor masked by a sugary scent.

"Hey, Google?" A pause. "Maria?"

I turn to Chris. "What?"

"They're all moving—the students. If we move with them, they could be good cover."

The teenagers pull away from each other, the girls smiling in a way I do not understand. The chatter rises, smacking into my ears, slap, slam. Startled, I look to Patricia.

"It's all right," she says automatically, trotting off what she's had to say to me now so many times. "Deep breaths. It's going to be loud and close, but I'll stay right by you, yeah? Chris is right—the students'll be good cover."

I nod, but my eyes are on the moving mass. "Their skin, their scent."

"Deep breaths."

Chris starts to move. "Let's go."

We dart in and out as ahead of us, the boarding gates appear. People, limbs, spit and sweat. Announcements hanging from the ceiling with flashing orange letters and numbers declaring the area our flight is leaving from. Our feet brush the tiles as we surge forward amid the slippery mass, sliding across the mirrored thoroughfare where the shoes of the students clomp down in hooves of plastic and leather, jostling, laughing, bumping into me. Head down, I bite my lip and try not to scream.

Hidden by the human cloak, we remain out of direct sight. Some meters nearer now, the men move rapidly, steady, their presence two dark monoliths against the landscape of pick-a-mix color. My heart rate rockets. We duck, weaving, as Chris keeps watch and Patricia spreads five fingers on her thigh, but every time someone's arm or leg grazes me, I flinch. Every time I smell their burger breath, feel the heat of their perspiring skin near me— deodorant, talcum powder, flowers, and musk—I want to scream at the top of my voice, curl up into a tight ball. It is impossible to switch off.

We finally approach the flight gates, Patricia to my right, Chris to my left. We drop our speed as the students slow down, skipping and laughing at each other, and as I risk a small glance, I find myself fascinated by their ease with each other, their calmness, happiness even, transfixed at the way in which their limbs seemingly absent-mindedly intertwine, vines of arms and fingers interlinking as if all branches from the same tree. They oscillate and flutter, and I imagine a shoal of clown fish swimming around a new reef, relaxed, loose, just another day hanging out.

I unpick my gaze from the students and inspect the two men. They are talking to each other.

"They're calling our flight," Patricia says.

The entrance to our boarding gate is drenched in sunlight from a vast glass and steel dome above. Glass, steel, huge masses of heavy concrete. I do the math in my head.

"If a bomb went off here, the glass would shatter and kill and maim the people beneath it."

Chris stares at me. "Seriously?"

"Of course."

"Oh shit. Shit!" Patricia whispers. "They're looking this way."

She's right. "Walk."

We stride, not running, not wanting to create attention. Backs straight, footing as sure as we can make it, we mimic three busy work colleagues eager to catch their business flight. Soon we reach the gate. Patricia's face is pale. Chris' fingers are tapping his phone.

"Good afternoon," the flight attendant says, his eyebrows two tapered caterpillars. "Boarding passes, please."

We hand over our travel documents and fake IDs, as from my peripheral vision I see the two men searching through the students, casting them to the side, one after the other. The lights above shine bright, the traffic of chatter and laughter pummeling the air. I count to stay calm.

"Hurry up," Patricia mutters, but just as the line begins to move again, everything stops.

The flight attendant looks to us. "Could you step aside for a moment please?"

"But we're getting on the flight," Chris says.

My teeth start to grind. Breathe. One, two, three. One, two, three. The men are moving toward us in the pile of students washing up near the gate.

"We have to run," Chris whispers.

"Negative."

"Yes," he insists, stronger now. "The attendant stopped us."

"They are nearer now," I say.

Patricia's eyes go wide. "Oh God."

"God has nothing to do with …" I halt. Something is not right. The men have stopped. Their movements—why are they now so still? Keeping my head as rigid as I can, I check the CCTV cameras, their small domed lenses, dark black caps, blinking in the nearby areas. All seems as it should, all cameras facing the correct way, all security staff, in the immediate zone at least, carrying on with their duties as before.

Patricia shuffles from foot to foot. "Shall we peg it? This is fecking MI5. Shit."

I trace the outline of the officers. They may have been trained, like me, to prepare, wait, engage. Is that what they are doing now? If I were them, what would I do next?

"Doc? Doc, I think we should move."

"Holy fuck," Chris says.

I look to him. He is staring at his phone. "What is it?"

"I've just …" A shake of the head. "No way. It's—"

"They're coming!"

We look up at where Patricia is staring. The second man, the one with the slightly narrower shoulders, is touching his ear, scanning to his right and moving slowly forward. I track his eye line, wincing at the sharp clatter of some tray that is dropped in the distance, my assaulted brain just about keeping it together. What is he looking at, the man? What can he see?

I force my brain to focus, to think clearly. Maybe Chris is right—maybe the flight attendants know who we are and have been informed to hold us back and make us wait.

I turn to Chris and Patricia. "We must go."

Chris points to his phone. "You have to see this email."

"Not now. We must leave first."

We all turn, ready to duck from sight and out of the airport, my mind already fast-forwarding to a next plan to hide, when the flight attendant calls to us with a bright white smile beaming on his face.

"Hello? I'm so sorry about the short delay." We hesitate. He gestures over to us. "If you'd just stand to the side and allow our late wheelchair passenger through, then you can board. Apologies for the inconvenience."

We look to each other, the three of us, our chests visibly deflating, eyes blinking in what: Shock? Relief? I cannot tell, but we watch a wheelchair board the ramp and, with one nod of the attendant, we follow it fast through the final doors that lead to the plane ahead.

Outside, the Madrid air hits me. Aviator fuel, warm concrete, the roar of jet engines, all of it colliding in my head. I grind my teeth and blink at the blue sky that swirls through clouds spun with cotton. I stay close to Patricia.

As we reach the door of our Zurich-bound plane, Chris stops me.

"I got an email." He swallows, catching his breath. "That's what I was trying to tell you before."

My heart rate shoots. Alarm bells sound. "From who?"

An attendant smiles. "Welcome to the flight. Boarding passes, please."

I thrust her my pass, ignore her, and turn to Chris. The woman frowns.

"Who is the email from?"

Chris pauses then, lowering his voice, he tells me what I didn't expect to hear.

"It's a reply from the UK home secretary—from Balthus' wife."

CHAPTER 5

DEEP COVER PROJECT FACILITY

Present Day

I'm not certain how I feel when I see Patricia held behind the screen. Shock? Fear? Nothing? I am too scared to answer.

Stepping forward, I observe my former friend as if she were a specimen in a lab. On her head are fresh red lacerations. Deep bruises strangle her neck. Her torso is clothed in a dirty gray T-shirt, ripped trousers hanging from her legs that lie crumpled at odd angles. She raises her eyes and calls out my name, but the officer kicks her in the stomach and her middle folds in, body collapsing flat to the floor. I want to slap my hand to my mouth, but something tells me that would be a bad thing to do right now.

"What do you see, Maria?" Black Eyes says, a crackle of something indefinable stepping across his voice.

"Patricia," I say, quick, as steady as I can.

"This O'Hanlon woman—she is not your family."

"No," I respond, "she is not." Patricia is looking at me with big eyes, but while before they were blue and clear and shining, now her eyes seem dulled and bloodshot.

He regards me, holding my face with his sight and I so desperately want to tap my finger, my foot, anything to help my mind deal with the intensity of the attention.

"You had two fathers," Black Eyes says, "adopted, biological. Now both dead."

A heartbeat. "Yes." My sight remains locked on Patricia.

He folds his arms across his chest, watching the scene behind the screen. The officer is hauling Patricia up, but her body must be weak, because her rib-caged torso keeps buckling, her legs bending, feet toppling.

"I lost my father, too," Black Eyes says, sight on the screen. "I was fourteen. He was in the SAS."

Beyond the window, Patricia whimpers. We observe, Black Eyes and I, riding for a moment in a slow seesaw of sound, left, right, left, right.

"Why is she here?" I dare myself to ask.

"She is here because she is the enemy. You do understand, don't you, that after everything that's happened, she is no longer your friend?"

Friend. I roll the word in my mouth, feel it, test it out. For a long time, I never really understood what having one meant.

"You made the only choice you could, Maria, by being here. Here is where you belong. Patricia O'Hanlon is the enemy because she does not agree with the aims and objectives of the Project. She does not agree with you being here. Yet this?" He stretches out his arms to the room. "This is where you belong."

"This is where I belong," I say, the words marching out of my mouth of their own accord.

"That's right. And you don't need people like Patricia O'Hanlon when the Project is our only friend."

He reaches forward and presses a button. The gray blind rolls down slowly, one centimeter at a time, but the movement of it must jolt Patricia awake as, suddenly, she raises her head, staggering up a little. She begins screaming.

"Doc! Doc! Help me!" She wobbles forward. "Don't listen to them, Doc! They're lying! They're all lying! They're going to …"

The officer hits Patricia on the skull with the butt of his gun and she crumples, falling unconscious to the tiles. Without thinking, I slap my palms to the screen, startled, as before me the officer starts dragging Patricia's clubbed-seal body out of the room.

"Where are they taking her?" I ask fast, pressing my face into the glass trying to see around the corner. "She needs help." I turn to Black Eyes. "Why did he do that? Why?"

I gulp in air as to the side of me Black Eyes rolls back his shoulders, snapping the bones that puncture his spine one by one. He regards me as I stare at the screen as the blind descends, then he steps to his desk and picks up the photograph that sits on it.

"When people we love die, it is often hard for us to cope with, would you agree?"

I blink, the image of Patricia still fresh and raw in my head, not fully comprehending what is happening or why. Black Eyes holds the frame closer to his face and as he does, I find myself staring at the picture of the two people in it, my brain prodded by some odd curiosity, a vague, foggy notion that they look familiar. Both female, the oldest appears to be in her thirties: slim, caramel skin, hair in long black cascades down a suited back, wide collar, wire-rimmed spectacles clutching high cheekbones and resting against thick branches of brows. Beside her is a girl, young, at estimate under ten years old, the same hair as the older woman, same features, just softer, plumper, the sharpness to her cheeks not yet defined, still hidden under an infantile cushion of baby milk and bread.

"Who are they?" I ask before I can stop myself.

He does not respond, seeming, at first, as if he will not say anything at all, but then he sniffs, takes a breath and traces one thin finger over the printed faces. "They are—were—my family." He swallows; the pointed triangle of his Adam's apple juts out, then sinks in. "They passed away a long time ago."

Returning the frame to its allocated slot on the desk, Black Eyes picks up the file from the table, clutches it to his chest, then stands and stares at the gray blind where Patricia once was. For a few seconds time is suspended, the air swinging in silence around us. I steal a glance at the photograph on the desk.

Ten seconds pass, until, raising his chin, Black Eyes strides to the door and, unlocking it, gestures to the white-washed gleam of the walkways beyond.

"Come. It's time I showed you something."

ZURICH AIRPORT, SWITZERLAND
28 Hours and 30 Minutes to Project Reinitiation

From: Harriet Alexander
    (Secretary of State for the Home Department)

To: Maria Martinez

Subject: Re: The Project

Dear Dr. Martinez,

Thank you for your email. I've had your message decrypted and have verified the details contained within it. This information now is for our eyes only and has been seen by only the most trustworthy members of my immediate staff. You managed to find my private email address, so I am responding directly from that—given the nature of the situation you have brought to my attention, I believe it's our most secure method of communication at this time.

Firstly, you have my gratitude for informing me of the true cause of death of my husband, Balthazar. Balthus was a dear husband and, while I did not know of your existence, I am sorry for the sadness I am sure you must be feeling at this moment.

I have reviewed your files on this organization called

Project Callidus. Please be assured that I was unaware that this group existed. I am currently seeking to set up talks with the chief of MI5 with a view to beginning an investigation, but, as I am sure you understand, timing with these things is everything and I have to be very careful and measured with what we do next. Your safety, Dr. Martinez, is paramount.

To that end, I would be grateful if we could meet. I understand this may be a complicated request, however I strongly believe that, after reviewing the initial data you relayed to me, a meeting between us would aid in the investigation in the Project and MI5's involvement in it.

Please do consider my suggestion. In the meantime, there is one more thing. After hearing of Balthus' status as your biological father, I was naturally curious about the woman he had a baby—you—with. You asked in your email about her grave and its location. I thought it only right and fair to share the information with you as to her status.

Her name, as you know, is Isabella Bidarte. She is from Bilbao, Spain. Her last known location is Weisshorn Psychiatric Hospital in Geneva, Switzerland. She was born in May, 1968. After your grave location request, I also assumed she was dead, however, after a confidential investigation by my closest team, I can tell you that Ms. Bidarte is indeed still alive, her residence understood still to be the Weisshorn Hospital in Geneva.

I trust this news is of value to you. This has been difficult for me, as I am certain it has been for you. I am sorry for the distress you have, over the years, I am sure, been caused at the hand of our security services. I hope this news of your mother contributes in some way to atoning for that.

Please do consider strongly my request to meet with

you in order to aid our vital investigations and put an end to Project Callidus operations. Let us keep secure lines of communication open.

Yours truly,

Harriet Alexander

I look up from Chris' computer tablet at Patricia, my hands shaking at the shock, yet my brain curious and elated at the email.

"She is alive," I say. "She is alive."

Patricia comes close to my side, the milk of her skin and the warm bath of her scent reaching my brain. "I'm right here."

She touches my fingers and my mind becomes a little calmer, small clouds of our breath billowing in the frozen air.

We are hidden by a wall outside Zurich Airport. Close by, the external glass facade of the busy building glistens by a freezing taxi rank and the pencil-straight road washed in paint strokes of sunshine, leaving weak yellow lines across fine snow-covered pavements. I pull out my notebook and the photograph Papa had hidden in Ines' Madrid cellar. I gaze at Isabella's face, at her river of hair, her flowing skirt, her baby—me—swaddled and held in arms so smooth and melodic they sing like swans. Could she really be alive? Could it be true? Or is the whole thing a fabrication? Quickly, I begin to write down the email contents, cross match for any patterns, hidden codes or messages, but no matter how hard I look, there is nothing secret to find.

Chris hurries over, cupping his hands and blowing on his fingers. "I thought spring was supposed to be warmer here."

Patricia rolls her eyes. "Wimp."

He stares at her, shudders, then looks to me. "Okay, so—" He sneezes.

"Bless you." He tilts his head at Patricia and raises one eyebrow; I have no idea why.

"Okay, so," he continues, "I've double-tracked the email on my system and it's from her all right—it's from Harriet Alexander."

I clutch the sepia-tone photograph in my fingers. "Are you certain?"

"Yep. The thing is, she said what she said, you know, about investigating the Project, but if MI5 are tracking her then they'll know she's talking to you." He points to the email. "They'll know now she's planning to investigate it all."

"Doc," Patricia says, "he's right. They'll follow you and then MI5'll want you dead and the Project will want you with them, just like before. The home secretary asked to meet you. Wouldn't that be the right idea? She's based in Westminster—it doesn't get much more safe than there. The Project and MI5 can't get you then."

"Hang on though," Chris says, "what if she knows something—your mom, Isabella?"

I turn to him. "What do you mean?"

"Okay, so, what if we find her and she can, I don't know, tell us something to really put the nail in the Project's coffin? Because the way I see it, you can't trust—"

Patricia shakes her head. "No. No way. Too risky …"

"A nail in a coffin?" I say, but Patricia continues.

"The police have our bloody pictures, Chris, for God's sake. They'll find us. And then MI5 will get to us before we get back to the UK and we're all stuffed."

"Wimp," he says. "We'll be fine."

Patricia rolls her eyes and looks to me. "Doc, I don't like it. It's risky. God, I'd rather we went to the safe house of Chris' in Zurich than go to the hospital in Geneva."

There is a wall straight in front of us. It is beige, bland, the grouting along the brickwork in neat patterned lines, each one with a clear beginning and an obvious ending. I calculate the length of the edges to help my brain to think straight in the midst of the plane engine roar in the air around me, the birds in the swaying fir trees near the network of roads and railways, the tremble of trolley wheels and the faint scent of distant cigarette smoke. Yet it is only when a lick of aviator fuel flicks my nostrils, jolting me upward, that the thought occurs to me.

The brick and the grouting and the definable end. I think about that word—end—how it sounds and what it means …

Slowly at first then faster, I study the photo in my hands then scan the dates scrawled on the back. "There is an end."

Patricia looks over. "What d'you mean?"

I spin round to Chris, my mind moving at speed. "Isabella's birth date and death date are both on this photograph."

He looks.

"If she is alive," I continue, brain planning now at lightning speed, "as the email said, why is the date of her death written here? It was written over two decades ago. The conclusion can only be that either my papa wrote down the date without it being true or—"

"Or the home secretary is lying," Chris says.

I look to him, his body stomping from foot to foot, his breath blowing small, white candy strands into the air, and for the first time since we arrived in Zurich, I feel a strong urge to turn to him and nuzzle my face in his neck and just smell him.

"I have to know whether she is alive or not," I say now. "And if Weisshorn Hospital was her last known location then that is where we will go."

Patricia stretches bolt upright. "Doc, no. I don't think that's a good idea. There's a high chance she's not there and then what? Why on earth d'you want to go there, Doc, when it's so risky? Why?"

I stare at Isabella's image. "She is the only family I have left," I say, quiet, soft.

Patricia's shoulders drop. "Oh, Doc." Around us, lace patterns of snow float to the tarmac and evaporate into nothing. Patricia wipes her eyes, but doesn't speak and when I inspect her left hand, I see her index finger and thumb pressing hard against each other so the skin is white.

"Okay, so, Google," Chris says. "Do you freak out on trains?"

I tear my sight from Patricia. "What?"

Chris leans against the wall and, fast, flips open his laptop. "There's the Goldenpass route to Lausanne in Geneva. It's long, but quiet, a tourist route, not busy at this time of year. We can lay low." He looks to me, hair flopping in his eyes. "Would you be okay with that? It would mean it's calmer for you to, well, to deal with."

I study the details he has pulled up on the journey. Wide-open carriages, large windows, space, clean mountain air, and no crowds. "We will have to change outfits so we are not recognized."

"No sweat. I've got untraceable credit cards that can buy us new stuff, and an uncanny ability to deactivate security cameras." He pauses, drops still for a moment, looks to the photograph in my hand. "Hey, we'll find her, whatever happens. We can go under the radar, figure out everything we can. We've done it before, we can do it again."

I watch his lips move, smell his scent. "Can you hack into the Weisshorn Hospital, track any data?"

His face breaks out into a grin. "For you? Anything."

Patricia coughs. "What—" she stops, swallows. "Sorry—what time does the train depart?"

"In one hour," Chris says. "We all ready to go?"

"Yes." I throw my rucksack on my shoulder. "But first, I need to use the toilet facilities."

"Oh. Okay," Patricia says. She slips her cell phone from her bag, checks it and slides it out of sight.

CHAPTER 6

GOLDENPASS RAILWAY LINE, THE ALPS, SWITZERLAND

26 Hours and 20 Minutes to Project Reinitiation

I am unable to pull my eyes from the palette of watercolor before me. Aching blue lagoons of sky sifting in a mist of citrus and orange peel. Carpets of green grass shoots sprinkled with sugar flakes of snow all scattered among petals of spring painted with brushstrokes of yellows and lilacs and multicolored confetti. Majestic mountains rise up, backs straight, muscles taut, mountains that, each time I gaze at them, each second I take in their strong, solid presence as they whisk past the window, a lump forms in my throat. When my sight drifts up to the fading turquoise of the sky, my breathing softens and I think to myself that no matter what happens, no matter what wars are raged, what lives are slain, what untruths are spewed and sewn, the mountains that soar high above us are always there. Solid, present, and true.

"Doc, you okay?"

I peel my forehead from the window. Patricia now wears a wine-red sweat top with a hood and pocket, and on her legs blue jeans the color of the night sea hug her skin. Her brown wig is still in place, as is Chris' blond mane as he sits by us hunched over his laptop. We are all now casually dressed but, despite the simple comfort of the clothes, the fresh cardboard cotton of the T-shirt I currently wear itches my skin, irritating me. It's unbearable, so I go to take it off, but Patricia reaches forward.

"No, Doc. Not here."

I stop. "Why?"

"People don't get changed down to their bras in public places."

I drop my hand. "Oh."

Scratching my stomach to bat away the clothing annoyance, I glance around the carriage. It is sparse. An old man with white hair wearing a pressed herringbone coat, black tie, cotton blue shirt sits two seats beyond reading a French daily newspaper containing headlines about the NSA and their surveillance of the German head of state. Near to him is perched a young woman, small birdlike shoulders hunched over a worn-out copy of Jean-Paul Satre's *La Nausée,* the dog ears of the cover touching the tips of ten porcelain fingers as she turns the page, nails bitten, faded black jeans on petite, slim legs.

The only other group in the carriage is a father in his early thirties with two children, both boys under the age of ten, one nestled under each arm. The children are swaddled in navy blue duffel coats sewn with eight toggles apiece and they sit across a wooden table, opposite an elderly woman whose stomach and chin rest in kneaded batches of dough, square metal-framed glasses perched on the tip of a podgy nose as, making conversation with the small family, she points out the various Alpine sights that trundle past.

I observe the father for a moment, watch the way he smiles each time one of his sons whoops or claps at spotting a random cow or a snow-covered mountaintop. A father, living, breathing. I hold my gaze on the family scene then, swallowing hard I touch the picture of my papa and the photograph of Isabella and her baby.

"Hey," Patricia says, leaning forward a little, "what've you done to your thumb?"

"What?"

"Your thumb—have you hurt yourself?"

I glance down at the small wound peeking out beneath a pale plaster still partially wet with blood. "I cut it."

"Where?"

"In the toilets in Zurich."

She leans forward. "Oof, that looks sore. Must have been some wallop you gave it."

I hide my hand out of sight and try to ignore the sting. "It is healing."

The train jostles on and I take out my notebook, careful to avoid contact with my thumb. I check our current location against the brief list I have compiled to help me tackle the journey. Places, times, exact locations, short, sketched scenarios.

Satisfied we are on schedule, I peer through the wide window again and breathe easier. I turn my attention to Chris and his laptop.

"Have you hacked the Weisshorn database yet?"

He nods his head. "Yeah, but it doesn't make sense."

"What does not make sense?"

Chris sits back, scratches his chin. "Well, okay, so I'm in their system, yeah—the hospital's—I still can't find Isabella's name but either way, there seems to be some kind of glitch with my computer." He swivels his laptop to me and points. "See it?"

There are a series of numbers, stretching across the screen and linking to the database Chris is trying to hack. "They are codes," I say.

He nods. "I know, right? And every time I click on them, the screen shakes, just for a second." He shows me, and, sure enough, it shakes.

Patricia leans in to see. "Why's it doing that?"

"No idea. I've checked the OS, but it's all fine."

"Can you not tell using a file or something and bypass the shake, or whatever you do?"

"Nope. My trace files won't open right now. No idea why."

Connections firing, I rip open my notebook and cross-reference my written data with the online file then sit back. Nerves prick my spine. Something is not right. I wait for a second, think through the program on the laptop with the details in my notebook from dreams long gone. The motion of the train back and forth, the rhythm and gentle chug of the sound and its predictable pattern soothes my brain, and I flip through my cerebral files, checking, referencing, interweaving the recalled data in my mind as if it were open in a book in front of me. Connections, link, numbers …

"There's a thread," I say finally, noting that just five seconds have passed.

Chris' eyes flip wide open. "Jesus, that was quick."

He's right—even for me that was fast work. The train, the lull of it, the empty white bowl of the mountains and snow—that must be enabling my mind to work at such speed. Patricia watches me closely, frowning.

"The thread," I continue, scanning the laptop, "is linked by an algorithm like this one," I swivel my notebook to him, "that attributes a line at the back of this hacking program into the hospital."

"What? You serious?" He peers at the page. "You got all that from there? But what does it mean?"

I try to think it through, but the woman with *La Nausée* breaks open a baguette of ham and cheese and the scent flicks at my nostrils. Butter, stale bread, sloppy ham with veins of fat, the sugary fug of processed cheese. I pinch my nose shut and, trying to focus on anything but the smell, look at Chris' laptop and the information from the hospital contained on it. The data merges together in my mind, line after line of it racking up a catalog of knowledge at such speed and with such force that I have to slam my palm down on the table to steady myself. I am aware of the stares toward me, but I ignore them, focus on the screen as, slowly then faster still, an answer begins to form, until, with fear, I realize what is happening.

"There is a tracker." I swallow. "It's linked to the program, activated when you connected with the hospital database." How did I come to that conclusion so fast?

"What?" Chris studies the screen, eyes wide. "Holy fuck! But if they've targeted my actual laptop it means that whoever's done it, whoever's singled this device out must have done it deliberately. They must've known I'd try to get into Weisshorn and as soon as I did, they sent a virus to my computer to locate it. Fuck."

"It may not be deliberate. It is common for servers to have an instant defense virus attack sent out when any hacking is detected."

Chris' shoulders drop and his features visibly soften. "Oh God, d'you think so? God, yeah, shit. I should know that—*do* know that. Sorry. I'm just ... fuck. This kind of stuff makes me nervous." He leans over his laptop, fingers moving fast. "I'll cut all links now to their database and get out of there. I have software that should stop any viruses, but it must have bypassed it."

Patricia watches us. "What if hacking into that database means they know where we are? I mean, they can do that, right? Find locations and stuff?"

We stare at her. Chris swallows. "She's right."

"So it would be better," Patricia says, "if we ... if we get off this train?"

Chris smacks the laptop shut, throws his hands up as if the computer were a hot coal, a burning ember. "Shit. Shit, shit, shit."

Panic wells inside me at the prospect of the Project finding us before the investigation can cull them. I steady myself, gaze out at the patches of snowflakes that stick on the window. Outside, deep lakes give way to fields of fir trees and sugar-dusted green pasture. Sometimes I imagine that if I look at nature long enough, it will make everything better and, like the snowflakes melting on the warmth of the window, it will all disappear.

I turn to speak to Chris, when a loudspeaker announces in French, German, then English that Brünig-Hasliberg is the next station up. At the barking sound, my hands slap to my ears while ahead, the two boys whoop and clap and tell their father that this is the best train trip ever, and can they have some sweets.

Patricia looks to me. "Doc?" She jabs a finger to her ears. "The announcement's stopped."

"We need to get off this train as soon as we can," Chris says. He is fidgeting—does that mean he is anxious? "I'll have to leave this laptop on here so they won't find us—it'll be full of the virus now." He fumbles over a paper map looking for a station.

I lower my hands. "Interlaken Station would provide a good place to alight the train as it is located between lakes Thun and Brienz. It will therefore provide more places to hide, and better access to more low-key transport opportunities. It is also a place popular with backpackers."

Chris nods "Okay, yeah—I see where you're going with this. If it's full of backpackers, we can slip right in, unnoticed. Awesome."

"It's not on our routine, Doc," Patricia says to me. "Will an unscheduled stop be okay with you? I'm not sure if you can cope."

"I can … cope."

Patricia gives me a flicker of a smile. I drink in her face, her soft smile, and feel happiness. Soon the train begins to ascend, lurching and heaving through the white dust of the mountain that yawns steep through the Brünig pass. As I observe the lakes laid out in mirrors of deep blue ice alongside our carriage of glass and gold, I worry about the tracker linked to Chris' computer, and so to remain calm, I watch Patricia and I tell myself how lucky I am to have finally found, amid this confusing world that changes in a heartbeat of time, someone whom I can truly trust.

DEEP COVER PROJECT FACILITY
Present Day

We walk along a white corridor with low-level bulbs that do not assault my senses. All is quiet.

Black Eyes strides by my side. In his hand is clutched his folder, and in the light that glows down in calm, controlled pools beneath our boots, his fingernails appear to glisten as they pinch the plastic edges of the documents.

We reach a junction and halt. Having witnessed Patricia behind the glass pane just moments before, I am jittery and my finger taps the side of my thigh where my combats skim my skin. The cold air gives me goose bumps. Black Eyes shifts his vision down. He regards my finger where it flaps and, with a flicker of a frown, he flares his nostrils and returns his chin to its upright position. No one speaks.

I count my breaths while we walk further to within the bowels of the building. I find myself, illogically, searching for Patricia everywhere. I try to stop doing it. I know it is wrong—no longer is she my friend and even though the memory of her skin beaten into blueberry bruises on her neck and arms and legs haunts my mind, I tell myself that the Project alone should be my only focus, that what they do is for the greater good. Yet still, images of her broken body enter my thoughts and I have to push them away, place one foot in front of the other and recite in my head as many birth dates of classical composers as I can.

Black Eyes remains quiet as we halt, and a familiar whoosh sound hisses into the air as, before us, a door bows open into a room that I have never entered before. I pause, suddenly nervous, but unsure why.

"Maria," Black Eyes says, extending a periscope of an arm forward, "please enter."

I peer into the room. It stretches toward a larger door three meters beyond. I walk in upon instruction then halt as told, and turn.

"Where we are about to go," Black Eyes says, "is all part of your therapy, Maria. Do you understand that?"

I nod, yet inside there is uncertainty building. I have so many questions but am nervous to ask them, and when Black Eyes looks at me, it feels as if he can see into my head, read my thoughts. I press my lips tight together. Nothing in, nothing out.

"Patricia O'Hanlon," Black Eyes says now, consulting his file, "should no longer be regarded as a friend, colleague, or anything else of significance by you. Do you understand?"

"Yes."

"Good." He lets out a sigh. "I know this part is difficult. We are accustomed to the trauma individuals feel—the assault of noise and thoughts and smells—so where I am about to take you will shut all that off and allow you to have no intrusions, help you to … come to terms with your situation, yes?"

"Yes." The room swims a little. I press my heels hard into the floor as an anchor.

"So, Maria, shall we?"

Black Eyes gestures to the next door and closes his folder, and as he does I catch sight of the photograph that lies on the main page: Patricia. Her skin is clear, before the cuts and bruises, her neck long and slim, and while the sudden image of her alarms me, what grabs my curiosity the most is the word *dangerous* stamped in red writing across her face.

I begin to move forward, normally, try not to show any eye movement toward the document while I work through the unexpected reaction in my head. I register an emotion—what? Anger? Hurt? For some reason unknown, seeing the word *dangerous* in relation to Patricia makes me cross, yet it is not directed toward the Project because of what they have done to her—I am cross, instead, at Patricia herself.

Blindsided by this sudden realization, I attempt to decipher what the feeling means, and the reason behind the emotion drifts within sight but then slips away out of reach.

We halt at the second, larger door and Black Eyes claps his palm on the folder. I jump. "In we pop," he says, and he opens the door.

I peer into the room beyond, into a place I have never before been.

"This," he says, "is the Chamber. In we go."

I hesitate then obey. Patricia's photograph peeks out from the white folder's edge.

CHAPTER 7

GOLDENPASS RAILWAY LINE, THE ALPS, SWITZERLAND

25 Hours and 31 Minutes to Project Reinitiation

As the train slows to the scheduled halt at Brünig-Hasliberg Station, Patricia unfolds herself from her seat and announces she's getting off.

Instantly, I panic. "Where are you going?"

She smiles, her back stooping over while her head skims the metal rod of the caged luggage rack above.

"I've read about this place," she says. "It has a little bookstall and everything. The train'll be here for ten minutes or so, so I fancy a little wander round, stretch my legs."

"Is that wise?" Chris says.

"It's only for a bit. I'll be careful. I just need to get some air."

She yawns and stretches her arms. I peer out. A small station with sloping roofs sugar-coated in snow rolls in front of us and lurches to a stop. It is constructed of brick, metal, and wood, and under the low-hanging eaves of the worn tiles are housed creaking oak shelves crammed with dog-eared secondhand paperback books of fiction and fact, a metal honesty box slotted at the end where the shelves fall away and the tall wide station doors yawn open to the ticket office beyond. It is quiet. To the left of the makeshift bookshop sits a jumble of bric-a-brac for sale and, feeling the need for stability, I count it all: three old radios, a peeling wooden horse, a stack of board games, twenty-seven ornaments, and fifty-two picture frames, items passed on, no longer needed. I count five people waiting on benches by the far right side, heads hanging over smart phones stuck to frozen white fingers.

"Do you have to go?" I say.

"Oh, Doc," Patricia says, "I just want to have a nosey around. I've never really been anywhere like this or, well, anywhere really. It looks really pretty."

"You have been to places," I say, thinking this through logically. "You have been to Ireland, to England, and to prison."

She bites her lip. "It's not the same, Doc."

"Not the same as what?"

She throws a glance to Chris then turns back to me. "I'll be just five minutes, okay?"

"Five minutes?"

"Yep."

I click the timer on my watch. She pauses, then breaks into a soft smile.

Patricia alights the stationary train. A late stab of sunshine rushes through the window, casting a buttercup glow on the tables and metal gray marled walkways of the carriage. I try to quell my worry for the safety of my friend by counting once more the passengers near to our allocated seats. I watch again the two young boys sitting with their father, scan the doughball woman opposite spilling from the edges of her chair. The boys have now shed their duffel coats and are squabbling over who is to have the last biscuit of what seems to be a discarded packet.

"Can't you just share, poppets?" the woman says.

The boys cease momentarily their squabbling and blink at her with four deep brown eyes.

The father leans in, scoops up the boys, his gaze on dough woman. "It's okay," he mutters. "They're okay. Thank you, though."

I watch them for two seconds longer, curious at the odd lump in my throat, then switching attention to my belongings, I lay out the old photograph of Isabella and I. Taking out a pen, I turn to a new blank page in my notebook and, starting from the top and working my way to the bottom, I scratch down the series of events, where, from hacking and investigating, we have discovered key information on the Project.

Chris leans over. "What you doing?"

"This is a time line of all the points where we have uncovered Project files."

"Right. Why are you doing it?"

"I am trying to define a pattern to pinpoint if the virus that attached to your laptop from Weisshorn is coincidental or deliberate."

Chris goes quiet. He slopes back in his seat, glances to Patricia on the platform. She is flicking through books. I watch her. She slots a novel back to the shelf then, pausing to glance left and right, she takes out her phone.

"Look, I'm sorry," Chris says.

I blink once more at Patricia then turn to him. "Why are you saying sorry?"

"Because if it's deliberate, the virus, then that means there's a high chance they've been in my laptop before." He shakes his head. "I've got protection and all, defenses and everything, but these guys." He blows out a breath. "They're in another league. It means, without realizing it, I could've led MI5 and the Project to the abbey in Montserrat—to you. And then they turned up and the Project took you away."

I watch him as he frowns. Sometimes I wonder if neurotypical people must be as exhausted with all the unfounded assumptions that they make as much as I am exhausted with trying to understand the inferences of their unfounded assumptions in the first place. Maybe, when we scratch at the surface, we're not so different after all.

"If I was not taken away that day," I say. "I would not have been in the Project facility in Hamburg and we would not have been able to hack into their system and discover the files that revealed how many people like me they have tested on. It means we would not have been in a position to contact the home secretary and potentially put an end to the entire Project via what will be an in-depth governmental investigation."

He drops his head for a second. "Thank you. You're ..." He stops, though it's not clear why. When he speaks again, his voice is low and a bit wobbly. "I'll do all I can to help you find your mom, okay? I ... I still miss my mom every day and it's been years since she died."

I feel a strange need to reach out and touch him, hug him, even, but instead, not knowing what the right action is at all, I have a go at arranging my lips into what I think is a sympathetic smile, then, picking up my pen, I channel my feelings into facts.

We work together on the Project file time line. The carriage is quiet. Every three seconds or so, one of the small boys whoops at some card game they are playing, and when the father looks at them, I notice crinkles by his eyes. When he ruffles their hair with a gentle hand, the pang that stabs me inside comes on so unexpectedly that I have to stop writing and try hard to prevent my thoughts from wandering to Balthus and Papa.

"Do you remember in my house in Montserrat where we found that kind of countdown thing?" Chris says after we've been working for a few minutes. "You know, the one with your age on it, counting it down?"

My pen hovers in the air as I look over to him and trip off the exact date, location and time of the occasion he is referring to.

He turns his tablet to me. "Well, d'you remember the timer thing? This?"

I study the screen. Dates, numbers, the tick of a clock. "Yes," I say. "That is the same one as before."

"I know, right? I kept a link of it on file along with all that Black

September terrorist stuff from 1973 that kick-started the whole Project in the first place. I thought, while we're looking for connections while the train's in the station, I'd go through all the stuff we've found since being at my place. But, the thing is—this clock definitely seems to be linked to something else other than what we found, only, I don't know what."

I look again at the screen and try to fit what I see to anything from the Project facility in Hamburg, but the only aspect that piques my curiosity is my allocated subject number that sits in the yellow square next to the countdown file. I point to it. "It states my subject number here."

Chris nods. "375."

The fir trees outside ripple. I watch the leaves bend from one branch to another until they merge into a single sea of pale mint green. A thought begins to form.

I turn. "Click on there," I instruct Chris, unsure why, but cogs turning.

"You've got an idea?"

Following my finger where it brushes the screen, Chris takes the cursor and hovers it over what appears to be a tiny gray square that sits in the corner by the age countdown flash at the very bottom of the laptop. He clicks on it once, twice, but nothing appears. The carriage sways a little as people alight and ascend, bustling in with them the smell of toffee popcorn and burnt sugar. Alarmed at the scents, I cover my nose with my hand and watch as the boys with their father pull at his coat and beg him for food.

"You all right?" Chris says.

I nod. Only my eyes peek out "My brother, Ramon, fed popcorn to me in the cellar at Mama's house in Madrid where he had me imprisoned."

"Ah."

Once the smell fades, nothing is still appearing on the gray square on the screen. I check my watch. Patricia has been away three minutes and one second now. I peer to the window. She is tapping her phone as, two paces from her, a woman wearing a plain navy baseball cap, blue sneakers, and tight black jeans steps out from inside the bric-a-brac shop and halts one meter from where my friend now stands. Why, I think to myself, is Patricia using her phone? It is for emergencies only. I drop my hand and press my face to the window to get a better view when Chris calls out my name.

"Maria, you have to see this."

I turn to see, on the tablet screen, numbers. Hundreds and hundreds of numbers.

Chris scans them all. "They just sprang through when I clicked the gray box again. Why's there a line through every single one?"

"They are subject numbers," I say, immediately, almost to myself as in my brain I am photographing each one and cross referencing it with the presorted data in my head until I am 100 percent certain. "Yes. I can confirm they are all subject numbers."

"How do you know?"

My eyes speed over each line again, but there is no mistake in the match. "They are the same numbers in the file we found in Hamburg. Then, 2,005 of 2,113 were marked deceased."

"So why are they crossed out? They weren't crossed out before." His eyes narrow. "It's as if someone's put a line through them all. I mean, you don't do that on a computer file, so why have they done it? It's like they want to make a point. Like the numbers, the people have ceased existing or something."

"As if they are all dead," I say.

"Shit." He blows out some air. "That Black Eyes guy, the one that came up on the screen, d'you remember? On my computer in Montserrat? Do you think he's behind this again? D'you think this thing is programmed, maybe, to match remotely, like, real-life events? You know, people dying? The Hamburg files said they were their subject numbers, right? So, are the rest now dying, too?"

I am about to answer when Patricia returns. My eyes track her every move as she rushes toward us clutching two worn books with cracked spines and tea-stained pages, catching, as she passes, the eye of the woman with the doughball chin and stomach.

"Doc," she says, breathless, slipping her cell in to her pocket and folding her legs and arms into the seat, "you have to see this!"

She shrugs off her coat, confetti flakes of snow floating from the sleeves and vanishing into the carpeted floor below.

Chris looks over. "What is it?"

"There was a woman …" Patricia gulps some air and slides onto the table a worn old book. "She …" Another swallow. "She gave this to me by the bookstore."

It is an English-language copy of *1984* by George Orwell.

Taking the novel in my hands, I smell its pages. Coffee, mothballs, mint, and lavender, each stain and rip and penciled etching depicting the tracks of the readers who have lived in these words, all of their movements documented and preserved in the multicolored cover and spine that now sit in my hand. I leaf through the old yellow courier typeface.

"Who gave this to you?"

"A woman on the platform." She pauses. "Doc, she said you have to read page ninety-seven."

"Okay."

"No, Doc. *You*—she said *your* name." She looks between Chris and I. "She knew who you were."

CHAPTER 8

25 Hours and 25 Minutes to Project Reinitiation

A tsunami of fear hits.

"Where is she?" I say.

Patricia scans the platform. "There. Doc, that's her! That's the woman who gave me the book!"

We all dart up. The train is beginning to pull away from the platform. We sprint to the door, watched by the father and his sons and by the doughball woman pressed into her seat.

"There, Doc, look! Do you know her?"

I scan where Patricia is pointing, but all I see are books and assorted junk and bric-a-brac. "There is no one."

She thrusts her hand ninety degrees west. "There!"

The train shudders to a temporary halt and I see her. The woman. She has buttermilk skin, a navy baseball cap with tiny wisps of chestnut hair peeking from underneath, blue jeans, red sneakers, chocolate-brown eyes, and a face I recognize. A gasp slips from my lips. There is a flash of memory inside my head: of Kurt, the Project intelligence officer whose real name was Daniel, passing as my therapist after prison, of the spiked coffee with the Versed drug that the Project used on me to transport me to their facility.

The woman who brought the spiked coffee to me.

"She is with the Project," I say, remembering. "She is the girl-friend of a Project officer who Balthus killed. She ... she was at Montserrat Abbey when the Project took me."

"No shit," Chris says, ramming his head to the window. "Fuck."

I grab *1984* from Patricia and scan page ninety-seven. At first, there is nothing obvious of concern, no code jumping out, no immediate message.

Chris scans the page too. "See anything?"

I search. "There are words."

"Yes, but anything ... unusual?"

A whistle blows and I jump, instantly clicking my tongue at the noise. On the loudspeaker, the conductor announces that there are cows on the line, which are finally moving and the train's departure will be in one minute's time.

"Doc, you're clicking—you okay?"

I let out a quick breath, count to ten, try to think straight. "There is nothing here," I say to Chris. "The words seem normal."

Chris reads the page then stops. "Wait. What's that there? I've read this book, like a hundred times before—that line shouldn't be there."

I reread. "You are correct," I say, amazed. "There is an extra line."

Patricia looks. "What?"

Together, Chris and I examine the page in front of us.

"There's a code," he says after a few seconds, voice low, eyes locked on to the book.

"Where?"

He goes to take the book but I am clamped to it. "Can I ... can I have it for a sec? Thanks. It's difficult to see, but if I angle it ..." He rotates the page ninety degrees.

I spot it—the code in the letters. The whistle of the guard, the bark of the train announcement must have stopped my brain from working at it before.

Patricia bends in. "What is it?"

"There's an extra sentence at the bottom of the page," Chris says, "exactly the same as the one above it."

"Not exactly the same." I trace the prose, mind firing now. "Here. It angles differently and there are three extra letters."

Chris narrows his eyes. "And two extra numbers."

I begin decrypting the code, as does Chris, his mouth murmuring the numbers we see. But I go fast, more rapidly than ever. I grab my notebook and tearing it open to the area I need, tracking fast the data that I have recalled in the past, I decipher the hidden code in Orwell's novel, catching my breath at the rate at which I work. Chris' lips move along the indecipherable words and numbers, his mind analyzing, as Patricia looks on, glancing from time to time to the platform book-store in the near distance then back to us, before slipping her phone from her pocket, checking it, slotting it back out of sight once more.

I examine the last section of the page, reading, rereading, but it's only when Chris mutters two elements of a code we both deci-phered from the files held within the Project facility in Hamburg that the idea forms.

"The code you just relayed," I say. "It connects."

He wipes his mouth, eyes flying over the numbers. One second passes, two, three until he pulls his head up and mutters, "Jesus."

"What?" Patricia says, glancing between the two of us. "What?"

"It's a warning," Chris says.

"Huh? A warning? A warning for what? Doc, what does it say?"

My eyes stay on the code, decrypting it again to be sure, but still, no matter how much I wish to deny it, the message is the same.

"It says the Project knows where we are." I close my eyes. "It says they are waiting for us at the next station stop at Interlaken."

The train starts to pull away and pick up speed.

DEEP COVER PROJECT FACILITY
Present Day

"This is an anechoic chamber."

Black Eyes nods to a white-haired officer as he opens a door. The officer presses a green button and 170 small LED wall lights ping into life in a room that stretches in a long, tubular shape like an airplane cockpit of a space.

I place one foot inside. When I inspect the initial area, I see that each light throws a soft blue glow on my skin, face, and hair, and when I twist my arm around to reveal the spongy underbelly beneath, a kaleidoscope of tiny rainbows dances along my skin in drunk, swaying circles.

"Please walk in," the officer says.

I hesitate, then step forward and the door behind me immediately whooshes shut, a draft of air sealing it behind me. I whip around, startled, and frantically scan the door, its metal whiteness, a cold block of ice that freezes out the world from me, from these lights and sounds. A shiver breaks out all over me.

"Walk three steps forward, please," the officer's voice instructs over an intercom.

"What is happening?"

On the curve of the wall there is a small, square window with a deep blue rim and, through it, I see Black Eyes. "This is the next stage."

There appears to be two sections of the chamber. I move my feet into a different space where the light is almost gone. My pulse pounds. When I look once more through the window I see the officer. Worry shoots up my spine.

"Stop there," the officer orders.

I halt. Unsure what is expected of me, I shift slightly to the side.

"I said stop!" he shouts.

I instantly freeze, staggering at the loud-volume assault. Black Eyes' voice swims in, ordering the officer not to yell.

"Maria," Black Eyes says after a fraction of silence has passed, his fingers, from the window, still clasping the file where Patricia's head lies, "this is a place that can help you. Take a breath, calm down."

I feel a strong urge to run away as fast as I can, to pound down the door with my fists, but manage to stay put.

"You see," he continues, "we have found that subject numbers sometimes need assistance in … controlling their feelings, their reactions to situations. Although, as I'm sure you are realizing by now, you, my dear, are … well, unique."

As he cranes his head and speaks directly to the officer, my brain sparks somewhere at something Black Eyes just said. *Other subject numbers.* I don't move, fear and uncertainty preventing me from barely breathing as I aim to think straight in this strange environment, attempt to locate what alarm is being triggered inside my mind. Why does the phrase *other subject numbers* suddenly tweak something in my mind, something distant, a hazy recollection of an event not long passed?

"Maria? Are you ready, Maria?"

"I think so."

"Good. Then let me tell you what will happen next."

CHAPTER 9

GOLDENPASS RAILWAY LINE, THE ALPS, SWITZERLAND
25 Hours and 20 Minutes to Project Reinitiation
With Interlaken Ost Station fifty minutes away, Chris grabs all his equipment, fingers shaking, and shoves it in his rucksack. Rising into the aisle, his full head height skimming the ceiling of the carriage, he rolls his shoulders and turns.

I zip up my rucksack. Legs jigging in my seat at the nerves of what's ahead, I afford a brief glance to the window. The early night air descending on the mountains has produced a low mist that merges from yellow to deep blue then black, and in the fields that yawn wide into the elbow of the valley below, the petals of the spring crocuses bob on the heads of their stems and sway in the breeze of the train as it rolls on by.

"Right," Chris says, eyes to the left and right. "The hard drive's erased. I've copied everything we need onto a file. I've tried using a signal blocker thing I have, but it's not working, so we'll try again later." He looks up to the far door of the carriage then back to our table. "How're we gonna do this? I mean, why would this book woman warn us if she works for the Project?"

"We do not have the answer to that at present. However, our priority is to reduce any threat level to us all, so the best course of action based on probability of harm or death is to alight the train and leave."

"Shit. What if it's a trick?"

"People, it seems, play tricks all the time," I say. "This is no different."

Patricia wrings her hands together over and over. She secures her bag to her shoulder, gripping it and, catching strands of her wig in the handle where it pinches her jumper, and stands.

Chris glances over to her. "You okay? You seem jittery."

She nods but keeps her eyes down, and when I look at her other hand, wondering how *jittery* appears, I see her thumbnail picking at the skin on the cuticles of her forefinger. I spread out my five fingers; Patricia looks at them and gives a thin smile.

I scan the train. I check the people and the families and the smattering of random, vague faces, observing life as it is: normal, regular, each person connected by an invisible thread of relationships. I glance to my two friends, slip my fingers into my bag and stroke, for one second, the spine of my notebook and rub the soft edge of the photographs tucked inside.

Breathing in once, and with the Project's mantra in my head—*prepare, wait, engage*—I withdraw my hand, secure my bag, and start walking. "We have to find a way off this train."

We negotiate the sway of the carriage and come to a stop by the door that opens up to the outside between the two cabins.

"Doc?"

I am scanning for the best exit. "Yes?"

"I'm not used to this kind of thing."

She chews her nails and I search for something appropriate to say. "It is highly unusual to be chased by a covert organization previously unknown to the UK government, who would kill you if they had to in order to capture your friend."

She lowers her fingers from her mouth and, taking this as a signal that I have delivered an adequate comment, I recommence examining the area.

I observe the eyes and the faces of each and every passenger. Patricia moves close by me now, nail nibbling again, and I use the partial cover her body provides to study the travelers. The old man is asleep in his seat, head hanging, brow tapping the window. The young girl has her face glued to her book, music shoved in her ears, while the father and his two boys, it seems, have fallen asleep, each body resting on the pillow of the other, the bread-faced woman opposite watching them, smiling. Nothing jumps out, nothing screams *run*. I breathe a little easier.

We move along one meter further to the far door where we are due to get off and consider our options of escape once on the platform. The train is moving a little faster now, not at great speed, but the chugging has increased in its ascent up a steep incline.

"Have you located any remote device trackers?" I say to Chris.

"I don't know. My phone's picking up some strange signal, not a virus or anything on the cell, but different." He searches the carriage. "I don't know where it's coming from. And look."

"What?"

"Well, after we realized we were being traced with the Weiss-horn virus, I quickly checked those subject numbers, you know, the ones crossed out. There was a link underneath the yellow edge of the countdown square."

Patricia looks to him. "I thought you couldn't get a Wi-Fi connection."

"I can't. I mean, you don't need one for this. It's just embedded code." He turns to me. "I didn't see it at first, it was hidden behind a series of encryptions that created the strike-through lines across the numbers, but I did a little digging and, well, it led to a place, just a file name header, but a place all the same."

"What place?"

He hesitates, eyes flickering to Patricia then back to me. "The Office of the Ministry of Justice. In Spain."

"Doc, isn't that where Ines used to work? Wasn't she a member of Parliament in that department?"

"She was the Minister."

"Well, the subject numbers," Chris continues, voice hushed, "whoever the people were—they seemed to have been, like, generated from there, from the Justice Ministry. What d'you think it means? Do you think it's all connected? Or is it just random, because Ines was always involved with the Project anyway?"

I grab his phone, examine the data, but no immediate answer comes.

"Er, Doc?"

I scan the data again. It seems valid, but how are the subject numbers linked? How can the government Ines used to help run be involved? It may simply be that Ines stored the data at the department. Only facts will tell.

"Doc?"

"Yes?"

"Doc, you need to look up, like, now."

"Why?"

"Who's she?"

Patricia is pointing to the dough woman, striding down the aisle at a speed that betrays her age.

Chris' mouth drops. "What the …?"

The woman moves quickly, unusually so for her height and build, her sight locked on us as she makes her way up the carriage. My pulse rises. I glance at the boys and the father where they lie asleep: the father's arm drops to the side, loose, oddly limp.

"What's that in her hand?" Chris whispers. "Is that … Oh shit—is that a gun?"

Prepare, wait, engage.

I instinctively slam my two friends out of the way.

"That is a Beretta 92FS pistol with a 9mm silencer."

Chris rams himself behind me. He is close, but I cannot let the confined space bother me, not now, not with my friends at risk.

"Doc," Patricia says, a wobble to her words, "I'm scared."

The woman looks like a harmless grandma, her chest a plumped, padded duvet encased in a lilac jacket, the armholes encircled with delicate flower patterns. She smells of boiled sweets and lavender. Nice, sweet—except for the gun.

"Do not move," the woman says. Her voice is a clipped typewriter of words, harsh, metallic.

I stay walled in front of my friends, arms spread in an iron fence to either side. "Who are you?"

"You know who I am *with*."

"If you're MI5," Patricia says from behind me, "you can fuck off!"

"I am from Project Callidus, not MI5, and there's no need for such language. There are children present."

I glance to the father and the boys. Do they know? Do they know who they have been traveling near? My heart races. I feel the bodies of Chris and Patricia behind me, their heat and breath, the shake of Patricia's arm, the warmth of Chris' torso. I have put my friends in danger again and at every turn they have found me, so if I run, will this never, ever end? But the email, the email we sent from Madrid airport to the home secretary—the Project will be investigated and culled.

"Who are they?" I say, gesturing to the father and boys. "Are they the Project, too?"

Her green eyes briefly flit behind her. "With the Project? Them? Oh, no, no." She sighs. "They are … collateral."

My blood chills.

"What?" Chris says.

"Children," she says. "They can just get far too inquisitive sometimes. It can cause … problems. Sweet little poppets they were, though."

"Jesus," Chris says. "You … you mean you killed them?"

"No," I say, panicking. "No, no, no …" My sight goes straight to the little family. The father's hand hangs over the edge of the seat rest, the boys' heads are slipping downward just a little more than sleep would normally allow. I start to sway, even though the train travels relatively straightly. "The Project is for the greater good. How … how can this be for the greater good? I have to help them."

"No." She slams her arm across the walkway, blocking my path. "It's time."

I stare again at the father, think of the way he smiled at his sons, ruffled their hair, the way his eyes creased when his lips turned up—a family, a real loving family. I clench my teeth, heart slamming against my chest, a rage in me burning. "I am not going anywhere with you."

She emits a small sigh, bosom rising then falling. "You have no choice, Subject 375. Project Callidus needs you."

"How do you know that number?

"Because I am here to see you back to our family. Our nickname—*Cranes*, remember?"

I do remember but, for some reason, I do not want to say.

"Not going to tell me, sweetie pie? Okay. Allow me. After World War Two, in Japan, a Crane came to symbolize hope and peace. A young girl—her name was Sadako Sasaki—she contracted leukemia after the atomic bombings. She knew she was dying, so she took to making thousands of origami cranes. Sadako died, aged twelve, and the world held her up as a figurehead for the innocent victims of the war." She fixes me with a stare. "Do you remember now?"

A chill runs down my spine. She is telling me this tale exactly as I have heard it before, the tale Black Eyes told me. And she is reciting his exact words, as if she were perfectly programmed.

As if Black Eyes were here.

"The crane Sadako made symbolized peace, Subject 375, as you know," she says now. "Peace. We, too, stand for peace. Cranes—our nickname—it means peace because that is what Project Callidus represents, that is what we are about, what we fight for: peace. We are the Cranes family."

"You are not my family."

She smiles and it confuses me—there are creases fanning from her eyes.

"Doc, don't listen to her."

Chris thrusts his head forward. "The Project is over. The British government has all the information on the entire program. It's not a secret anymore."

The smile remains on her face, but now her eyes droop downward, making the creases deepen. I try to decode it, translate what it means. Eye creases with a smile mean happiness, doesn't it? So, is that what she feels upon seeing me? Content, whole? If so, why?

"Leave us the fuck alone," Chris says now, moving forward a little. I feel his warm, moist fingers link between mine; I surprise myself by not pulling away.

"The home secretary—she has an email," he continues. "An email with all the files stretching back thirty years on every twisted little thing the Project and MI5 have done."

"You mean this email?" The old woman's words are cashmere soft as she slips her hand into her pocket, pulls out a phone and holds it aloft with the email and file sent to Harriet Alexander when we were in Madrid.

Chris shifts forward, looks. His mouth hangs open. "What the fuck?"

The woman switches her gaze to Chris. I do not move. The old man in the carriage ahead is absorbed in his newspaper. The young woman has earbuds in connected by a thin white wire to her phone.

"Mr. Chris Johnson," she says, "the way you encrypted that email to the UK home secretary, well, you gave us a hard task to decode it. If you are game, we are very interested in acquiring your special … services. Better to have you onside than off." She smiles. "Still, we found you all. Eventually. But of course, we did have a little help."

"Fuck you." Chris spits at her.

She glances down to the saliva on her coat, then points her gun to Patricia's head and looking at me, says, "I'll make the choice for you now really very easy: come with me or I kill your friends."

CHAPTER 10

GOLDENPASS RAILWAY LINE, THE ALPS, SWITZERLAND
25 Hours and 1 Minute to Project Reinitiation

"Doc, don't listen to her," Patricia says, her voice shaking. "She doesn't mean it."

The woman thrusts the gun toward Patricia's head. "Oh, but I do."

The train begins to slow down. Outside, the landscape passes by in gray and black and yellow, pinpricks of lights glowing in the distance against the slopes of the white mountains, flickering as the wooden chalets and guesthouses and bars switch on for the evening.

I look at the woman and feel disgust, anger at the sight of her. "Leave."

"I'm afraid I cannot do that."

"You know I have been trained," I say. "You know what I am capable of."

"You think I am on my own?" She shakes her head. "We are everywhere, Subject 375. They are waiting for you, so we can either make this easy or hard."

The air feels clammy. I catch sight of the dead family, the innocent little boys and their father. I can't let anyone else die. I uncouple my fingers from Chris and prepare.

"You do not. Touch. My friends."

She exhales. "I did warn you."

She aims the gun.

Engage. My hands launch into action.

Whipping up, fast and around, I slam the heel of my palm straight into the woman's throat, throwing her off course, sending her stumbling to the side. The old man ahead, now looking up, hangs his mouth open and stares; the young woman is still oblivious, earbuds and music plugged in.

I lock the old woman's head with the hook of my elbow and kick her feet out from under her. Patricia gets hit by a fist, staggers back, as Chris blinks, shaking his head, muttering, "Fuck, fuck, fuck," as the train grinds to a near halt, then begins groaning, lurching forward again, picking up speed.

The woman squirms; I crush her neck tighter.

Chris rubs his cheek over and over. "Ask her … ask her if anyone's tracking us."

"Is there a tracker on us?" I demand. "Where is the signal transmitting from?"

Her eyes are wide. "I don't … I don't know what … what you mean …"

The train, its momentum restored, races on toward Interlaken station. I squeeze the woman's throat. "Did you send her? Did you send the woman who was your intelligence officer's girlfriend to give me the book message? His legend was Kurt. Real name: Daniel."

She chokes. "What? No. How did she …?" Her eyes drift one millimeter after another to the right until they land on Patricia. "Her."

"What?" Patricia's eyes are wide. "What? Doc, why is she looking at me? 'Her,' what?"

"We will always find you," the woman croaks. "The next station … we will … we will be there. The Project is your only family. The only one you can truly trust … There's no escape."

I look again to the dead boys and their father. Papa and Balthus are gone, but somewhere, my own mother could be alive and, if I find her, I could find answers. Answers to the Project. Answers to who I am meant to be. Answers that could end the whole nightmare.

"Open the door," I say fast, gesturing ahead to Chris.

"W-what?" He glances from the lock to me.

"I said—open the door."

She moves, the woman, tries to slip from under me. I tighten my grip.

"Doc," Patricia says, "you're going to hurt her!"

But I ignore my friend's cries and instead find myself solely focusing on the task at hand. "Before the lock light turns red," I say to Chris, "open the door and jump. They are waiting for us at the next station. We have to get off now and find answers."

"Jump? I can't jump!"

"You have to. The Project is waiting for us."

"Doc," Patricia says, "this is crazy. Let the woman go. Maybe … maybe she can help us."

"No," I say to her. "They will kill you. I cannot allow that to happen."

Chris swallows, pulls at his collar. "I … I can't do it."

"Yes, you can. You surf, you snowboard—this is easy."

"Right." He gulps, nods frantically. "Right."

"Doc, can we stop for a minute and think about this?"

The woman squirms in my vice. "There is no time." Ahead, the old man shuffles forward, his head craning forward.

Chris looks over. "What about the locking system?"

I gesture to the crease of the door. "There is a manual override."

He crouches a little. "It … it seems to be on green." He bends forward just as the train lurches, sending us crashing to the right. The woman falls on top of me, rolls to the side and my arms fly out as I see her hand searching for her gun, but Chris spots it, gets there first and, grabbing the weapon and hauling himself up, points it straight at the woman.

"Stay," he pants, "the fuck. Still."

I look at him, sweat glistening on his face, shoulders heaving.

He leans over and gives me the gun. I take it.

"Thank you," I hear my voice say. Patricia glances between us both.

I grab the woman back in a vice and feel the train slowing down. I look at Patricia. "Are we approaching the station?"

"I … I don't know."

"I need you to look."

Fingers trembling, she pushes down the window. A cold wind whips in and licks my face.

"I can see it," she says. "It's tiny, though, Doc. Far away still."

I turn to Chris. "Have you unlocked the door?"

"Not yet."

I check the carriage. The young woman is on her cell phone now talking rapidly. Nerves jangle. Is she with the Project, too?

"You … are one … of us," the old woman says.

"No."

"Yes, you are." She swallows. "*Maria*, that is your name." She smiles, one with eye creases fanning out. It unsettles me for a second. Why is she smiling at me in that way? "I remember you when you first came to us, when your mother, poor soul, handed you to us."

My grip loosens a fraction. "You know my real mother? You have met her? Is she alive?"

"Yes," the woman says, her neck slipping beneath my palms. "I saw the other one who came to take you—Ines."

"Doc?" Patricia calls from the window.

"None of them care for you like the Project does," the woman continues, faster now. "Th-There is work we must do. And that includes ensuring you are okay. You …" A cough. "You have felt different recently, haven't you?"

"What?" How …?

There is a sudden blast of air, sharp, cold.

"Maria!"

Chris has wrenched open the door, the snow and peppered

green mountain grass flashing by faster and faster. "I've done it! Should we go now?"

But I can't stop thinking about my real mother. "Where is she? Where is my Isabella?"

"I … I don't know."

"Maria!" Chris shouts.

The door, the train, everything is flying by at speed—wind, snow, leaves.

"We will find you," the woman says now. "There's no point in running away from who you really are. You … you can't trust these people."

Patricia, Chris. "They are my friends …"

"Maria, if we're gonna jump," Chris says, "we have to do it now!"

"Doc?" I look at Patricia. "We need your help!"

"What? Yes. Yes." I hold the woman down with one hand and unloop the belt from my trousers with the other. Patricia helps me use the belt then to handcuff the woman to a metal bar by the toilets.

Done, I pause. "Do not hurt her," I say to the woman.

"Who?"

"Isabella," I say. "My mother."

The trees and outbuildings beyond are smeared in a painter's palette of color. I secure my rucksack to my back. Chris and Patricia are staring wide-eyed at the ground spinning beneath the open door.

"Doc," Patricia yells above the roar of the wind, false hair flapping against bright pink cheeks, "do we have to jump? Is there no other way?"

I glance to Chris, his broad shoulders, sunken dark face. His eyes are watering where they flicker at the fast air. He opens his lips to speak, but an alarm sounds. I flinch at the unexpected shrill sound.

"You okay?" Chris shouts. "It's just the alert, because we've opened the door."

I nod at him. "We have to jump," I say above the noise. The woman is still tied up, but for how long? I shove away the screech as much as I can and we prepare to jump. One hand, two, each of us sizes up the land racing below our feet.

"Patricia first!" I say, my voice carried away by the outside howl. "I will jump last."

"No!" Chris shouts.

"Yes. I have to make sure the woman does not come near either of you."

Chris hesitates, hair flying every which way, then finally, he nods. The train judders, wind and debris roar. I smell the pine-soaked scent of mountain air, the slick grope of engine oil, the cold pinch of ice-cold running rivers.

"One!" I yell. I look to Patricia. "Go!"

She hesitates then jumps. Her body rolls down the embankment, collapsing in on itself, her scream following her.

"Two!"

"I can't!" Chris says.

"You have to!"

He swallows. "You must jump too, deal?"

"Yes!"

He holds on to his bag straps and looks once more at me. He does not say a word, but his eyes are the size of plates, hands shaking, teeth clenched so tight the vessels in his neck protrude, great long blue balloons of veins bulging out from beneath the tan of his skin. He throws himself off the train and disappears out of sight.

I move next. My fingers grip the side rail, the woman's gun in my other hand, head desperately trying to deal with all the aspects of the loud situation. I take one step, two. My feet inch toward the edge, brain acutely aware how fast the ground is moving, how much speed the train has picked up, how my friends are there, waiting. I go to jump when something grabs my ankle.

I look down. The old woman has freed herself and has hold of me.

I try to kick her off, but she grips me tighter, her fingernails digging into my leg. I slide over but she rolls with me, her arms fat and strong wrenching me down, and the gun slips from my hand and away. I try to smack her skull into the metal rail nearby, but before I can, she punches my side, bearing onto me, her face, mouth, peppermint breath showering onto mine. I cough, thrash my head from side to side. The gun lies just to my right.

"Don't trust anyone," she hisses. "She is not your friend."

Her mouth is so close to mine and I can barely breathe.

"Remember that, Maria, yes?" I wriggle a leg free, flex my quad muscle. "Only trust the Project. We're on your side. We need to check that you are okay."

The train is set on its course. The Project could be waiting at the station. With one huge force, I kick the woman hard, high in between the legs, my shin making direct contact with her pelvic bone. There is a crack. Pain radiates through my leg as I scramble up and snatch the weapon, stumbling toward the open door, securing my rucksack on my shoulders. A guard from ahead is racing up the carriage now, his palms slapping each seat rest as he goes. The old woman yells, "Help!" in French and German, then turns her attention back to me, and it's in that split second that I make the decision I am trained to do.

I aim the gun and I shoot.

The bullet hits her head clean, creating a small, crimson hole. She slumps backward, dead. Her fur boot–clad feet hanging loose from the wide open door.

Wind whipping my face, I inhale and with the guard now running toward me, I throw myself from the train.

CHAPTER 11

DEEP COVER PROJECT FACILITY

Present Day

"So, Maria, the lights will be switching off soon." He is not in view of the window, so how can he can see what I'm doing? I look and spot a camera in the corner.

My pulse rises. "Why will you be switching off the lights?"

"To help with the therapy process. It's okay," he says. "You'll find it soothing." A pause. "Trust me."

I hear the clack of his finger where it must tap his file then a shuffle of a seat before his voice slices into the air once again. "Sensory deprivation is what you are about to experience, Maria. It is a crucial, advanced phase of your reinitiation."

"What will happen?"

"You are going to be deprived of all sight and sound, because, you see, Maria, your attachment to your friends, to what you think is your family, is too strong, and we need to break that down so you can be who you really are. You are not them and they are not you. We are your family now." He coughs, then recommences. "We have to strip you back, if you will; we have to strip back everything you once thought you were so we can reassemble you, assimilate you into what we all need you to be, before"—a breath, a heartbeat of time—"before it is too late."

"Too late—too late for what?"

"Never mind that now, you just need to focus on the sensory deprivation chamber. I expect you know all about them."

I don't want to speak about them, want to press him again on what might be too late, but, despite my will not to, despite my fright and uncertainty, the words and explanation trips off my tongue, the information in my head simply too much to be contained within the confines of my skull.

"In 1954, a man called John C. Lilly experimented on the effects of sensory deprivation," I say rapidly, the sentence falling over itself to be heard. "He used a device called a flotation tank, a space that simulates the appearance of an enlarged bath. This device here," I say, taking in my surroundings, "is not a flotation chamber."

"No, no it is not," he says, his voice echoing across the intercom. "This is an anechoic chamber. Our unit is free of water, but, as with the flotation tank, there is no noise in the chamber. The sound pressure therefore, as I am sure you have ascertained, is below the level of hearing. Peace and quiet—perfect for you."

I tap my foot. Why do I not feel safe here? Why, if everything is calm and controlled, do I feel I am standing on the brink of utter chaos?

"Flotation tanks are filled with 27.94 centimeters of water," I say aloud, hoping the facts will calm me, "water that has been saturated with up to 500 kilograms of magnesium sulfate."

When he does not immediately answer, a bubble of fear pushes up inside me.

"You remind me so much of her," Black Eyes finally says, his voice low, barely audible.

"Who do I remind you of?"

"My daughter. She was … she was so young when she died. Like you, she loved to play the piano, knew all the composers …" His voice fades away. When it returns it sounds scarred, cracked. "Not in the same prolific way as you, though, Maria. My … my wife was quick, too, supremely intelligent, as you are."

I don't know how to respond. He is not in the habit of discussing anything about himself—no one at the Project is. We deal in numbers, facts, tangible data, not the past, assumptions, or emotions.

Black Eyes clears his throat, the sound ringing in the intercom. I wince. "You'll find that the metal casing," he says, his voice flatter this time, "is created to form smooth acoustic boards. In between the walls," Black Eyes continues, "the inner and outer casings, the substantial blocks of them, are fabricated with fiberglass." There is a hesitation, a ripple of silence before he speaks again. "I thought you'd like to know because I know how much you love details, Maria, you appreciate the more complex aspect of technical assimilation." I hear the smallest swallow. "My wife was just the same."

There is a beeping of what must be buttons or a screen console of some sort that springs into the air now and my breath quickens and as it does, oddly, my mind twists to an image of Patricia. I am struck by the unexpectedness of the image and as I slowly focus on it, I realize it's not a picture in my head of Patricia here, beaten and bruised at the Project, but instead it's a memory of her from another time, one where her face is clear, unmarked. So what is it? A passing thought? Or something more significant?

"Please sit," the officer's voice in the air above me now instructs.

There is a chair in the center made of soft brown leather and wood. It has a tall back and big, thick arms. I sit as ordered, yet my mind insists on returning to the image it has just seen and, gradually in my head, a clearer picture begins to emerge. I see a tavern. I see Patricia in a tavern with warm light, hot red wine, and a fire.

"Maria, can you look at me?" Black Eyes says. "Look at the window?"

My sight slowly rises to meet the level of his. It is hard to achieve, the contact, the direct line of vision as, in my head, the memory burns a little brighter and I start to see flashes of Chris and

Patricia, all of us shaken, slightly hurt as if … as if we had jumped from somewhere.

"I need you, today, to begin the true process of letting go," Black Eyes says now. "Letting go of your friends, of your family, of what you were."

"Why?" I hear my voice say.

He pauses, levels my vision with a gaze. "So you can discover who you *really* are."

The memory of the tavern flickers then, as if doused in water, the whole thing goes out and disappears into whips of smoke before I can fully grasp its meaning.

"Are you ready?" Black Eyes says.

Above my head, the lights are switched off.

GOLDENPASS RAILWAY LINE, THE ALPS, SWITZERLAND
24 Hours and 23 Minutes to Project Reinitiation

Chris hobbles forward. "Ouch. Fuck."

Chris has twisted his ankle. It is preventing him from moving with ease, and each time we shuffle in the growing darkness, he winces and swears. I examine our surroundings. A steep grass shoulder is behind us, the train far away in the gray horizon now. The daylight near faded, above our heads I can just about make out the peaks of the frozen Alps beyond. An oil slick of navy and black seeps across the sky, covering up the last splash of orange from a sun that has now long slipped behind clouds. Scents of crocus petals, snow, fern leaves, and defrosting rivers drift by.

I shiver and wrap my arms around myself to stay warm. While we have coats on our backs, a lack of sufficient insulation in them means that our bodies are feeling the cold, goose bumps and shakes and chattering of teeth, and when we press our feet into the dusting of snow, wetness seeps into our shoes creating wet patches on our skin. The frost clamping our mouths, we walk in silence for some time until talk inevitably turns to the events on the train.

"Jesus Christ," Patricia says. "Who the fucking hell was that woman?"

"She knew my biological mother," I say, stepping over a rock and counting to three to keep myself calm. In the far distance, yellow lights flash and flicker too fast for me to feel comfortable with.

"Seven hundred and twenty-one," I say.

"Huh?"

"Ahead in that village," I say to Patricia, pointing, "there are seven hundred and twenty-one lights."

Chris looks to me. "Your brain's running like a race car, Google. You okay?"

I nod, but the truth is, I'm not sure.

We trudge forward like this for the next hour. Our muscles are seizing up. Each time Chris takes a step, a small whimper slips from his lips and even though he takes turns leaning on us, my senses getting oddly used to his closeness and scent, the trek is a struggle. After thirty-three minutes of dragging feet, we arrive at a small wood cabin and use the opportunity to rest for a moment and check we are not being followed. The cabin is closed with a padlock on the door, but with roof eaves that overhang enough to provide relatively dry, soft ground underneath, it offers a quick place away from the frozen trail.

Spotting an upturned crate tucked behind the back, I grab it and ease Chris down to sit. Crouching in front of him, I pull up his trouser leg, scoop up a handful of snow, wrap it in a cotton handkerchief from my bag, and press it into his ankle.

He winces. "Ouch! What are you doing?"

"This is an ice pack. It will reduce the swelling."

"Oh."

There is a light outside the cabin, weak but yellow, shining from the right-hand corner of the hut where cobwebs hang in white cotton strings of snow, and, satisfied Chris' injury is tended to, I take out my notebook from my bag and start scribbling.

"What are you doing?" Patricia asks.

"Writing down everything the woman said to me. She said she wanted to ensure I was okay—she asked if I was okay. She said that time is running out."

"She did? But what does she mean by … wait … what?" She stretches her neck forwards to my face. "Doc, is that … is that blood?"

I touch my cheeks; the woman's blood is on my cheeks in tiny speckles.

"Did … did you shoot her, that woman on the train?"

I wipe my cheeks with the heel of my sleeves. "Yes." I wait, as I say the word, expecting to feel shame, regret, and yet all I feel is relief: there is now one less person from the Project to chase us and to hurt my friends.

"But, Doc, why?"

I carry on writing. "After you jumped, she attacked me. She was going to hurt me." I pause, lower my pen. "She was going to hurt you and Chris. She killed that father and his boys. They were innocent. Another father who was … who was innocent."

"Oh, Doc." She tears off her wig and slumps against the wooden slats of the cabin, rubbing her face. Under the lemon light, her skull, now uncovered, shines in small iron filing regrowths of hair that pierce through her scalp where she hasn't shaved for a while.

"Are you okay, Doc?" she says. "I mean, do you want to talk about it?"

"No."

She waits for a while in the night and the snow. "What's going on?" she says after a moment. I raise my head from my notebook. "I mean, the home secretary gave us the information she did, and you chose not to go to her. And I said you should—you'd be safer there. And now look—the Project and God knows who else are after us."

Chris looks on, phone in his hand, the other one holding the snow pack to his swollen ankle.

Patricia emits a sigh. The air hangs heavy and cold. "Doc, I just worry, that's all," she says. "I mean, if you killed that woman, Doc, that means they'll be after you. And not just the Project and all them lot—the local police will be looking for you, too. They'll have your face on camera from the train."

"She's got a point," Chris says. "As soon as I get a secure connection, I'll check the local police lines, see what the chatter is."

I look at Chris, at Patricia. I don't feel remorse at the killing, but I do feel guilt at the danger my friends are in. At the danger those two boys and their father were unknowingly subjected to. "People die because of me."

Patricia shuffles forward, her wig swinging from one hand, her other laid out in five star-shaped fingers. "Let's get going," she says. "We can find somewhere warm, hide out for a while, maybe in that village over there, plan what to do next, yeah?"

Chris nods. "Then I can try and fix the signal-blocker device and start figuring out if anyone's transmitting our location."

Patricia swallows. "Sure. Yeah." She shoves on her wig. "Good idea."

As Patricia gathers her bag and Chris frowns at his phone, I briefly find myself thinking of the Project woman on the train and what she said.

Don't trust anyone.

We all stand, ready to leave, and in the bulb that blinks above us, two moths fly close by. One flitters away, escaping into the looming night sky, but the other lands on the hot glass, stuck, trapped, singeing its legs first then torso and wings until, three seconds later, it is dead.

CHAPTER 12

UNKNOWN VILLAGE, THE ALPS, SWITZERLAND

22 Hours and 17 Minutes to Project Reinitiation

We reach a small tavern tucked away on the edge of the village we had seen in the distance earlier. I walk in, register it all, and stop. Candle flames, rugs, and the clink of glasses. Beer, bottles of spirits, and the bubble of hot, spiced wine. A log fire and the crack of its flame, the charred whiff of burning wood and the lemon-stung scent of pine tree walls, a singer on a stool strumming a song.

"Hey—he's playing Nirvana!" Chris says. "That's … yep, that's 'Come as You Are.' Awesome!" He looks to me. "You coming in?"

Patricia coaxes me in by finding a table in the very far corner where a moose head hangs on the wall next to two skis mounted in a cross by a portrait of an old man snowboarding in a bear suit. Everyone at the bar stares.

I clutch my rucksack, stay close to Patricia and slip into a leather-clad alcove that smells of cheese and cinnamon. I breathe out, deep and long, not realizing until this moment that my body was tired, worn, my muscles tense and sore.

"Drink?" Chris says.

"I do, yes."

He laughs.

I go rigid, immediately looking to Patricia for reassurance. "Did I tell a joke?"

Patricia smiles. Chris shakes his head and flattens his hand to his chest. "Sorry, sorry. You're so great. I meant, would you like me to get you a drink?"

"Oh." My shoulders loosen a little. "Yes. Something red."

"Wine?"

I think about this. "Yes."

He grins. "Well, okay then."

Chris limps to the bar through a small crop of tables where eight sweater-clad people sit huddled in hushed conversation around glasses of steaming cinnamon wine and floating fruit. To their side stands a tall, red-bricked chimney stack over a fired stove roaring in the center of the room, its shaft creating a pillar for me to hide behind. I scan the faces of the customers, trying to pinpoint anything unusual, odd, but no one looks up, no one presses any buttons on a phone or stands and stalks toward us. With all for the moment safe, I allow myself to rest a little.

"This is nice," Patricia says, popping on a smile of soft apple cheeks and feather-down eye-creases.

I try to connect with what she means. There are thick, water-proof ski coats hooked on the back of wooden chairs, hot chocolate drinks in beige mugs, bottles of gin and vodka and tanned, golden whiskey behind the bar. I click picture after picture in my head, try to compare them with filed memories of other places to which people have referred to as *nice*.

"That woman, the one on the train," Patricia says after a moment, stretching out her arms then bringing her chin down to rest in the heel of her palm. "What she said bothers you, doesn't it, Doc?"

From my rucksack, I take out the two photographs and my notebook, and setting them on the table, I feel a pang of sadness and worry.

"What exactly did she say?" Patricia asks.

"Why do you want to know?"

Her face flushes pink, two petal patches blossoming on her cheeks. "I just …" She stops. Her fingers fiddle with her drink, but I'm unsure what this means. Is she simply touching her glass or does it signify something else, an unspoken sentence? I scour my learned behavior actions, wonder if she is nervous? But what could she be nervous about? Being on the run?

"I just want to know so I can help you," Patricia says now, head slightly down, fingers fallen by her side, out of view. "I … you're my friend. I want to know you're okay."

I consider her words and as I do, a feeling comes over me, of what? Of guilt? Of thinking something about her that may not be accurate? Maybe. I'm not used to having friends, to having people who genuinely care about me. Perhaps I should relax a little.

"The woman on the train said that she knew my mother's name," I say after a moment. "She used the present tense when referencing her. She answered in the positive when I asked if Isabella was alive."

Patricia reaches forward and touches the photograph with the tip of her fingers. "Doc, I know I've said this before, but don't you think, given everything that's happened—the woman on the train, the Project tracking us—don't you think the best place to be now is in England?" She glances to where Chris is leaning on the thick wooden bar.

"I have decided already that I have to find Isabella. I have no …" My words falter as I look at the picture of my smiling papa, feeling unsteady. I reach out my fingers and touch his strong face, move then to Isabella and her long Rapunzel hair. "I have no family," I say after a few seconds. "Isabella is my family. She may have answers that will help."

"But, Doc, she's never tried to get in touch with you." She sighs. "You've got to ask yourself why she's never tried to contact you."

"There are many answers to that question: she may be dead. She may believe I am dead. She may not have been allowed any access to communication devices. She may be imprisoned. She may be—"

"Okay." She holds up her hands. "Okay, I've got it."

"Got what?"

Sighing, she spreads out both palms so her fingers lie in two fans on the table. "Oh, Doc, we'll figure this all out, and besides"— she gestures her head toward Chris who's now hobbling back from the bar with a loaded tray—"you've got this fella here, haven't you?"

Unsure what she means, I follow her eye line to see Chris crashing into the table, drinks clattering as, heaving up his leg, he slumps into the seat beside me. I shoot a glance to Patricia—her fingers are still spread in a star shape on the table.

"God," Chris says, "it's boiling in here."

Alerted to his words, I immediately assess the temperature. "It is not boiling. That would require water and a temperature of one hundred degrees Celsius at a sea level pressure. However, as you increase in altitude, water can be boiled at a lower temperature."

"Rrrright …"

"The optimum room temperature is twenty-one degrees Celsius, which this tavern seems to be at."

He nods at me and I think I did a good job at conversation there, so, buoyed, I try something else. "What level of discomfort is the pain in your ankle?"

He holds his drink. "Huh? Oh, okay. Swelling's not so bad now."

"That is because I put snow on it."

He grins. "You did."

"It reduced the swelling."

He keeps grinning. "Good."

"Good."

"Good."

I can feel my cheeks get hot as a rush of blood hits the skin. "Good," I say again, smiling now, copying Chris' wide grin, but not completely sure why.

We sip our wine and, for a while, we do not speak. The bar lulls in the enveloped warmth of pine wood, candle flames, and, by the fire in the center that crackles and spits, the guitar man continues to sing the Nirvana song Chris likes so much.

"Okay, so," Chris says, wiping his face and pulling out his computer tablet and tapping the screen. "Let's see what we can find out. By the way," he says, sipping his drink and wincing, "that vin chaud is strooooong stuff."

Patricia shifts in her seat and studies what he's doing. "I thought you said that we couldn't risk being tracked?"

"We can't," he says, clicking the tablet, "that's why I have this little thing." He waves a small plastic box, matte black, only five centimeters in length and nearly as slim as a credit card. I reach forward and snap it from his fingers.

"Who gave you this?" I say.

"Huh? What? Oh, I made it."

I pause. "You?"

"Don't look so surprised. I can do stuff, you know."

I watch him, wondering what my surprised face looks like. There is a mirror on the far-right wall and I look into it and study my features—cropped hair, same worn wide eyes, olive-tanned Salamancan skin—but no matter how hard I trace the contours of myself, I cannot determine what constitutes surprise.

Refocusing back on the table, I study the black box. Wires thin as cotton are embedded into the spine of the back and, when I flip it over, there is a smooth section into which I can slip the tip of my finger. "This is a button?"

"Hmm? Oh, no, but … I wonder if that's the connection I need to get it working. I was going to put something in it but …" He rustles in his bag and withdraws a tiny black circle, same slit thread and mirrored surface. "Here. This would do it."

Patricia looks on, clutching her wine glass. "What will it do, this thing of yours?"

"Block any trackers on us, any remote signals," Chris says. "I hope."

Patricia's chest for one small second ceases to move then, taking her glass, she downs a big gulp and sets the drink back down.

I examine the card. It is well-made, sturdy, with grooves embedded on each corner. I check its sides, its outer skin then, without consciously thinking, without analyzing in advance what I intend to do, I begin to pick apart the box. I can hear Chris protest, but it is just white noise in the background of my brain as my hands move fast, my fingers flipping and flying as, at quick speed, I unpick the device, fitting the button, rerouting wires and reinserting each minute item until, within eleven seconds, the entire mechanism is back together. I thrust it to Chris. "Now it will work."

He opens his mouth to speak then closes it. He takes the card from me and begins testing it. "Holy crap. You're right—you've done it. It works. It fucking works!"

"That is what I said." I pause. "Though without the swear word."

Chris' smile seems to cover his whole face as he stares at me but then, it drops, changing instead to a frown. "Hey, your nose— it's … it's bleeding."

I dab my face and see blood smeared on my fingertips.

Patricia leans forward. "Oh, my God, Doc. He's right."

"It is okay. It is simply a nosebleed," I say, except, when the words come out, I doubt them. I have never before in my life had a nosebleed, even when, at fifteen, I walked into a glass door because I was too preoccupied with reading a book about Mozart.

"Here. Take this."

I look at Chris and accept the ball of table-dispenser tissues he is thrusting at me. I hold out my fingers—they are trembling slightly.

"Press the tissues in hard," Patricia says.

I want to say that I am a doctor and so I know what to do, but the blood is rushing out too fast. I pinch my nose just above my nostrils, leaning forward, trying to regulate my breathing to drain the blood so it won't hit the back of my throat, reeling at the taste of metal in my mouth. I count until it stops. An unusual headache is forming at the base of my skull; I decide not to say anything about it.

Chris watches me. His face is drained white, even though it's me who had the bleed. "D'you want to lie down or something?"

"No. Remaining upright reduces the blood pressure in the blood vessels and will therefore stem any further bleeding."

"Oh. Right. Good … good." He blows out a long breath. "Jeez, you had me—sorry—you had *us* a bit worried there for a sec."

Patricia helps me wipe away the last of the blood. "Doc, this isn't right. You know that, don't you?"

"It is nothing."

"Nothing? No way is this nothing. Has this happened before?"

I hesitate. "Why do you want to know?"

She throws up her hands. "Because I worry about you!" Then, sitting back, she shakes her head and bites down hard on her bottom lip.

I glance to the black box device, touch my nose where the blood is already drying in small lines around the edge, and I start to think. "Your mechanism," I say to Chris. "I reassembled it very quickly. The codes I have decrypted recently have been at great speed." I glance to Patricia. "Could the nosebleed and my ability to think faster be … be related?"

Patricia looks at me but says nothing.

"They gave you drugs, right?" Chris says, shrugging. "You know, all your life? Maybe they're making you ill."

Patricia stares at me, at Chris. She is still biting down on her lip and when I look to her fingers, I see her clutching her cell phone. With her right hand, she picks up her glass, drains it then stands. Her head almost skims the ceiling and she has to stoop to avoid brushing the fake vines that twist and turn around the pine roof rafters.

"I need a drink," she says. "Anyone else want one?"

Chris shakes his head. I say no, but as the word comes out, I hear a crack, a crackle, because of what? Because of worry?

Patricia begins to walk away and I start to tap my foot.

"I … I am sorry," I say after her, not sure why, but somehow knowing that it's the right thing to do. "I am sorry I do not always say … always say the things you wish to hear."

She turns her body to mine and even from here I get lilacs and linen and freshly laundered cotton sheets. For the first time in the light where she stands, I notice dark shadows under her eyes, a drawn-in pinch to her skin. This, I tell myself, is what worry looks like.

Her eyelids flutter shut, briefly for one, two seconds of time only as behind her three women, an assortment of ages, hair colors, and heights, step up onto a small wooden stage, each of them clutching an acoustic guitar slung in soft leather straps over checked shirt shoulders.

"I'm your friend," Patricia says finally, opening her eyes once more.

"I know."

"I … I'm tired, Doc. I just get tired sometimes with it all. If you know you're my friend then you have to act like it, you have to act like you know what a friend is. I know it's hard for you but …"

I open my mouth to speak then halt, stunted, mute at what to say. What does a friend act like? Where is the blueprint for the role? Where are the manual and the instruction book?

Patricia slips her lips into a thin smile and I notice that her cell phone is still in her hand. Unsure what to do, I hold out my five fingers and, to my relief, Patricia reciprocates. "Are you sure you don't want a drink?"

"No." I pause. "Thank you."

She keeps her smile on me for a second longer then, dropping her arm and slipping her phone into her pocket, she turns and heads toward the bar.

Chris fiddles with the signal-blocking device, eyeing the band ahead as they set up. "Electric guitars do belt out some wattage. I should know—I play myself."

Wanting to avoid the odd lump in my throat, avoid the confusion I feel, I watch Patricia take her phone from her pocket and switch it on. I turn to Chris and, keen to try my habit at conversation, I pluck some facts from my brain. "Electric guitars rely on a ratio between wattage and decibels. Wattage is the power developed from current and voltage. For example, using the equation—"

Chris holds his palms aloft. "Okay, okay." He sighs. "I get it. I understand."

"You do?"

"Yup."

We sit in silence. Chris fiddles with the black box, I leaf through the copy of *1984* from the train, tracking any pattern I can find, tracing over the words, imprinting them to my brain. My fingers linger on the worn edges, old, weary.

After a minute passes, Chris lifts his head, eyes flickering briefly to Patricia. He shifts his body forward and I smell on him bread, spiced cologne, warm wine. "Maria?"

"What?"

"I've been thinking about the Weisshorn database." He clicks the button on the black device and a green light glows. The soft, silent rhythm of the beat.

"You have now blocked our signal?"

"Yep. No one should be able to hack into my system this time." He gulps his wine and shivers. "But I think there's a problem."

"What problem?"

"Okay, so, you remember on my laptop on the train when I was in the Weisshorn database and I thought they'd sent me a virus and that's how they found me—us?"

"Yes."

Again he shoots a glance to Patricia at the bar. "Well"—a shift in his seat, a slight shake to his normally steady fingers—"you see, once you fixed my blocker thing here, it gave me a chance to quickly look into exactly what had happened, you know, safely check the virus origin and everything so I could make sure it didn't happen again."

A strange ball of nerves builds in my stomach. "What is your point?"

"Well, I thought they might have known it was me on their database."

"That was an unsubstantiated assumption. An automatically set virus can penetrate any computer."

He shakes his head. "No. No, see that's the thing." He takes another, bigger mouthful of his drink, winces, then sets it down and when he speaks again his voice and his head are lowered. "That's the thing. Sure, there was a virus, but … there was something else, too."

A glass falls and shatters at the bar. We both jump.

Chris slaps his hand to his chest, swallows hard, and watching for a moment the tired bearded barman waddle to the front and sweep up the broken glass while muttering in French under his breath, he continues. "Okay … God, that made me jump. Okay, so … ah, yeah, the box. Right, well, the box, even though it couldn't block anything until you fixed it, it could still pick up signals. And now I've been able to access the data on it …"

He pauses. My palms sweat, but I don't know why. It's warm in here, but there's something else, something intangible that I'm strangely too scared to touch.

"Maria, there was also a separate signal transmitting to us from an actual device."

"Separate?"

"Yeah."

The room feels as if it's standing still while my brain does a rapid assessment of what the separate signal means. In the bar, the rustle, the guitars, the chatter—all of it falls away to just white noise as I begin to realize the implications of the transmitter.

"It is …" I falter, scared at the conclusion. "The signal is caused by another tracker."

Chris shuts his eyes. "Yes."

My breathing accelerates, pulse quickens. A tracker. Another tracker. Words, codes, numbers, and sounds. They all collide, one, two, three, bang, bang. Tracker. Tracker, tracker, tracker, tracker. When I finally part my lips and form words, my voice is scratched and torn and filled with fear.

"Are there cell numbers on—"

"Are there cell numbers showing up on the device?" A beat, a drop of his shoulders. "Yes." He throws a glance to where Patricia is now tapping her phone.

I direct my eyeline to my friend, to where she is staring at the band members who are getting set up to play. "Why … why are you looking at Patricia so much?"

He rakes a hand through his hair, once, twice. I tap my thumb, catch the band-aid on the edge of the table, a sting of pain shooting up my arm. Time feels suspended, a loud clock. Ticktock, ticktock.

Chris shakes his head, and when he finally speaks, even though I'm prepared for it, it shocks me to the core.

"One of our phones has a tracker on it." A beat, a pulse of time. "I'm sorry, Maria, but Patricia's phone could be it."

CHAPTER 13

DEEP COVER PROJECT FACILITY

Present Day

Air like thick, black ink oozes around me in the chamber.

"Hello?" I shout. Nothing. I try shouting again, louder this time, but still no one answers. The only vibration in the air is the rasp of my own breath.

Panic rises. Am I being imprisoned? Have I been tricked and this, now, is where I am to stay, like before at Goldmouth Prison in London with the guards and the hands and the sweat and the screams? I start to count to keep myself steady, up to ten then back down again, over and over, but it doesn't work and my heart rate rockets in a cascade of sticky perspiration.

I close my eyes and try to focus on something, but the air seems to press in around me, on my skin and face, up through the canals of my nostrils, and my voice shrieks out, yet it doesn't resemble my own, and I find myself thinking, why? Why is this happening to me? What have I done? My shoulders drop, exhaustion, resignation, the complete silence and blackness seeming to conjure in my head the faces of my family, dead, shrieking past me, and I am overcome by an almost overwhelming sensation that I'll never really have the energy to fight anyone or anything anymore. Adoption, Papa, the Project, the years of lies and exploitation. It all just seems too much. I am only one person in a sea of strangers.

My eyes open, but all I see is black. Heart rate shooting up again, I count: one, two, three, four, five, six, seven, eight, nine, ten. This is supposed to calm me here, now, this type of environment. I am finally free from sensory assaults and having to deal with them, and yet why do I feel more threatened than ever?

I don't know how much time passes, the chamber utterly disorientating with only my thoughts to fill the void. I think of Mama, of Papa and Ramon, then of Balthus, and though it pains me to see their faces, they appear normal as they always used to. But then my thoughts begin to change. I grip the edge of the seat, nails digging in, recite the Project's mantra, *Order and routine are everything. The Project is your only friend.* Yet still they come, the images—a river of colors and shapes.

At first, it is just Black Eyes I see. His face, his tree branch frame, appear in my mind as if they are real, as if here, now, I could reach out and touch him and feel the coarse sandpaper of his skin. But he is not looking at me. Instead, he stoops over a reclined leather surgeon's chair and in it lies a woman: the same woman from the pictures in his office. But her hair, instead of waterfalling down her back, is tied up in a ball high on her head, loose cotton tendrils falling down her neck to the caramel skin where her shoulder meets her arms. She is sweating. Her breath, when I listen, appears in short, sharp bursts and when I study her arm, I see a tourniquet, thick and brown, tied tight around the nook of her elbow.

Black Eyes stands and wipes his face, tears streaking in tiny columns of gray down his cheeks, and when he turns, the woman looks toward him with sleepy eyes and a complexion of wax and ash. Black Eyes flips open a folder and scratches out some notes then returns his attention to the woman.

"Samuel?" the woman's voice suddenly says, floating into the air like a smooth petal. I listen, silent, dark, feeling as if I'm eavesdropping on a conversation I should never hear.

"Samuel, is it working?"

Black Eyes. Dr. Carr.

He is Samuel.

Black Eyes swallows and his Adam's apple protrudes then sinks back in.

"Sarah," he begins, then trails off. He dabs sweat from his brow with a cornflower-blue handkerchief, hemmed with gold-colored thread. The woman's hand reaches out, forefinger and thumb landing onto the corner of the fabric. "Aisha gave you that."

He smiles, weak, thin, then slips the silk away into a pocket.

The woman's hand drops, arm falling, drifting down to her side. "Our daughter," she says. "They killed her, Samuel. This has to work. We have to stop it all happening."

"My love, you are not well."

She swallows a sip of water that he now holds to her cracked, dry lips. Done, her head flops back. "I am thirty-three. No one has ever made it to …"

Her words falter. I lean in, although, in the cavernous dark, there is nothing to lean in toward. No one has ever made it to what?

"Rest now," Black Eyes says, stroking the woman's brow. "We will run some more tests. There may be something that …" He clears his throat, smears dry his face. "There may be something we can do. Something the Project can do."

She smiles, but there is a sallowness to her cheeks, a slack weight to her chin and jaw. "My darling, there's nothing left to do. We've seen …" She coughs. Tiny specks of blood pepper her hand and when she tips back her skull, the rim of her nose is red. "I haven't got Asperger's, that's why it's not working on me … the drugs." She takes one more drop of water. "Aisha—she was the one it worked on." She was like … like you."

"But she was not Basque, not fully."

"Exactly, my darling, exactly. That's why we have to keep moving forward. The girl, the one the Ines woman gave to us."

"Maria."

"Yes. She is it, my darling, the test child."

"It was you," he says now, his head tilted so it suspends in the air; I think of a child's balloon floating in the sky, a lone head bobbing above water. "You were the one who predicted that people like Maria would be the key. Your blood—our blood, me, you. Basque people." His vision moves to a photograph nearby of a young girl. "She only saw the death." He smooths his fingers around the frame. "Our daughter's death."

"Help us all," the woman says.

He smiles, tears trickling. "I promise I will get the girl to the age we need her to be."

"Thirty years of age, Samuel—we need to get her past that. Treat her like … like the daughter you—we—lost." She coughs but when he goes to help, she bats him away. "In one breath we lose, and in another, we gain." Her shoulders drop and a breath, deep, pungent, expels from her chest. "We gain."

He cries now, Black Eyes, openly, tears rolling down his cheeks in small, glass balls that look as if they were blown with gold and silver foil.

"Don't cry," the woman says now, her voice weaker, more distant. "Make it work. I know you can. I married you because you are amazing."

"But you're the brains, my love. You helped set it all up—the Project."

"And you will continue it, Samuel, you. I know you will. Turn the Project into what we know it can be. Work with MI5, but watch them."

"I will."

They smile weakly at each other, Black Eyes reaching down, his calloused skin touching her satin-sheen palm one fingertip at a time until all five touch. I squint, bend in. Are they …? I inspect their fingers, the way the five of them are close, laid out to communicate a silent message, just like the way … just like the way …

"Patricia," my voice says, and as it rings out, the image of Black Eyes and his wife wobbles in my subconscious, flies and flits until it fades entirely to be replaced by a thick black screen of nothing.

My breathing becomes heavy, its rise and fall the only sound in the gloom.

"Patricia," I say. "Patricia." And I see her face, her lily skin, her broken, beaten body, and her head turns to mine on a cool tiled floor and whispers, "Nothing's ever what you think," as her fingers uncurl and from them floats a photograph. The same photograph on Black Eyes' desk. Of the woman and the girl.

Of his wife and daughter.

UNKNOWN VILLAGE, THE ALPS, SWITZERLAND
21 Hours and 35 Minutes to Project Reinitiation

Chris begins immediately to rip apart our phones, but I simply sit there, numb. I cannot unpeel my eyes from Patricia. She is still at the bar. Her face, her skin, her hair, her nails. Separate elements that join together to form one person visible from the outside and another hidden within. The world continues around me, the smells, the sounds, spinning on its axis, day turning to night, sun rising, moon fading, yet still I sit and think and worry.

"It could be her phone," I hear myself say amid the guitar music that now whispers through the air. "It could be her phone."

Chris briefly glances up to me, holding the torn phone items in his hand then gets back to work. By the time he has pulled apart every section he can, I feel numb. My eyes stumble down to the metal pieces in front of me and I instinctively count every item, murmuring the numbers of each small section, creating a rapid in-brain itinerary, but no matter how hard I search, no matter how many times I check and recheck the mechanical and electrical elements that create the cell mechanism, I cannot locate anything that indicates a clandestine transmitter. Our two phones are clear.

"I've got nothing," Chris says, throwing his torn phone to the table. The cover spins toward me; my palm reacts immediately, slamming down to halt the revolution. I then take the cell and lock it shut.

Chris watches me. He leans back then forward then bites down on his lip as if he is about to eat it. "We have to check."

I jump, lost in my own world of thought as if he were never there at all. "Check what?"

"I'm sorry, but we have to check Patricia's phone."

A deep, unidentifiable knot tightens in my stomach. I force my eyes to study my friend. Patricia's chin is propped up by the heel of her hand, and her elbow, where it attaches to the end of her long, milky limb, rests on the wooden bar where a half-empty beer sits, the bartender behind a wooden table wiping a glass with a white cotton cloth.

"She's not really your friend—that is what the woman on the train said to me." I look to Chris, a pocket of heat swaying between us. My cheeks burn. "Who was she referring to?"

He sighs. "I don't know. Patricia? Or maybe … maybe Isabella?"

"But why would she say that?" I anchor the tips of my fingers to the edge of the table. "I … you." I stop. "Why?"

He opens his mouth to speak, then lets out a long, slow sigh and, raising his fingers, rakes them through his hair. "I don't know."

"What do you not know?"

His sight locks on my fingertips. "This." He moves to spread his fingers to mine then seems to hesitate, and instead he picks up a SIM card. "All of it."

My eyes stay on his fingers before switching to the innards of the cell phones on the table. I don't know what to do. My friend. The tracker. None of it makes sense and it hurts. It hurts me—the thought of it, of what it could mean, that I am even now suspecting my friend, my first true friend among all of this.

My eyelids feel heavy. I am tired with it all and yet there is no end in sight, no stop or halt or slide to the finish, just an infinite line of lies and corruption. Both Chris and I take it in turns to stare at the ripped-up cells and Patricia.

"Inside," I find myself saying as the music sways around us, soft words, "I think, we are all made in the same way." Chris looks up but remains silent. He feels near to me, even though he is sitting on the other side of the table. I pick up a bit of cell phone innards. "I think we are built, like these devices, from the same blueprint; it's just that from time to time, adjustments happen and circuit alterations occur. So, does that make us different? Does that explain the reasoning behind people, behind their thoughts and actions and the things that they do? That they are simply wired in a similar yet unique way?"

Chris shakes his head and lets out a long, deep sigh. "We have to ask her."

"What?" Panic floods. "No." I shake my head. "No."

"Yes."

"No."

"Why?"

"Because … because it might not be her." A rush of heat and anger hits my head. "She is my friend."

"Okay, okay. Sorry." He holds up his hands, five fingers a piece, and for a moment this calms me. I sit back, leg jigging at it all, unable to make eye contact.

"Look, Maria, if—" He hesitates, bites on his lip, glancing at Patricia who is looking our way. Chris leans in, lowers his voice. "I'm sure, if there's a tracker on her phone, there's a good reason, okay? I mean, shit—the Project is fucking everywhere. They … they could have got hold of her phone at any time."

"How?"

"What?"

Jig, jig. "How could the Project snatch her phone? Our cells are with us all the time."

Chris opens his mouth to speak then closes it.

"I do not want my friend to be upset," I say after a moment, a moistness to my eyes that takes me by surprise.

"No." A beat. "It will be okay, you know."

"How can you know? *We* cannot predict the future, just wish for it."

"No, but I think it'll all be okay."

"How can you say that? Are you a mind reader? A time traveler?" I feel my pulse rise along with my voice. "Are you? Well, can you—"

"Maria, shh!" Chris' hand is on mine. He immediately whips it away. "I … I'm sorry."

I touch my hand where his fingers have just been as Chris rakes through his hair and mutters chastisements to himself. Skin. Another person's skin on mine, I realize with a jolt is not a sensation I am familiar with and yet, I miss it. Odd. How can you miss something you have never known?

I set down my hand and look at the primary-colored copy of *1984* on the table as a possibility strikes me. "She could be in trouble."

"Hey? Who, Patricia? In what way?"

"The woman at the station who gave her this book"—I pick up *1984*—"she could have planted something on Patricia."

"I guess, but how would there have been the time, you know, to place the tracker?" He pauses. The door to the tavern opens and closes, a small flurry of snow blowing in. "We can't say anything, you know."

"I do not understand."

"I mean … I mean we can't say anything about the tracker to Patricia, not just yet." He starts to sweep away the pieces of our phones, clip them back together. "We know there's an issue, so we'll be careful, and I have the black box to block signals, but we don't want to … worry her. Not yet."

I consider his words. Why do I feel as if I want to cry? "She …
she does have a propensity to worry."

"Exactly. So"—he searches my face—"we won't mention it for
now, until we know more. Deal?" He snaps my SIM card into place,
slides my phone to me. "Maria?"

I begin to reply then stop, because in my head I cannot help
but try to calculate an answer, attempt to compute how a tracker at
the station could have been secretly planted on Patricia's cell. But
in the end, all I come up with is speculation until, desperate for
something, for any lifeboat of an idea, I look to my friend where she
nurses a half-empty beer at the bar and yet, despite all I do, despite
my intelligence and my order of facts, I come up with nothing.

"You okay?"

I look to Chris as he checks on me, and even though I want
to reply, I am numb, unable to articulate myself. His words as he
speaks to me, as he repeats his request on my status, evaporate into
the air, and in the center of the room, the fire burns and the wood
in the grate chars to black.

CHAPTER 14

DEEP COVER PROJECT FACILITY

Present Day

The door to the chamber flies open. I blink, eyes assaulted by the sudden bright light that floods in.

"You can come out now," Black Eyes says. The officer stands close by.

I do as ordered, wobbling a little so I have to hold the heel of my palm to the wall.

"Just a side effect of your treatment," Black Eyes says. "Nothing to worry about." He flicks his fingers. "Come."

I step into the main room, a strange ripple through my muscles and spine, and sit in a leather chair the color and texture of butter.

"Tell me what you saw in there." Black Eyes draws in a long line of oxygen, his chest swelling beneath the cloak of his white coat, rising then dropping as, pen in hand, he clicks a fingernail to the metal part of the chair.

"I saw … people. I … I saw things." I rub my brow—odd, woozy. When I blink, the room sways and I think of the drugs I am being given, the Typhernol. Is that affecting me now?

Black Eyes sits upright, his mouth cut into his crinkled skin and I try to focus on him, to stop the tide of nausea that now comes. I slap my fingers to my nose. There is a stink, thick, overpowering, of medical swabs and clinical sutures.

"I want to know exactly what you saw, Maria. Time to us is crucial now."

I want to ask him how his wife died, where his daughter is buried, but something is warning me not to.

"Subject 375—Maria—I require you to answer my question." He leans in. "This is for you, here. This is your therapy."

He sits back, clicks the steel of his pen. "You must now talk."

UNKNOWN VILLAGE, THE ALPS, SWITZERLAND
21 Hours and 27 Minutes to Project Reinitiation

The guitar music drifting in waves in the warm air, Patricia wanders over and slips back into the seat next to me and smiles. Both Chris I and remain silent. Our cell phones are reassembled, all pieces slotted away. I want so much to tell Patricia our findings. I want to speak to her and converse with her and tell her how worried I am, how this tavern and its spiced wine smell and hearth is fuzzing my brain, how, when Chris speaks, I have such a strong urge to nestle into his chest that it almost overwhelms me, and most of all—most of all—I want to ask her about the tracker and have her tell me that she has nothing to do with it, that it was planted and that everything is going to be okay.

But I don't do that. Instead, I watch her, scan her body and count in my head as a nervous ball of elastic tightens in my stomach. The gaps in her teeth. The three black holes in a rosebud mouth, a mouth that, when she moves, seems to shine in the glow of the low lights that pulse out yellow and orange across the wash of wood entombing the tavern. One second of time, two. She is supposed to be my friend but now I am too scared to admit to myself what the opposite of that could mean. Is enemy the only option?

"Hey, Doc," she says, "look, I'm sorry about before."

I snap out of my reverie and, for a moment, I am temporarily confused. "What … Sorry for what?" Chris flicks me a glance then quickly looks away.

"For the way I … the way I walked away, you know, before." She shifts in her seat, pulls at her ear.

"But you did not walk away. You walked to the bar. To get a drink."

She breathes in, a frown fixed on her face and for a second, it seems as if she may say something, may even get cross, but then her features break out into a smile, a smile that fills not only her face, but, it feels, engulfs the whole room.

Spreading her fingers out to mine, Patricia remains close to me then, exhaling hard, she slips her phone from her pocket and places it on the table. I touch it and notice, oddly, that it is warm, as if it has been used for a prolonged length of time. Chris catches my eye and this time I do not look away until a bleep sounds from his computer tablet.

An alarm bell rings inside me. "What is it?"

He scratches his cheek. "I'm … I'm not sure." He swivels the tablet round. "So, I ran a quick program on this earlier, you know, just to check everything's okay, using the blocker, double-checking for any more viruses, when, well, look—this came up."

The alarm tolls loud. "It is the age clock timer again."

Patricia immediately looks over. "What? There's two of them? But, I don't get it, how—"

"There's a duplicate clock."

"Shit." Patricia stares at the tablet. "That … that doesn't sound good." I glance to her hands; her fist is clenched white.

A prickle of concern travels over me as I study the clock. "Where has it come from?"

Chris punches out a breath. "I have no idea, but there's a number code linked to it every time I hover the cursor over. I don't want to click on it yet in case it triggers another virus."

"Yet the black transmission device, the blocker you have, is working?" I ask.

"Huh? Oh, yeah."

"Then how did this new clock appear here?"

In the tavern, the fire flames lick the hearth, the barman pours wine into small glass goblets, and to the side, the band on the stage beyond plays a low-slung song with lullaby voices made of silk scarves and chocolate. My brain registers it all, filtering it, checking faces for familiarity, my foot tapping slightly to skim off the anxiety inside me. I feel uncentered, as if everything I thought was set has suddenly been blown to pieces.

Patricia slides nearer to me, and giving me a small, compact smile that I cannot decipher, she points to my notebook.

"Doc, why don't you check in here, see if there's anything that can help? If the Project is after us"—her eyes do a loop around the tavern—"we'll have to go soon. There probably isn't much time left."

"What makes you say that?" Chris says.

"What d'you mean?"

"How d'you know we haven't got much time left?"

"What ... how ..." She stops. "What the fuck are you on about? I just meant there's never any time left. Jesus ..."

My brain sparks at her penultimate word. "Time."

Patricia turns. "What?"

"Time, time, time," I mutter to myself, tearing open my notebook and locating a page where an algorithm sits from a dream I had in prison. "Time." I run my finger down the page, over the words, past the drawings and sketches then look straight to Chris.

"Talk to me, Google."

"Two thousand and five—the number of deceased subject numbers from Hamburg." I jab at the page open in front of me. "Read this."

Chris looks at the notebook. I can smell his sweat, the sugary baked-bread of his skin, and think again of how much I like him, without fully understanding why—or what to do about it.

"Is this what I think it is?" he says after three seconds pass.

"Yes," staring at the dark hairs on his skin, counting their pattern. "It is something I dreamt of a long time ago, a time frame algorithm I used in prison to break into MI5's database. We can use it to get through the duplicate clock without being found."

"It could work."

"Yes."

"Can you do it?"

I pause, a mild headache forming between my eyes. "Yes."

He spins the laptop round to me. "Go for it."

It takes me ten seconds. No more. My fingers are rapid, tapping at such a speed that my eyes barely register what they are doing, my brain working so fast that my breath has to catch up, and when I am finished, when I flop back and blink at the access I have created, I start to shake.

All together, we peer at the screen as, before us, the seconds tick down and down to a date when I was born to a woman I have never met, whom I may not ever be able to know or trust.

"Hey," Patricia says after a few seconds, "what ... what's that?"

Chris frowns, leaning in a little further as, slowly, an image rolls onto the screen pixel by pixel. A face. Familiar, well-known. "Jesus. That's what the duplicate links to?"

Patricia's mouth drops open. "Oh, my God."

My whole body has gone rigid, chest barely inhaling, because the face staring back at us is someone familiar, someone we have to try and trust.

Harriet Alexander. Balthus' wife.

The home secretary of the United Kingdom.

DEEP COVER PROJECT FACILITY
Present Day

I do as Black Eyes says and talk.

One word after another, I reproduce every single detail of what my mind saw in the chamber—the photograph, the wife, the daughter, the words spoken. When I finish, I notice my hands are shaking, my skin is perspiring, and my foot, when I glance down to it, is tapping rapidly.

"Here," Black Eyes says, leaning forward and, a flask in hand, he holds out a cup of steaming hot coffee. "Take it, you are cold."

I reach out and clasp my fingers around the metal, feeling the sting of the warmth. I take a sip. The liquid slides down my throat.

"Better?"

I swallow. Hot, strong, good. "Yes."

"It is a good therapy for subjects, the deprivation chamber, helping you to have time out from the everyday sensory overstimulations."

He regards me for a while, not moving until I drain the cup, and, handing it back to him, he screws it back onto the flask, placing it to the right side of his chair.

"You know," he says now, a small smile drawn on his lips, "the brain creates its own reality in the darkness. When there is no sensory input whatsoever, the brain guesses what it can see, hear. When our senses no longer give our brains any new data, it continues to use what it knows." He pauses. "In the chamber, your brain generated its own reality."

I touch my scalp. "But what I saw felt real …"

"What you saw was the brain creating a world to replace one that didn't, for that short moment inside there, exist."

"I saw the photograph. It was the same one as on your desk."

"Yes, and your brain recalled that and then used it when all other sensory input was nonexistent, to create a new vision for you to see. Even though there was nothing to see at all."

Heat rushes up my spine, to my neck, head. "So I saw … a hallucination?"

"Correct."

"Did you take Project drugs as I do? Did your wife?"

His eyes flutter shut for one second then reopen, glistening. "Maria, what you saw was not real. It's what our minds do. What you saw was made up, make-believe." He reaches forward and I think he's going to touch me when, instead, his hand lands on his knee. "She was real," he says after a moment. "My wife, the one you saw in the photograph. She was, once, the love of my life. But what your brain conjured in there?" He delivers me a direct stare. "That was a complete hallucination."

Make-believe. Unreal. I contemplate the words, run through the dynamics of the theory, yet no matter which way I turn it, no matter how much I attempt to extract some clue or secret unearthed from deep within my brain, the only conclusion that can be reached is that he is right. Black Eyes is right. I look back to the chamber, find myself oddly wishing I was back in there, hidden by the sensory barrier it provided, enclosed in the peace it gave me away from the regular world, when I begin to recall something. A thought … No. So, what? A memory?

At first, it appears as simply a flicker but then, a second or two later, it is a fully-fledged flame that burns bright in my head.

Chris, Patricia—the three of us in the Alps. Something about a timer … no, two timers and the face of someone I know. I try to pinpoint the memory, grab onto it, but the effects of the chamber, the Typhernol I am taking jumble me up and it's hard to lock down what I recall.

"My age," I say, the word tumbling from my mouth, unexpected, rogue. "The woman—your wife—she was the same age as I am now."

"That was just your mind playing tricks, Maria. As I said."

"No. No, I remember a clock."

Black Eyes' knuckles run white. "What clock? In the chamber?"

"No."

"Where?"

"I ..."

"Where?" he asks, louder.

I flinch, trip over my words. "In Switzerland." A heartbeat of recollection. Chris. A computer device. The warm fug of wood and wine. "Why is my birthday important?"

"It ..." His teeth clench then release. When finally he speaks, there is a glaze in his eyes, a steel tip to his tongue. "Maria, enough now. I have explained to you that everything you saw in there was nothing but your brain generating its own show. You have just been under sensory deprivation therapy. You are on Typhernol to help you relax." His eyes narrow and when he speaks, his voice slithers like the hiss of a snake from his lips. "Stop insisting on asking these questions when there is only one answer. Do you understand?"

I shiver. Chris. The scent of baked bread and aftershave. Patricia. Her broken, bloodied body—the enemy. A clock ticking loudly in my head. The number thirty-three. They all collide together in my mind in meteorites of thought that want so badly to connect.

"Subject 375! I said, do you understand?"

I jump, grip my seat tight. "Yes."

His shoulders drop, and from his mouth billows an invisible cloud of stale garlic odor. "I shouted," he says. "Please, forgive me."

I look left, right, not knowing what to do, the worrying part of me suddenly very frightened.

"Maria," he says, this time softer, slower, "do you understand that what you saw in the chamber was a trick of the brain, not real?"

I swallow. "Yes."

He nods and presses a yellow button. "Good," he says, exhaling in the cold air. "Good." The entrance bell buzzes and the intelligence officer from earlier strides in. He leans to Black Eyes and whispers in his ear. I sit, wait, contemplate the prospect that what I saw in the chamber was not real, and yet, each time I do, my mind struggles, for a split second, to believe it was far from a hallucination and instead was a memory, a real, true memory from the past.

From my past.

The intelligence officer moves to the side as Black Eyes now unfurls himself from his seat and raises a finger in the air. "Come, Maria, there is a situation—we are needed."

CHAPTER 15

21 Hours and 1 Minute to Project Reinitiation

Patricia's mouth hangs open. "Oh, my God. What's Harriet Alexander doing on the bloody screen?"

Chris is flapping his hands, trying to figure out the situation. "It … it. Shit. It connects to a live feed to her office. How the hell did that happen? Shit." He panics and tries to shut down the computer tablet, but it remains stubbornly intact. "It's not working. Why's it not working?"

I snatch it from him, do what I can, but still the image of the home secretary remains on the screen, and even when we clamp the computer shut and reopen it, the picture is still there.

"Oh fuck. There's an eye and it's moving," Chris says, voice high, "just like the one that sprang up back at my place in Montserrat. Oh fuck, oh fuck."

"You are panicking," I say, tapping the keys, not looking up. "You need to lower your voice and take a breath. Cup your hands in front of your mouth and breath."

While Patricia calms Chris, I work quickly and quietly. Chris is right. There is an eye on the screen just like the one in Montserrat, but this one is different. I track it. I follow the groove of the skin that creeps under the socket and, when the lashes flap and the black pin of the retina widens, I lean in, inspect everything I can see. The picture of the home secretary appears to connect to a live, real-time feed somehow in her office, yet what we are seeing now is just a still image. Sweat trickles down my spine to the base of my back.

I look to the camera. "Is this on?" I say, tapping the webcam at the top of the device.

Chris drops his hands. "What? Oh. What? No."

"Turn it on."

"So we can … so we can see in her office? Nah." He shakes his head. "No. No way."

"Yes. There is an eye on the screen similar to the one that linked last time to Black Eyes and the Project. Accessing the home secretary's office, therefore, may be helpful."

He tracks the outline of my face, flips his eyes to Patricia and her cell then looks back to me. "Fuck it." He sits up, straight and quickly. "Okay, this," he says, grabbing the tablet and tapping the lens, "means … okay so, it means we can see in, but, trouble is, use it and we risk being seen ourselves."

"Can you ensure we are not detected in the government system?"

He leans back a little and rubs his head. "Hmm, I did devise a program once that can get you into webcam systems undetected. It *might* work here."

"Guys, no." Patricia says.

"Do it," I say, ignoring her, a ripple in my gut.

Patricia blinks at me. Chris blows out a breath. "You sure?"

"We just witnessed the home secretary of the United Kingdom appear on your device and the image merge with the same one we saw on the computer at your house in Montserrat. If the Project is in receipt of the knowledge that Harriet Alexander possesses the file that incriminates the entire program, she could be in danger. Do it."

Chris chews on his lip then circles his gaze around the bar; everything is as it was before. Warm wine, half-finished glasses of beer, licking flames and a now-silent band chattering indecipher-able small talk over a drink before they play their next song. "Okay. Let's do it."

"Doc," Patricia says, whispering just to me, "do you really think this is a good idea? I mean, this is the home secretary—this is risky."

Normally, I would answer immediately what I think, but I am spooked. Is this what it is like for neurotypical people? Second-guessing each other's intent based on words that aren't spoken, on gestures that are and are not made? Chris says that he has safely readjusted the camera lens via a program to what we can see on the screen. Relieved to not have to speak, I lean in, study it, and when I do, it is not the eye or a code or even a series of complex algorithms presented to us, but the plush mahogany and leather office of the UK home secretary.

"Jesus Christ, Chris!" Patricia says. "What the fuck have you gone and done? What's that?" She points to a small green box to the top right of the screen.

"Huh? Oh, that's a program that automatically accesses her emails when she logs in."

She rolls her eyes. "Sweet Jesus."

"What? It's just a small hack."

Why did Patricia roll her eyes? What does that mean? Does that mean she is hiding something or does it mean she is … is annoyed?

"Small?" Patricia is now spluttering at Chris. "Small? Fucking hell, you've hacked her computer and that's her bloody office. In. The. Government!"

Worried what everything signifies, I lean in and look at the well-dressed figure that crosses the screen like a shadow. "Can she see us?"

Chris shakes his head. "Nope."

"Is the connection secure, undetectable?"

"Yep. Pinged around the world, backed by my program—we're as good as invisible."

I hear Patricia swear. I am concerned that she is angry, unsure as to why she would feel that way, but all the time my eyes remain on the screen. Harriet Alexander is typing on her computer, the activity log of it tracked by a small green light that flashes in the corner of the visual. Her long flame-red hair licks round her shoulders, coiffured, no gray for her fifty-five years, Parisian-smart. She is wearing a cream blouse and a crisp navy blazer with gold buttons and neat stitching. Her skin, alabaster white, is sprinkled with a crop of freckles that butterfly across her nose and cheeks, and when she scratches her brow, fine crepe-paper lines fan out in delicate feathers over a heart-shaped face. She pops on a pair of thick, square glasses with a dark brown frame.

"What's she doing?" Patricia asks, slinking back into toward the table. Her fingers linger on her cell.

Chris surveys a program open on the top right of the screen, a scanner that tracks usage. "Reading files," he says, cross-checking something. "But I can't tell what. Hang on …"

He taps the keys, blows out a puff of air that makes a stray strand of hair billow upward then remain there, stuck in a one finger salute to the screen. I suppress the intense urge to reach forward and dab it back down.

"Oh shit."

"What?"

"It's … no, that can't be."

I lean in. "What?" He looks up, his face drained suddenly of color. "Is your leg hurting?"

"Huh? What? Oh, no. It's just that …" He scratches his cheek where the stubble, once shaven for camouflage, is now pushing upward. "She's been hacked."

"Uh, yeah—duh," Patricia says, "by you."

"No. Well, yeah, but no. There's …" He halts, stares at Patricia, flips to me then, swallowing, squints at the screen. "All we have to do … Oh fuck. There's someone else in her system."

I feel the nerves in my spine sprint at speed. Patricia moves in too, asks what's going on, and I find myself confused, wondering whether the reason she wants to know what is happening may be different to mine. "Can you see what they are accessing?"

Chris shakes his head. "I don't know … I … wait." He reads fast, taps the screen program. "Okay, so there's someone else who's hacked in and … Jesus …" He looks up. "Whoever it is, they're reading the email, the one I sent from Madrid airport, you know, the one with all the files from the Project? They're reading it right now."

"Stop them," I say.

"Doc, no, that's dangerous. You can't just—"

"Wait!" We turn. "Her phone's buzzing."

Chris swivels the tablet as, bending in as far as possible, we all watch Harriet Alexander pick up the vibrating phone on her desk

"This is daft," Patricia says. "And private. Turn it off."

"They're still reading her emails," Chris whispers. "Whoever has accessed this is still in there."

"Find out who they are."

"I'm trying!"

The home secretary clutches the phone to her ear. "… No, I haven't spoken to Ruth Quo yet …"

Patricia mutters, "Jesus, that's the head of MI5."

Chris' head whips up. "What did you say?"

"What?"

"Just now. You said 'head of MI5.' How do you know that?"

"What? Like I shouldn't know that? Everyone knows that. How do *you* know that?"

The two of them stare at each other for one second, two, Patricia pulling her sleeve over her fingers and fiddling with the thread, Chris just glaring at her, and I am unsure what to do, what to say. I only breathe out when Harriet Alexander's clipped tones break the silence.

"… They are trying to eliminate her," the home secretary says now. "Her name is Maria Martinez … Yes, yes, that's what I said in my email to her, that we know her mother's alive …"

"I've got the number of who she's speaking to," Chris says. He taps some keys. "It's … the deputy prime minister."

Patricia's fingers cease pulling her sleeve. "Are … are you sure?"

"Yes."

Nerves ripple inside me, making stronger and stronger waves. Something is not right—all these people, the tracker. I breathe, count to three, try to center myself, and as I do, I am surprised to find my sight locking not on Patricia for an anchor, but instead on Chris. "Is someone else still hacking the home secretary's files?"

He nods. I inhale his scent and feel calmer.

On the screen, the home secretary, phone still fixed to her ear, now has a frown cemented to her forehead. I watch her, attempting to determine what her facial expressions may mean, but no matter how hard I try, no matter what learned aspects I recall, I reach a blank, the human face a code I'll never be able to crack.

Ms. Alexander's voice floats back into the air. "… We have to investigate this, Geoff. Yes, now … what? No. We keep this between us until we have all the evidence we need, then we involve the prime minister's office. The more removed he is from this right now, the better, but we have to help this girl, she was …" She falters and presses together her lips. "I'm sorry. It's just that she was Balthus' …" She pauses, inhales. "Look, I feel I owe her, this Maria. I feel I should … help her … but look, the woman at the Swiss hospital we have the chatter on—Isabella Bidarte—intelligence is saying she's in trouble. And I don't know if we can keep her safe. She may be crucial to the investigation."

I grip the table. My real mother is in trouble and this woman wants to help me, us. This woman who was married to Balthus, who I have never met, gave me what I wanted all along to hear—that my biological mother is alive, but now she says may not be safe. But

I'm unsure. I look again at Harriet Alexander's face on the screen, her eyes downturned, her brow creased, hair sliding in red ribbons down her shoulders. A face can speak a thousand sentences without ever uttering one word, and yet each, to me, is a foreign language. On the camera, the home secretary is talking on the phone now about the budget deficit and the treasury.

"I'm in," Chris suddenly says.

I glance round. "In where?"

"See this?" He points to the live program square on the tablet. "So this? This tracks the entire thing, you know, Harriet Alexander's emails, who sees them. It's like a worm—burrowed deep, so far you can't even tell it's there, and when it's in, it grows big and fat. I've set up a tracker here so when it finds who's hacking her stuff, we'll see them straight away."

"A tracker," I say. Chris fidgets in his seat, eyeing me, eyeing Patricia, but I don't mention the word again, and I wonder if I have been so burnt by the truth in the past that I'm too scared to face it in the present. I focus on the screen. There is a small blue oblong at the bottom left corner of the screen and next to it a series of numbers. "The numbers cast a link directly to the hacker."

Chris smiles. "Yes. God, how d'you know so much? Yeah, it's like a fishing line—as soon as they bite, the link pulls them out of the water and we see who it is."

Harriet Alexander continues talking on the phone. Her voice is deep, gravelly. I think of fast cars and diesel engines. "… No, no, I want to lead on that … Yes, I'll be in touch with MI5 and find out what they know. No, this all has to be kept quiet for the moment while we investigate …"

"Whoa," Chris says.

Patricia looks. "What?"

"Maria," Chris says. "We have a bite."

"A bite?" My eyes fall to where he points at the bottom left of the screen. At first, there are simply digits appearing, fast, rolling in a continuous stream within the confines of the box, but then they change, pixelating into lines, then letters.

Then words. Two solitary words.

"Weisshorn Hospital," my voice says into the warmth of the tavern air.

"Doc, isn't that the one—?"

"Where her mom's being held," Chris says.

I look at him. "That is who's in the home secretary's system right now—the Weisshorn Hospital?"

"Yes."

The blood drains from my face. "The Project is there," I say, a shake to my voice. "They are at the hospital where my mother is."

On the screen, the home secretary is reading an email, her eyes wide.

"Doc, you definitely can't go to the hospital now," Patricia says, words whipping out fast. "This Alexander woman said she wanted to help you, but if the Project is at the hospital in some way or another, Doc, you can't go there. Please. Harriet Alexander may know the head of MI5, but the Project is way worse. Go back"—her shoulders drop, thumbnail digging into her forefinger—"go back to London. You'll be … you'll be safe there."

Chris taps his phone. Patricia frowns.

I look at them both, confused at what their faces and actions signify. I try really hard to interpret it, but it's all too much. I pick up the photograph of me from the cellar, a baby in arms. "Everyone has died," I say, my voice detached from me, floating, as if it's not mine, not a part of me. "I … I cannot let her die, too."

"Doc, you can't save everyone."

"I do not want to save everyone." I touch the outline of Isabella's sunlit hair. "I want to save my real mother. And you heard what the home secretary said—Isabella may be crucial to the investigation, the investigation to cull the Project."

"Guys?" Chris says, cutting into my thoughts. "Um, look." He has the screen turned to us. "I know the hacker's in there, but my program allows me to read emails." He wipes his mouth. "I can read the email the home secretary's looking at right now."

Slowly, the message Harriet Alexander is reading scrolls open on the screen in front of us one line at a time until, finally, the entire script appears.

Chris glances to me and slowly, we both stare at the message on the screen then we look to Patricia.

We look to the woman who says she is my friend.

CHAPTER 16

"They're blackmailing her," Chris says. "The Project is blackmailing the home secretary. Holy fuck."

"This has to be wrong," Patricia says. "Chris, you're not supposed to hack like this and find out—"

"Hang on!" Chris scratches his cheek. "Let me see if I can …"

He taps the keyboard and, after two seconds, the email appears in a blue square by the top right corner. Harriet Alexander's face stares forward with cheeks drawn and teeth biting down on red lips.

Patricia reads aloud from the words that appear on the computer. "We know about your deceased husband's affair. We know he had an illegitimate child with a woman he was not married to … If you …" She halts. "Holy Jesus. Can they do this? They can't do this." She looks to Chris. "Can *you* do this?"

"I can."

I nod. "He can. He did." I point. "See?"

"What? No, Doc, I meant—"

"If you begin any investigation into Project Callidus or any of its activities, we will leak the story," Chris says over Patricia, continuing to read the confidential email. "If you contact MI5 about the file that you have from your husband's illegitimate daughter, Maria

Martinez, we will leak the story. If you do anything that implicates any member of the Project, past or present, we will leak the story." Chris stops, flops back to his seat and exhales hard. "My God, this could ruin her. I mean, this could ruin her career."

I read the email again, uncertainty and worry colliding. "I do not understand. How could you draw that conclusion?"

"She's a politician. She is—was, sorry—married, happily, by all accounts, so if this story got out, that Balthus had an affair that ended up in an illegitimate child—in you—never mind the whole Project connection, well, that kind of secret can wreck a career, especially for someone so high up in politics."

It still it makes no sense. "Why would the fact that I exist damage the home secretary's career?"

"Doc, because people care about what other people think of them. People think that we all should behave in a certain way."

"Why? Why should it matter?" I genuinely am flummoxed by this.

She sighs. "I don't know, but it does."

"It should not matter what people think of each other."

Chris nods. "Well said, but not everyone is immune to the bullshit that is society, like you are."

"Then more people should be like me."

A smile breaks out on his face. "Maybe they should."

I stare at him, at the sunken contours of his cheeks, at the stray hair on the cling film sheen of his skin. Why, when I am near him, do I feel the intense propulsion to draw back his hair from his eyes and bury my head in the nook of his neck?

"So," Patricia says, "if the home secretary's reading the email now, all the implications of it, the shit storm it throws, tell me: why is she not reacting?"

I watch the screen, curious. "I do not understand. What do you mean by 'she is not reacting?'"

Patricia points. "Here, see? Her forehead? If you're concerned about something, worried, say, you kind of frown, right? And that means you get crinkle lines on your brow. But her?" She shrugs. "Nothing. Her mouth's not even moved or anything."

I study Harriet Alexander's face. "So what does that mean?"

"It means," Chris says now, head tilted, observing the screen, "she's somehow not surprised at reading any of the information on the blackmail message."

"D'you think she knows more than she's letting on?"

Chris looks to Patricia. "It's definitely possible."

I observe my two friends, consider carefully their words. How can so much be interpreted from so little? Is such whimsical body and facial language meaning not open to wild—and dangerous—misinterpretation and then I think: is that what I have done with Patricia, just in my own way? Have I analyzed the facts, slotted data together and let myself be convinced by Chris that Patricia could be linked to the tracker? And if so, what are Chris' motives and why? Did Balthus really know who Chris was? Do I really know who Patricia is? Aaaaargh. The questions fly around me so fast until they spin at such a speed that it gets too much. When the music from the band starts again and combines with the clink of distant glasses and the beep of the computer tablet and the fire flames and the slurps and the crunch of crispy baguettes, I start to rock a little in my seat and raise my hands to my ears.

"Doc? Doc, what are you doing?"

When I can't reply, Patricia drops her voice, spreads her fingers. "Doc, can you hear me? Breathe. There's just a lot to take in, but just breathe through it. Count. You can do this."

I watch her lips, eyes flit to Chris and the frown on his face, see his fingers too are fanned to five, and my chest starts to slow, my brain rattle decreases. When, finally, the information in me settles, I inch my hands from my ears.

"A little better now?" Patricia asks.

I nod.

She smiles, but there are no eye creases, so I can't tell if she's happy or sad or something else. She turns to Chris. "Harriet Alexander knew about Maria's mother at Weisshorn. She told her Isabella was alive."

"Yeah, well," Chris says, flicking one last key. "I reckon she took a risk there to tell Maria that because ... Oh no."

Patricia frowns. "What?"

"Oh shit."

"What?"

He swallows, points. "This."

On the tablet screen, emails, one after another, are flying onto the screen inbox from Harriet Alexander's private online account. Each one of them contains another threatening message, linking to my existence and to the existence of my biological mother.

"Jesus," Chris says, "no wonder she wasn't surprised to get that email. They've been blackmailing her for ages." He squints at the email subject lines. "So the one we've just seen probably came as no surprise to her."

Patricia sits very still, eyes wide. "That's why she didn't react shocked or anything."

"Maria—look." Chris jabs the screen. "I've run the program on the emails and they all seem to originate—every single one of these messages—from Weisshorn, just like the email to her does today. And ..." he hesitates when he glances to Patricia, "I found this."

An image of a face emerges on the computer, pixelated at first then sharp, and as it comes to full view, I intake a sharp breath at the unexpected sight.

I lean in and read the name that sits underneath the image. "Isabella Bidarte."

"Oh, my God," Patricia says, "is that her? Now? Is that your ma?"

I take the old, worn photograph and flatten it on the table. My fingers are shaking a little.

Chris watches me. "Hey, want me to hold that?"

But I am unable to speak, concerned that if I do, I may yelp or yell. I scan the image of my mother on the screen. Her hair, still long, now flows over her shoulders and down her back in gray and silver streams, her skin once pearlescent, now muted and flat, and over her brow and mouth and by the jowls of her jaw hang wrinkles in strings of skin that wash up against the receding hairline of her scalp. Gone is the skimming skirt, the bare feet on stones, and in their place is a pale blue jumpsuit of cord and burlap, a rough cut of fabric that bunches by swollen ankles connected to feet encased in black boots so thick that the leather appears as if it has been stitched with thread made of metal.

My throat feels rough, dry, and when I swallow the now-lukewarm wine I feel a strange lump in my esophagus, small and round, like a pebble.

"Is it her?" Patricia asks me.

I carry out a rapid facial recognition match in my brain comparing the image here with the one from the cellar. "The two faces are the same person."

Chris and Patricia share a look as my sight, now oddly watery, remains locked on the face of the old and tired woman who peers out at me with eyes that once sparkled but now stare in downturned ovals of washed-out gray.

"Well," Chris says after a second, "at least when we get to Weisshorn, you'll know what she looks like."

Patricia shakes her head. "No. No way. We're not still going."

"Why?" Chris asks.

"What? Because it's too risky, that's why."

I keep my eyes on Isabella's face. "We have to go there."

"Doc, no."

"Yes."

"What are we going to do about the blackmailing?" Chris says. "If the home secretary doesn't order an investigation into the Project because of it, then we're back to square one."

I touch my notebook. All the codes and dreams and distant

drugged memories—they are the origins of who I am, the very beginning of the Project. I contemplate the thought, roll it over in my mind until the answer, the solution appears bright, fresh, and fully formed.

"It is all connected to the source. If the emails are being sent from Weisshorn, by going there we will be able to destroy the source. And if, as we predict, the source of the blackmailing messages is someone from the Project, then if we eliminate them, we eliminate the blackmailing."

Chris grins. "You're a genius."

"Yes," I say, matter-of-fact. "My IQ is higher than that of Albert Einstein's."

He blinks at me for a second, mouth half open. "Um, so if we go"—he clears his throat—"if we go to Weisshorn where the Project is and we stop their blackmailing source, like you say, then we can redirect the messages."

Patricia starts tapping a finger on the table. "What d'you mean?"

Again Chris hesitates. I try to interpret his facial expression— the way his brows wrinkle, the way his mouth hangs slightly open and then his teeth bite down on his bottom lip.

"We compile new messages," he says now, "so it looks as if they're halting the blackmailing, backtracking on it. We can send the home secretary an email that looks like it's from the Project, via Weisshorn, saying that, I don't know, something huge has happened and they need her on their side so they won't be blackmailing her anymore. That way, she's free to investigate Callidus."

"But why would she just go, 'Sure. Okay,'" Patricia says, "and accept that explanation out of the blue?"

"What? You'd rather stall and do nothing?" A beat. "Why would you want to do that?"

"I never said I wanted to stall."

"But you're questioning what I'm doing."

"You're questioning what I'm doing."

"No, I'm not."

"Yes, you are."

Chris blows out a breath, flicks his eyes to me then to Patricia then shakes his head, throwing up his hands. I watch, unsure what is happening.

Patricia holds her chin high, whips a nod then speaks. "How about if the message has a clause that says they will keep the illegitimate daughter story out of the press if, say, the investigation the government carries out is kept away from the public arena. It can acknowledge they know she's already been talking to the deputy prime minister, and that, for the Project, that's serious shit. You know, so the message can say she can investigate, but the Project tells her to just keep it, well-hidden from view, away from the public eye, that way it seems as if the Project is cooperating, finally, but not too much, not so out of the blue. Surely that seems more plausible?" She stares at Chris. "And *not* stalling at all?"

Chris rolls his eyes. "I guess … I guess it's a good idea."

"Thank you."

Another eye roll. "So, you're talking about asking a politician to keep secrets from the voting public?" He shrugs. "Yeah, I'd say it's plausible."

We look to the screen, to Harriet Alexander's ivory freckled face.

"So, we're going then?" Patricia says after a moment, "We're going to this Weisshorn place in Geneva?"

I nod, "Yes."

"And there's no way … there's no way I can talk you out of it?"

I start packing up all my belongings into my rucksack. "No."

She presses together her lips but doesn't reply.

As Chris shuts down the computer, Patricia shakes her head and sighs, then, tutting, begins to gather her belongings. Done, she stands. "I'm going to nip to the loo first. Doc, you okay? You got everything?"

I stand, too. "Yes."

"Okay." A glimmer of something crosses her face, but I'm unsure what look it is. "See you in a sec."

Chris watches Patricia leave and, as soon as she's out of sight, he pulls himself up and turns to me. "We mustn't say anything about the tracker yet, agreed?"

I glance to the toilet door, to the band where they're too now packing up, to the fire and the flames and the old man behind the bar. "She may have nothing to do with the tracker."

"I know. I know but …" His shoulders drop, he moves closer; I find I don't move back. "Look, the block is on, and the Project, if it's them who're involved, won't think that's unusual—they'll be expecting it. So we're safe. Kind of. And yeah, you're right, it might not be anything to do with Patricia—why would it be—but … it's kind of like … I guess we have to be careful."

"Careful."

He watches my face. "Careful."

We stand there, the two of us, the table by our side, my eyes on his shoulders, unable to make eye contact, and curious, keen, but scared, unsure. There's a spec of fluff on his shoulder; I reach forward, pick it off.

Watching me, Chris smiles, then, oddly, stumbles a little as he tries to move—I assume his injured leg must hurt. "I … You … My bag …"

I blow the fluff from my fingers, letting it free, watching it float for a moment then fall. I secure my rucksack and watch Chris gather all his belongings and turn, and I feel a strange sense of calm.

"How about," he says now, slotting a SIM card into his phone, fingers shaking, "we check the tracker situation when we get to Weisshorn, say to Patricia that we have to test everything's okay before we go near there and so we need to check her phone."

"We have to test everything?"

"Well, no, but—"

"Then why would we lie?"

"To, well, to save her feelings."

"Oh." I think this through, unsure what it means. "Feelings."

"Yeah."

I think. "Is this the same as with the home secretary where what other people think of us matters?"

He hesitates. "Yes. No. Sort of."

I battle with the concept. Despite my IQ, nothing, sometimes in this world, makes any sense at all and after a moment of contemplating what it could possibly all mean, Patricia bounds back, slightly out of breath. "Ready?"

Chris throws me a glance and this time, I catch his eye. Patricia stares at the two of us. "What's going on?"

Chris' face flushes red. "Huh? What? Nothing."

I watch him. Is he doing that thing he talked about? Lying to protect other people's feelings? I decide he must be and so try the same. "We were just staring at each other for a longer than expected amount of time. It is common when people like each other for the blood in their faces and cheeks to rush at greater than normal speed to the surface of the epidermis." I halt, look between them, satisfied that I have played my part.

Patricia bites her lip, pushing down a smile. "Okay."

I begin to stride to the door. "Do you have the book from the woman at the train station?" I say.

"Huh? Oh, yeah." Patricia taps her rucksack. "In here."

We walk over to the exit, past the wall made of wood and fresh pine, through the fug of beer and vin chaud and sweet cinnamon scent, past the singers and their guitars and their checked shirts and pianos with soft lullaby melodies about love and friendship and not being afraid anymore. I shut down my ears as much as possible to block out the assortment of it all and keep my body as close to Chris and Patricia as I can bear for protection. I suck in the last pocket of warm air before the outside comes in.

As he opens the door, Patricia walking through, Chris turns back for a second and looks to me. "You ready?"

I find myself nodding and, for some reason, feel an odd happiness that he is here. "Ready."

We step out into the silent snow-sprinkled night. The air is crisp and the black sky is punctured by silver fairy lights tinged with twinkles of blue and yellow. When I look to my thumb where the bandage on it cuts into my skin, I spot blood on the edge.

"Doc," Patricia calls to me, five fingers outstretched to me, "let's go."

I look at her hand, at her pillow-soft face. She can't know, can she, about the tracker? She is good to me, kind, how could I think otherwise?

"Google? We gotta go."

Quickly pressing my palm into my thumb, I check the dressing is fixed to the wound, then looking ahead to where Patricia and Chris now wait under the wooden eaves of the old tavern, I pack up my thoughts and walk out, cold and shaking under the deep cover of the night and into the sharp slap of Alpine snow.

Behind me in the tavern, the flames in the grate lap warm at the hearth, and the people at the tables tuck cozy into their drinks and laugh with each other as the barman cleans his glasses and serves baguettes and plates of oozing cheese.

CHAPTER 17

DEEP COVER PROJECT FACILITY

Present Day

I am led to another room by the perimeter of the facility by Black Eyes and the officer. Once we stop, the officer walks away.

Everything in the building is neat and in order and, while my brain is reassured by it all, the hallucination or memory or whatever I saw in the sensory deprivation room is playing in my mind over and over, and no matter how hard I try, I cannot shake it away. The woman, the daughter, deaths, and the age: thirty-three.

A door is unlocked and I pass a silver plate on the wall that reads SITUATION ROOM. Black Eyes gestures for me to enter and as we do, I am presented with a cavernous airplane hangar of a space. It yawns wide open to reveal what appear to be rows upon rows of subjects dressed in soft cotton clothes of gray and black, all of them stretching out before us into the distance, each attached to a laptop and communications pod, tapping on keyboards, swiping data on screens, and talking into devices linked from their ear to their mouths.

Black Eyes strides ahead and instructs me to follow. The lights, as we move, are low and cream, no flickering of what would be normal bulbs within the glass encasings, instead they are consistent, calm, long lines of light subdued for subject brains to cope with. The room has been designed, as all have in the facility, to mute the extent of sound, to soften it and make it easier for subjects to deal with, yet, I have never before, until now, seen it work in such mass action, the robotic nature of it, the neat, prim, far-reaching order. I have never before seen so many subject numbers together at one time. When I observe them now, their steel-straight spines, their nonexistent eye contact, their fast calculations of infinite and complex numbers, something about them bothers me, creates inside me an alert that, despite my training and control, I find hard to ignore. The hallucination from the chamber whispers in my mind.

I arrive at a platform that sits at the far end of the hangar and wait. There are no windows for air, no pictures on the wall. Nearby sits a series of sheet reels on a table made of solid metal that, even from here, I can see clearly. Numbers. The reels contain line after line of numbers presented on whitewashed plates of paper, which, initially, appear as if they're cell phone contacts. But as I scan further and decode it all, reassemble them, they reveal themselves to be not purely numbers, but geolocations of small towns and villages across central Europe.

"Subject 375?"

My head snaps up, heart slams against my chest.

"This is number 277," Black Eyes says, gesturing to a man in his twenties who sits in front of a complex bank of computers and screens on the platform where we stand. "Subject 277 leads the situation room and is working on a program for us that is tracking a terrorist cell we believe is working out of Hamburg and London."

The subject glances to me without catching my eye. He is short, stocky, stomach board-flat, face peppered with angry red pimples, hairs on his arms so dark that his pale skin looks pebbled black. And as I look at him, as my eyes input his physical description to photographic memory, it hits me. The odd feeling. The element of being present here in this vast, computerized space that bothers me, that puts me on alert. I look out beyond to the lines of young men and women working at speed on devices and keyboards and I know what it is.

Their age. The subject numbers' age.

Every single one of them is younger than me.

LAKE GENEVA, SWITZERLAND
6 Hours and 27 Minutes to Project Reinitiation

We have managed to hitch a lift in a truck. It is smelly and loud. In the breaking morning that slides yellow across the midnight-blue sky, we begin to see Lake Geneva stretch out ahead of us, its deep water twinkling in the early sun where warm rays bounce off gentle waves lapping the far lake shore in an early spring breeze.

The truck jostles us from side to side and I try hard to ignore it, but it's difficult. My brain is wired. The smell of the vehicle is a mixed soup of fish and castor oil and old rope. I find myself looking at my friends, focusing on the soft yet defined contours of their now familiar faces, the routine of their very being offering me comfort, providing me with a regulatory vision that my mind can latch to so for the moment, all is okay.

At approximately 0700 hours, we arrive at our destination. Crumpled and bleary, we jump down from the truck, Patricia thanking the driver. Our feet sink into a shallow layer of snow and new grass shoots, broken flakes of ice scattered on the roads and paths making the morning appear like a frosted cupcake.

"Hey, Doc?"

I look around to Patricia, blink in the sunlight, adjust my rucksack and assess our position. We are further west now than Lausanne, our original destination where the Goldenpass rail line yawns outward, and as I look north, my vision stretches far to the shore of Lake Geneva that now languishes out in front of me, yawning wide at the start of the day. I catch my breath at the sight. It is magical, cool, and glistening. It dances before me, and I hear the lake rippling in a vast, endless, undulating bowl within the valley of the snow-capped mountains.

"The hospital's further down this part of the lake," Chris says now, turning outward, pointing. "About five kilometers, I think."

I follow his line and register it all. Hansel and Gretel chalets sit in multicolored chocolate boxes on the hillsides beyond, each one nestled with warm pinewood and sheltered by doorway arches that jut far into the air immediately in front. Along the lake, jetties stick out into the water, long fingers of them dusted with icing-sugar snow where birds, small and plump, jitter and jump on the grass shoots, digging for worms, while nearby a small scattering of people wrapped in assorted scarves and duvet jackets, stride on, on their way to work, to friends, perhaps, to their normal, unfettered lives.

Patricia walks over. "Er, guys, we'd better move. There are two police officers over there."

We keep our heads down and hurry on to a copse of trees approximately three hundred yards from our drop-off point. There, Patricia and I wait by a low steel fence as, ahead, Chris buys hot coffee and pastries from a small wooden hut with yellow and green lettering. It is hard not to say anything about the tracker as we wait. Chris' words run through my head. Patricia asks if I am okay, her flat forehead crumpling to wrinkles, but I elect not to answer, unsure what I would say if pushed, uncertain as to what is happening or how or not she is involved. A world shaken upside down and I can't find the exit.

Returning, shoulders hunched, Chris blows out white clouds of breath and hands over our breakfast. I take a moment to realize that, without me asking, he has remembered that I only take my coffee black. Clutching the cup tight for warmth, I sip the beverage, eat the sugary, glazed pastry and stare at the fir trees where melting snow hangs across the branches in tinsel of white and silver.

Chris wipes croissant crumbs from his chin. He takes out his phone, consults a map and switches on the black signal box to search for the best route to Weisshorn Hospital. Patricia gulps coffee, smiles to me, unbuckles her bag and, scrambling inside for something, takes out the Orwell novel and sets it on the fence post where a robin pecks then flies away. I continue to stare at the trees, trying not to ask myself why she wants to take out that novel now, what her motives are. Something about the trees calms me. Their leaves, limp and loose, strain under the weight of a winter now in retreat, spring whispering on a faint breeze that it's on its way. It is soothing, the pattern of it all, the predictable nature of the seasons, and when my eyes scan the vista beyond, I see folds of snow sitting on white open book pages across the roofs of the chalets that lie wedged into the solid mountain slopes.

Snow, leaves, trees, paint strokes of color—nature's own artwork. It all blends in my brain, dancing, waltzing around in a gentle lullaby of rhythm until, gradually, one by one, it begins to merge, to connect in a way that makes me completely stop. My coffee midair, about to take a sip, I think fast as my gaze locks on the forest, on the roofs of the chalets where the snow hangs. My sight flips from there to the fence where Patricia stands and the novel from the woman at the train station sits as before. And as I look at it all, flitting back to the gaze of the trees, a thought begins to form.

"Voronoi," I say to myself. I set down my drink.

"Huh? Doc? V—what?"

"Voronoi … Voronoi …" I stride to where Patricia stands and, taking the *1984* novel, I inspect the cover. "Hey! Doc!"

Chris looks up. "You found something?"

My fingers trace the pattern on the book, the colors spread in hard, sharp angles across the surface. "We thought this book simply contained the code we found on the page and nothing else."

"Yeah."

"We assumed that was all that was in here."

He is alert now. "What are you thinking?"

"We were wrong to assume." I trace the bright cover of the

book. "The Voronoi diagram takes a pair of points. It uses these points, which are close together, and draws a line, which is equidistant. This line runs perpendicular between the points to the line joining them, which means all points are of equal distance to the closest two origin points."

He inspects the book. "You mean, this cover mirrors the Voronoi diagram? You mean the thing to do with the division of planes? That math thing that links to leaf patterns?"

I hesitate. "Yes. How did you know that?"

"Let's just say that when I was locked up, the prison library only had a limited selection of art and math books. But what's the Voronoi diagram got to do with anything?"

I blink at the book, rest my fingers on it and allow them to slide along the black lines that divide in walls between each block of color. "The woman at the station was from the Project. She was the girlfriend of the officer who interrogated me. Why did she give us this book?"

Patricia shrugs. "Doc, we already know why—to warn us that the Project was at the next station. It was on the page in code."

The tracker. Don't mention the tracker. "There must be another reason."

"How do you know for sure? Maybe you're tired, Doc—it's been a long journey and it's cold."

But Chris shakes his head and peers once more at the book cover. "They're used in technology and science, these diagrams, the ones that look like this artwork here." He looks to me. "Are you assuming a Euclidean distance when you calculate or a Manhattan one?"

"Manhattan."

"Hmmm." He studies the page; I feel a strong urge to shout out, *thank you*. "So you're using the Manhattan assumption to measure the distance between points?"

"What on earth," Patricia says, "has this got to do with anything?"

I turn to her, stalling for a moment, and I am shocked to realize my hesitation is because I'm wondering if I can trust her to tell her the truth. "I think … I think there may be a hidden message on the cover."

"Oh." Patricia's coffee suspends midair. "Jesus."

I look to Chris. "The formula for this is $d[(a1, a2), (b1, b2)] = |a1\text{-}b1| + |a2\text{-}b2|$."

Chris smiles at me, broad lines reaching out from his eyes.

I clamp my lips together, oddly nervous. "What?"

"Nothing, you're just …"

"What?" I cannot read his face. "Have I quoted the formula incorrectly?"

"No." He smiles again. "No. You're just right."

I hesitate then continue. "If we use the formula I have recited and apply it to a city, it can provide an approximate estimate on the district and number of the street the diagram in this instance is relating to."

"I can't see what … how can you pinpoint that answer?"

"Here." I show him, tiptoeing my fingers across the cover. "The nearest pair of points is the key. They relate to two adjoining cells in the Voronoi diagram. So, when you apply the formula, calculating the equidistance, you arrive at the numbers …" I perform the equation at rapid speed in my head. Five seconds later and I'm done. "376, 10,014, and 3621."

"Whoa—that was fast. Okay, okay, so I see what you mean, but you said, 'if you apply it to a city.' That'll require knowing what city it is. These could be numbers from anywhere."

I grab his phone, turn it to me and, tapping in the coordinates, wait.

"Doc, what are you doing?"

"I am using the Manhattan assumption. The distance, the diagram on this cover, the one it assumes—it has been selected for a reason."

Chris shakes his head. "I don't understand."

What I am searching for finally springs up on the cell. "Here.

The distance point equation is the Manhattan version for a reason. Number 376 is the street name. 10014 to 3621 is the postal district of—"

"New York," Chris says. He looks to me. "Manhattan. Holy shit. I know that place."

We look at the address in front of us to which each of the numbers correlate.

376 Hudson Street, New York. The home of the USA Passport Office.

The secret home of the covert division of the Central Intelligence Agency.

Patricia stares at us both then takes one noticeable step back.

CHAPTER 18

LAKE GENEVA, SWITZERLAND

6 Hours and 5 Minutes to Project Reinitiation

"The CIA," Patricia mutters almost incoherently. "It links to the fecking CIA?" She starts pacing, her fingernails digging into the coffee cup so it almost buckles. "Shit, shit, shit."

Chris watches her. "You okay?"

"Yeah. What? Oh, yeah …"

He whistles. "Because this is big, man. I mean, shit, why would that woman from the station tell us this? What does it mean? Do you … do you know?" Then he stops.

"What?" I say.

"The guy, the other one at the Madrid airport who was following us with the MI5 dude. The one I couldn't place—what if he was CIA?"

"That is an assumption, not a certainty."

"But a possibility, right?"

"Probable," I say. "It is probable. Probability is the chance that something will happen—how certain it is that some event will occur. It is measured often in percentage terms. What percentage of probability would you say that the man you saw would be from the CIA?"

"Huh? Oh, um, I dunno. Seventy, maybe eighty percent?"

"Seventy, maybe eighty percent. Based on what assumptions?"

"That he looked similar to the MI5 guy, you know, he was focused, kind of. I don't know, based on that this whole thing is a mess and for all we know, every crazy country could be involved."

"I do not believe every crazy country is involved. And countries cannot be crazy."

"No, but yes, but, wait, no …" He exhales. "I don't know, it just seems odd, you know, when I saw him. Off. A hunch."

"A hunch." I try to interpret how this would work. *Hunch.*

"Yeah. Don't you get those?"

"No."

His face drops. What does that mean? Sadness? Sometimes I really wish I knew what people were thinking. "I am sorry that I do not get a hunch."

He smiles. "It's okay. I'm kind of glad you don't."

I feel happy at his words, yet my reaction confuses me, so I study the diagram, tracking the hidden code that now sits in my hand. "There is one more link."

"What? Where?"

I reach into my pocket and pull out something I have not looked at since we left the tavern. The photograph of my biological mother with me in her arms as a baby. I pause, a tightness burning in my chest. I turn over the image. The address, the geolocation coordinates on the back. I run the figures through my brain, connect and calculate and, each time I do, I arrive at the same, inevitable conclusion.

"The numbers correlate," I say.

"What? Let's see."

I show him. "There is a pattern connecting the two."

Chris squints, reading, muttering the connections under the lisp of his breath. I catch myself thinking that I want to find somewhere warm, lie down next to him, back flat on the floor, and not move, only our five fingertips touching.

"What if she knows something?" he says after a few seconds.

"What if the woman who gave us the book knows something about your mother, and the CIA is a connection? The two locations have similarities in their patterns, so it's highly possible. Maybe Isabella, maybe she's been forced to, I don't know, work for them—for the CIA—or something and the Project have found out and are using that information. If the Project's blackmailing the home secretary, they could be doing the same to someone within the CIA for some reason."

"You mean this is where what people think of each other matters and can be used to as extortion? As with the home secretary?"

"Yeah, sort of, but this all means the CIA is involved in the whole thing. The question is why? How? I mean, Jesus, if the CIA is involved then the Project goes way beyond the UK. This thing, the whole cover-up of it, who's really involved, could be huge, could be global."

I look at Chris, look at Patricia and the creases on her brow, look at the way her teeth are pulling at her top lip, her eyes in the air, and I think. Places, people, feelings, movements, how they all connect, how each of us is inextricably linked by an invisible thread, a thread that spans age and race and creed and color. I look at my hands, spread out my fingers just as Patricia does to me, watch each one spider outward in the cold air, skin turning slightly pink in the morning chill, amazed at my own limbs, bones, nails, at what they can do, at how—when they are combined with the power of my brain, with its rewired uniqueness—they can carry out tasks and actions that I never thought possible. And yet here I am. No matter what I do, no matter how high my IQ, I am still part of the Project, still linked by an indecipherable, invisible thread.

"We have to go to find Isabella," I say after a moment. "Now. She could be in danger."

Chris nods. "If the CIA is involved, who knows how far this goes." He shakes his head. "What do they do in the Project, the CIA? D'you think they run it, too?"

"Um, guys?" Patricia says. "The police are coming back, just up ahead."

Chris looks to me. "The woman, the one you killed on the train. The police could have our pictures. They could be looking for us."

We scan the distance. Two officers, a man and woman dressed head to toe in thick blue jackets, are wandering by the path at the shore of the lake where a large white hotel glistens in the morning sun.

"The Swiss *polizei* carry guns," I say.

Chris secures his bag and draws up the map to the hospital on his phone. "Then, I don't know about you, but I think it's best we were going."

Grabbing our belongings, we dart under a low-hanging tree that dangles diamonds of ice in the early sun, and follow a dirt path half hidden under a light carpet of snow leading to a forest beyond. Patricia lags behind then jogs to catch up with us but as she tries, in the rush, to ram the Orwell book into her bag, her feet trip on the root of a tree covered by a paper-thin layer of snow. She stumbles and the novel flies far from her hand, thudding to the ground in a ripped open heap among the twigs and ice and mud.

Chris goes to get the book, but Patricia stops him, grabbing his arm. "No!" She gestures up ahead. The police are scanning the area, much nearer now to our location, questioning passersby.

Chris glances to me, to the novel, then looks back to where the police are scouring the road near to the coffee hut. "Damn it." He goes to turn.

"No! We must retrieve the book," I say, distressed at the thought of leaving evidence.

"Doc, the police are just there. We have to go, it's too risky."

I hesitate, my sight darting between Patricia, Chris, and the torn, dirt-streaked novel. The police ahead begin talking to the coffee shop vendor.

"Doc! Let's go."

I look to Chris, desperate to read a signal from him of what is the right thing to do.

"Doc," Patricia calls to me, "there's no time! We're best to just leave it and go!"

I'm torn. The police are nearing now; if I ran to get the book, I could be spotted, but the book is valuable evidence, a vital link.

"Doc! Come on!"

I take one last glance at the novel on the ground, scattered with snow and dirt. I try to imprint all the Voronoi diagram information to my brain, then securing the worn picture of Isabella tight in my hands, I duck into the tent of trees and hurry out of sight.

DEEP COVER PROJECT FACILITY
Present Day

Black Eyes talks to the pimply faced subject number in the situation room while, around me, I scan the area as much as I can without drawing any attention to myself. I was right. Each subject who sits at one of the consoles in the vast, windowless hangar of a room beyond cannot be more than thirty years of age, indeed far under it. Their unlined skin, their late pubescent acne, their colt-like limbs. They resemble, as I consider it now, my own frame and face and stage of bodily growth when I was younger and taken to the Project against my will.

"Subject 375?"

I jump, not having heard Black Eye's voice initially, so focused was I on the area in front.

"What were you doing?" he asks. He regards me for a second, frowning, and I have come to learn that, with him, this is not a good sign. But is he cross or simply mildly irritated? I cannot tell.

"I was counting the subject numbers," I reply, "to remain calm, as I was trained to do." And as the words come out, while they are in part, true—my mind has in moments been counting the subjects present—it has not been in order to keep me calm. So why did I feel the need to lie?

"We have intelligence from the field," he says finally, his nostrils sucking in to the bridge of his thin nose as he inserts a breath. "It indicates an imminent threat. 277 here is helping us use the data you've just seen to track and eliminate an attack. 277?"

"Sir. We have narrowed the list down to within a three kilometer radius of the target's location."

Target. What target?

Black Eyes draws his full height upward and points to the computer screen. Green lights flash to the right of the console. I count every one. "This is the data we are awaiting analysis on, am I correct?"

Subject 277 nods. "Yes, sir."

Black Eyes turns to me. "This data here will provide us a link, a way in to a situation we want to … rectify. But, Maria"—he coughs—"Subject 375, we have not found that way in yet. I need you to analyze this data, tell us what we are missing."

I am drawn instantly to the numbers and facts and reams upon reams of precise information. I begin to track it all, faster, it feels, than ever. Dates, phones numbers, transcripts of personal emails, all of them one after the other presenting themselves of free will.

Black Eyes paces then stops. The heat of his body is only centimeters away from mine and I am alarmed to realize that I find this fact comforting. As I track the figures, Black Eyes circles me, swooping around the platform.

"This is all personal, private data of individuals," I say, analyzing.

"Yes. We, along with the Americans and every other first-world proactive agency under the sun, have been dealing with this kind of data for years. There is no such thing in the modern world as privacy."

Americans. The word filters in to my head as I continue my analysis, momentarily distracting me. Why would the word *Americans* alert me so much?

I focus back on the task in hand. Sight on the screen and on the documents that stack to my side the whole time, I read email after email, fast, scanning so quickly that a knoll of a headache begins to form at the base of my skull. I read about feelings and emotions of people, random, anonymous people anywhere in the world, their personal communications hacked, stolen without their consent, so I, now, can pilfer through them on command of the Project.

Black Eyes turns to me. "Have you found anything yet?"

But before I can answer, Subject 277 spins his seat around. "Sir, I have the next set of transcripts."

Without saying a word, Black Eyes nods and the Subject slides across a new set of files. I take them, start scanning each one. It seems futile. What I am flicking through are only words, words talking about emotions and feelings, words that, unlike binary code, are not going to …

Wait. Is that it? Is that what they're searching for? "Here." I say, fast.

Black Eyes immediately looks. "Tell me."

I trace my finger toward an email that tracks through a series of metadata. "This is not a personal email," I say, "but a business one, but look here." Black Eyes leans in. I swallow as my nose detects garlic, stronger than normal, in small clouds of warm breath. "There is a code hidden here in the personal message that tail-ends on the metadata information bulked over it."

He reads the screen then frowns. "Explain."

I try to recall emotions I have learned in training. "People talk in … hidden meanings. This message is no exception. At first, I thought the code we were searching for, the answer, was in the meta-information this man required for his website launch."

"Get to the point."

"The code is not hidden in the metadata. It's instead in the main text. The words he uses—they are different."

"How?"

I point. "The vocabulary here is irregular. In his previous emails, which I have scanned at speed, he uses a consistent regularity of written words, of style and form, but this communication differs. It follows a unique path and in fact, it is very clever. See?" I trace my fingertips over the area of concern.

"They are words."

"Yes. They are words that translate into a code." I pause, touch the back of my head. "They are a message."

Bringing up a separate spreadsheet page, I begin to tap in the words and execute a file run across each one. At first nothing changes, the letters and numbers hanging static in the air, filling the room with a heavy silence only punctured now and then with the clack of 127 keyboards in the hangar beyond. I launch a fast program using the metadata link from the actual email online, then wait. I sit back as, before my eyes, flashes of information speed across the green screen.

"Is that …?" Black Eyes drags over a chair, sits, stares at the screen then, shaking his head, claps his hands and smiles, a smile that makes creases prickle out all across his face. It is so sudden, so unpredictable and unprecedented that the entire control room floor of subjects stops what they are doing and turns to stare.

"Maria, you did it!" he exclaims. "She was right." He smiles. "She was right."

His cheeks swell into two pink apples fattening up a face that usually resembles a skeleton's sunken skull. He slaps my shoulder, the touch taking me completely by surprise, then, in an animated fashion that I have never before witnessed on him, he picks up a blue phone on the side of the console. He turns to me.

"That is the attack there, in code, is that correct?"

"Yes."

I watch his face, comparing it to pictures of expressions I have recorded before. He is happy, I think, happy with me, perhaps, and yet, why does this not please me? Do I not want to be the best subject I can? Am I not a member of the Project Callidus family? A family who cares, who actually has my own interests at their heart for once in my life? Is that not what we all want, as human beings— to be part of something … something meaningful?

"Subject 375?"

"Yes?"

"I want you now to tell me exactly what you have interpreted from the metadata you uncovered."

I nod, prepare to decipher and speak. And as I do, as I begin to decode the data in front of me, my eyes flit to the right and I see 127 subject numbers look up, blink at me, then return to their work.

CHAPTER 19

WEISSHORN HOSPITAL, LAKE GENEVA, SWITZERLAND

3 Hours and 50 Minutes to Project Reinitiation

We arrive at the outskirts of Weisshorn Hospital hidden by a line of fir trees decorated by baubles of ice. It is quiet. There is a road to our left, gray and winding, cleared of snow for vehicles to pass, and when I sniff the air I detect damp pine needles, a forest bed of earth and the fresh scent of spring water running across river rocks. The sun peeks over the horizon as day fully breaks, the sky a soup of morning mist. Birds jump from branch to branch while squirrels scurry up tree trunks from a forest floor of fat white and lilac crocuses and small beds of wild flowers the color of chalk drawings.

"So," Chris says, checking his map, "the hospital is just one hundred meters through these trees."

We trek until we reach a final clearing where the wide road has been replaced with a narrow side one that dips down on each side into a hidden ditch. I count every step so I know the exact distance and time back to the main road. Patricia exhales, drops her bag to the ground and wipes sweat from her brow. "Whoa—is that the hospital?"

To our right looms a large white building. Constructed with oblong concrete blocks and guarded by a perimeter of antique brick wall topped with corkscrews of barbed wire, the hospital lies nestled under a canopy of trees, huge towering firs swaying in the breeze. In front loops a long driveway laid with gravel and pebbles.

I take out the photograph of Isabella from my pocket and blink at the image in the shine of the sun. "It is the same," I say. "Papa knew she was here."

Chris comes over. "Okay, so I've done a scan on the perimeter and it's blocked."

I look once more to the photograph then focus on Chris. "Is there an electronic surveillance system?"

He opens up his tablet device, switches on the black signal box and taps the pop-up keyboard. "Running a check now."

As Chris works, Patricia stands by me and points to the photograph. "What d'you think you'll do when you see her, Doc?"

I glance up. A robin lands on the barbed wire ahead then immediately flies away. I stare at the fencing then look to the photograph in my hands, to the contours of Isabella's skull, to her blond flowing hair, her smooth, unblemished skin. "She is older now."

"Yes."

"She could be in danger."

Patricia shifts from foot to foot, leaving small prints of her shoes in the snow. "Look, Doc—and don't take this the wrong way—but d'you really think it's wise to go in there, into the hospital?"

"I do not understand what you mean by, 'take this the wrong way'?"

Chris taps his computer. I watch him for one second; he shoots me a glance. I turn back to Patricia for her answer.

She sighs. "I just want you to know that I think you're strong, okay?"

"Okay." Why is she telling me this?

"But you've been through a lot, you know." She bites on her bottom lip and I start to think: why does she do that? "The train," she continues, "being held at the Project, being trapped in the cellar. The Project will be after you if you go in there, into the hospital. It's more of a risk for you than Chris. So I thought that … well, how about Chris goes in instead?"

"No," I say immediately. "It will be me. I have to find her. I have to find out who I am."

"But you know who you are." She swallows. "You … I know who you are, Doc. You're … you're my friend, and I think it's a mistake you going in there. This is the Project, for God's sake. They don't mess about. They could … they could hurt you."

"Friend," I say aloud.

"What?"

"A friend is a person with whom you have a mutual liking."

"I … Yes. Doc, are you okay?"

I am unsure how to respond, not entirely certain of my own feelings. Chris looks toward me, and for the first time, I feel the need to match his gaze, to keep my eyes on his, no matter how much it makes me want to scream, want to run in case he can see what is inside my manic mind. After a few seconds, I drop my lids, count to five, and try to push the tracker and the Project to the back of my thoughts. Patricia moves nearer to me; I take one step back.

"I'm in!" Chris suddenly says.

I blink an odd wetness from my eyes and turn. "You are in their system?"

"Uh-huh." He swivels the laptop our way. On the screen is a detailed map of the hospital: rooms, black lines, a warren of corridors and computer links. I snap a photograph of it in my mind so I can recall, when I am in there, every nook, turn, barrier, and window.

"I will enter via this door," I say, pointing on the map to an area at the side of the building.

"What? Oh no. I can't disable the alarm there, but here," he indicates a low-hanging roof area to the left ahead side, "this one I've managed to access, although be careful—I think there's another sensor there. If there is, and you spot it when you're in there, text me and I'll link into your signal and see what I can do." He pauses. "Here's where I reckon she'll be, by the way, your mom."

"How do you know that's where she'll be?" Patricia says.

"Oh, because that's the older patients' wing from the plans, and I guess, well, I guess Isabella will be old now."

I stare at where Chris' finger hovers over an area of the map separated from all others and try to imagine the face of my real mother today. There is a cordoned-off section of the hospital ward system that appears on the map in the shape of a scorpion's tail. Each segment seems to consist of a locked-in partition and when Chris clicks on one of them and taps some keys, a series of numbers springs up, quick fire across the screen.

"Binary units," I say instantly. "These are names and numbers that correlate exactly with the ones I found in the Project Callidus facility in Hamburg."

"That's what I thought—and they're just like the ones we accessed via the Weisshorn database when we were on the train. Plus, look—there's one number here: 375."

Patricia squints at the screen. "Doc, that's your number."

"Exactly," Chris says, "and I thought, okay, so they have Maria's subject number—sounds about right if the Project is emailing the home secretary from here—but then I got thinking: what if you input Isabella's full name, date of birth, and geolocation of country of origin and run it through into numbers divided by—"

"Divided by the number of subject numbers who have died."

"You got it."

Patricia stares at us both. "What on earth are you two on about?"

"You arrive at Isabella's number: Subject 21," I say.

Chris nods. "Subject 21."

We look now to the screen where the map pulsates beneath the fingerprint-smeared glass casing, as there on the point of the scorpion's tail is a room with a number of the occupant inside allocated to it: Subject 21.

"D'you think it could be her?" Chris says now.

A sliver of sun bursts through the tree tent, splashing, momentarily on the screen of the tablet, flashing everything on it yellow and white, blurring temporarily the thick black bars of the hospital map, and for a second, my mind is cast back to Goldmouth Prison, of being locked in solitary confinement, of being pressed in with no room to move or hide or curl up away from everyone and everything, of London and of running and being chased by the Project.

"Maria?"

I jump slightly, look to Chris.

"I think it could be Isabella. I know you don't like to assume anything, but it's … it's a logical conclusion. Whatcha reckon?"

A subject number. They gave my biological mother a subject number too. How far does the Project's hold stretch? "I think … I think you could be correct."

"Good. So I think the plan should be first to sort out the email thing—send the message we agreed to the home secretary saying the Project will compromise, you know, promise to keep the investigation out of the public eye, blah, blah, blah—then get to Isabella after that. That way, we're cutting off their blackmailing source before they can do anything to harm your mom."

Patricia looks to me. "Doc, you okay with that?"

But I find myself ignoring her and focusing on Chris. "Where do I go to check if the Project is indeed the email source from this location?"

"Here." His finger sits on a small room three corridors away from that of Subject 21. "Once you're in, contact me and then, just like we did in Hamburg at the Project facility there, I'll lead you through the hacking system."

"But we cannot access their second-layer database."

He shakes his head. "We don't have to. If, from what I can tell by looking at their system so far is right, I can jump through a couple of hoops in their initial firewall and slot a worm virus in."

"They will detect a virus."

"Nope, not this one. It has an outer casing, making it untraceable." He stops, stares directly at Patricia.

"What?"

"Nothing."

Chris watches Patricia for two seconds, then turns to his computer.

Tapping the screen once more, he hacks into the hospital map and its internal alarm system. It all works well until, in the frost that floats between the trees and snow, gunfire rips through the air.

CHAPTER 20

3 Hours and 23 Minutes to Project Reinitiation

Fireworks of gunfire explode around us.

We run, dart into the trees, the forest flying by our eyes in a blur as we tumble into a bush, thorns ripping into our skin, cheeks, and hair. The noise fires around us screeching into my head, hammering so loud through my ears, it feels as if my skull will explode and bits of my brain will be splattered all over the snow in red diamond flakes of congealed matter.

"Doc! Doc!"

Patricia presses herself next to me. Her skin slick with sweat gives off her scent, of talcum powder and baby bath bubbles, and for a moment it calms me, but then I think of the tracker, and the gunfire tears through the air again and I thrash my head down, ram my palms to my ears, curling my neck into bent knees, my lips emitting a low moan.

"What the fuck is happening?" Chris asks, his voice fast, frantic, but Patricia does not reply, instead her hand is in her bag, fumbling for something I cannot see.

Chris crouches in the brambles, the frost pulling at his coat. "I can't see where the hell this is all coming from."

The bullets fire out for three more hellish seconds then, as fast as they began, they cease. All falls still and silent, only the birdsong dancing on the breeze that blows through the leaves of the fir trees. The thorns digging into my arms and face, slowly I lift my head and lower my hands from my ears. The hospital building glistens white and yellow where the early spring sun falls in innocent, oblivious rays, and I blink at it. The thought of it, the regular, continue-on-no-matter-what order of it helps me lift my head further, an ache in my neck throbbing where I must have wedged it tight between my knees.

Patricia pulls an empty hand from her bag and crawls nearer to me. "Oh, Doc, you've got thorn marks all over your face."

I touch my skin and feel small warm trickles of wetness, and when I hold my fingers to my eyes, I see their tips stained bright red with my own blood, my Basque blood, blood that the Project wants, blood originating from the real father and mother that I never knew about until recently. I turn to Chris and, forcing my brain to think and to perform logically, I scan the area.

"Where … where are the shooters?"

"I don't know," he says, also scouring the horizon.

The barbed wire twists in spirals on the roof of the wall as before, but there are no snipers visible, no guards to be seen. The wild flowers of pastel and cream ripple in the wind.

"I reckon it was random shooting," Chris says now, turning back to us and crouching down so his knees jut out and touch his chest. "We must have tripped some sort of wire or … or switch or something. I don't think they've actually seen us or they'd be out here now hunting us down." He stops, catches his breath.

I examine the forest bed, tracking the entire area. "When I go into the hospital, I will aim to disable any controls for external trip wires that I find."

Chris nods. "Good call."

"Nope," Patricia says. "No bloody way."

"What?"

"No. Uh-uh. No. Doc, you are not going in there, not now."

"Yes, I am." I brush the blood from my face, but instead it smears into one round mass of pink paint.

"Doc, how do you feel right now?"

"I do not understand what you mean."

"We just got shot at with loud gunfire and you had to roll into a ball and cover your ears to cope with it. And look at your face—"

"Do you have a mirror?"

"What? No, Doc, no. That's not what I mean. I—" She throws up her arms and exhales. For a second or so, she bites her lip, shakes her head and momentarily flutters her lids shut. I am unsure what to do, uncertain as to what I have perhaps done, what she has done. Usually, I find when people stop talking midsentence, despite not being interrupted, it can be a bad thing.

When Patricia finally opens her eyes, they glisten with fresh tears that threaten to spill over. "I worry about you, Doc."

I say nothing. Instead, I listen, not comprehending at all what is expected of me, not knowing what to say, what to keep hidden. I glance to Chris; he is scanning the hospital perimeter and checking on his phone for any alarm alerts, and I so desperately want to join in with the routine, with the mathematical shelter it provides.

"What if you go into that hospital and there's some big alarm that goes off and makes a huge noise?" Patricia says now. "Or ... or, I don't know, what if there's more gunfire? I mean, you just covered your ears and hid in a ball, Doc. How are you going to cope?" She shakes her head. "How did you ever cope on the operations for the Project that you say you went on?"

Chris bolts up like a meerkat. "Why?"

"What? Why are you asking—?"

"I was drugged," I say quietly, perhaps more to myself than them. "They gave me drugs to deal with operational situations and numb me. Then they gave me Versed to forget it all. Except, no drug can deal with me, with what I am." I pause, tired suddenly, exhausted.

Chris looks over; Patricia drops her head. Above in the clear snap of blue in the sky, a black kite bird of prey circles the air, scavenging for scraps.

I unzip my rucksack and, taking out my notebook, rip through the pages until I find a blank one. The thoughts and fears and anxieties collide in my head creating a mashed-up jumble. It's only when I grab my pen and scratch ink to the page of facts and figures—on the lives of composers, on the pattern formation of the snowflakes that lie on petals and leaves, on the names of all the people I have known and their meanings—that I lose myself for a few seconds and my mind has a clear space to breathe and think.

After a small while, Patricia sits down and crosses her legs. She looks at my hands where they work on the notebook, fingers now forming diagrams and calculations on the trajectory that the enemy bullets may have made. Chris looks too, craning his head to see.

"You think the gun shots came from over by that outbuilding?" he says, narrowing his eyes as he follows the line of the fully formed sketch of the entire hospital plans on the page. "How in the hell did you manage to draw all that so fast? Actually, no, don't answer that."

I go to speak to him, to explain my findings when there is a pain in my head, sharp and pointed, spiking into the back of my skull where my spine dips in a well between my earlobes. My fingers fly to the pain source.

"Doc?" Patricia unloops her legs and scrambles forward. "Doc, what's the matter?"

The pain radiates outward, tentacles of it whipping up toward the crown of my head. I ram my eyes shut and hear my mouth moan, but it doesn't sound like me: wild, an animal caught in a trap.

Patricia is near. I feel her, the warmth of her hands, Chris too, the baked-goods scent of his tanned skin, but none of it makes the pain go away. My body remains folded in on itself until one full minute later, the pain finally recedes and the shores of my mind return to still waters.

I flop back, exhausted, aching, the blood in my veins pumping so hard, my heart beats in big fist bumps against my rib cage. I grab my notebook, try to record the final trajectory that I was formulating in my brain before the headache took hold, but when I go pick up my pen, it slips from my fingers and clatters to the ground, only rolling to a stop when it hits a thick wall of plump crocus stems.

"I have to go ... go to the hospital to find ... to find Isabella."

"No, Doc."

I lift my lids to hers. "Yes."

She looks to Chris. "Please, can you go instead? Look at her—she's in no state right now to be sneaking around from the Project." She turns back to me. "What's caused the headache, Doc?"

"I ..." I wet my mouth, my lips dry. "I do not know."

"Has it happened before?"

I hesitate. Do I tell her? Does the truth make life better or are lies there to protect us?

"I experienced a similar headache on the way to the tavern," I finally decide to say. "However, it was not as severe as ... as the headache which has just now occurred."

"Right, that's it," she says. "Chris, you're going in."

He looks to me. "Are you sure?"

"No," I say, trying to pull myself up, then falling back down.

"Yes," Patricia says, snapping out the word. "Chris, you're going."

"You seem very certain of that."

"What? Jesus. If Maria goes in there, she'll set off an alarm or something. It's too risky. Nosebleeds before, now headaches—Doc, what's going on?"

I open my mouth to answer, but then realize, with worry, that I don't have an answer. Why is it all happening?

Chris chews on his lip, glances around the area for a moment, to the barbed wire and to the outbuilding where the gunfire came from. Looking back to us, he slips out his tablet.

"This program here connects to my phone," he says, tapping the screen then handing the device to me. I take it. Colors and black-and-white maps spring up on the screen, the interior skeleton of the hospital building.

"The sections here," he continues, pointing, "these are alarm area triggers, I think. Remember in Hamburg at the Project place there, you were stuck and I disabled the alarm inside remotely?"

White corridors, guards chasing me, my skin blue from bruising. "Yes." I touch my arm, roll up my sleeve a little then a little more, pulling at it until it reaches my elbow.

"Well, this is the same system. Watch." He shows me what I need to do, how to cut any alarms that he may set off, allowing him, hopefully, if our calculations are accurate, to access not only the email system and therefore the blackmail source to the home secretary, but helping him to get to the room of Subject 21. To Isabella.

Chris looks at me. "Is that okay? Do you need me to run through it again?"

"No. I recall every aspect of it. Is that not why you call me Google?"

A smile breaks out on his face and for a split second, it pleases me.

"I'll go in," Chris says, "but you stay safe," he whips his eyes to Patricia, "out here."

"Oh, my God. Doc!"

Patricia is peering at my arm where my full sleeve is finally up revealing the flesh of my upper muscle. "Is that the tattoo Black Eyes gave you in Hamburg, the one he scratched out with the fountain pen?"

Chris slaps his hand to his mouth. "Jesus."

We all look down now at the words scratched into my skin by Black Eyes as he held me down while I screamed: *I am Basque.*

I blink at the scar, at where the skin still smears in red rings around the letters. "He said he etched this on me so I would never forget who I am, yet I am unsure who I truly am, and the woman who made me, who gave birth to me is in there."

Chris exhales, shakes his head. For a moment, it seems as if he may turn away, but then, quite by surprise, his eyes with a strange moistness to them, he reaches forward. And with the most gentle and unexpected of actions, he touches my cheek with his fingertips where my blood lies dried and smeared. To my surprise, I don't flinch.

"We'll find her," he says.

Patricia looks between the two of us. Chris' fingers linger on my skin for three seconds, and as he climbs out of the bushes and drops down to a ball and scurries out of sight toward the hospital, on the breath of the breeze that floats through the crisp early morning air, I can still smell his scent on my skin.

CHAPTER 21

DEEP COVER PROJECT FACILITY

Present Day

"Subject 375," Black Eyes says to me, "can you explain aloud what you have deciphered from the data provided to you."

The lights from the control area in the muted situation room blink in soft focus as I look to Black Eyes. The room is still. Beyond in the wide hangar space, the ant-worker subject numbers continue diligently at their consoles, but every now and then I notice one look up. With the light and the data and the intelligence information to interpret in my mind, I cannot quite make out their faces.

I turn to Black Eyes to deliver my findings. "There is a bomb," I say. "It is a medium-size bomb, due to explode in a crowded shopping center in the Södermalm district of Stockholm at 1300 hours tomorrow morning. The data deciphered indicates that the organizers have deliberately selected a Saturday, as it is a time when the city will be filled with people and tourists."

"Good," he says. "What else?"

I glance for less than a second to the hangar. One lone female subject number is looking at me. "The bomb will be contained in a white mail van. The van will have the company name *Post Bokstäver* on the side. Yet this is not a real mail van. It contains a bomb that can be detonated remotely."

"How?"

"Using a cell phone."

"Did you decipher the cell's number?"

"The data was unavailable."

Subject 277 leans in. "Sir, this has just come in now."

Black Eyes takes the transcript proffered by the officer. "This contains the data, you think?"

"Yes, sir."

Black Eyes hands the document to me. I take it, scan it straight away, gorging on the lines and lines of numbers that salute neat and still on the page. Within nine seconds, I have the answer. "The number is 07210 546 810."

Immediately, Subject 277 begins tapping in the cell phone number to his system. The screen flashes as data and more numbers from people across the globe fly in, all connected by thin black lines.

"We have the ability now to block signals remotely to practically all types of mobile communications devices," Black Eyes says. "We have advanced technology that we want you, Maria, to be a large part of. If we cut off the terrorists' communication networks, you see, jam them, we cut off their ability to plan attacks. We cut off their ability to detonate bombs."

He looks to the officer. "Subject 277—status?"

"All communication lines now jammed, sir."

"Good. Send a communiqué to the relevant security teams; give them the report on the threat with instructions to lock down immediately the van and all persons connected. Understood?"

"Yes, sir."

The subject number scratches his spotty skin then dances his fingers on a keyboard that sends a message about the information I have deciphered.

"Well done," Black Eyes says now, turning to me, his head tilted and the bone of his shoulder jutting out under the thin stretch of his woolen sweater. I shiver, but I don't know why. "Project Callidus, you see, exists for the greater good. 'Cranes' is our name for peace—and you just saved countless lives, Maria."

"Four hundred twenty-one."

"Pardon?"

"The amount of lives estimated that could be killed from a bomb of such magnitude is four hundred twenty-one. This is deduced from analysis of maps and retail and tourist footfall data for the seasonal time of year in the area."

A wide smile springs up on his gaunt, skeletal face. For a moment, it looks as if he is about to cry, small globes of tears threatening to break free of their moorings, but then he sniffs, swallows hard, and clears his throat.

"You know so, so much," he says after a moment, his voice so low, so quiet, I strain to hear it among the whir and hum of the computers in the huge situation area beyond.

He goes then to move, indicating that it is time to leave, but there is something else I have to inform him of.

"Dr. Carr, there was further data I deciphered in the data given to me."

For a second, it feels as if time stands still, but then he raises his chin, measured and pointed into the air. Again, unsure why, my body trembles a little. "Tell me."

"There is a gunman."

"How many?"

"One."

"What?"

"One."

He sighs. "Maria, there is always one gunman."

"This is different than simply one gunman."

He bores his gaze into mine, gone the smile, gone the warm, welling tears, and in their place a cold tundra, a looming blizzard. "Explain."

I hesitate. Why do I feel uncertain? Nervous? I glance to the hangar; the woman who was looking before shoots me a gaze then whips her sight back to her screen, then rises and leaves. Something about her sparks something in me, but her face is obscured and I cannot place it.

"Subject 375—I said, explain."

"There are multiple towns and villages located on the data spools," I say, robotic, steady. "On their own they simply signify geolocations, places. However, the second series of intelligence gathered indicates significant activity."

One second, two. "Continue."

"There are a series of lone gunmen. From initial findings, they all appear to be members of the same terrorist cell and—"

"Do you know the name of the cell?"

"No. Not yet, but—"

"Continue."

A mixture of irritation at his interruption and worry at the snap of him mixes inside me. I move it aside for the moment and carry on. "The cell is communicating, but they are not using phones or social media or any other lines of electronic discussion. So far, I have not been able to determine their exact method of information exchange facility. But I have identified that they are aware that secret government services are blocking signals and they know these intelligence agencies are becoming increasingly sophisticated at jamming cell phones and GPS satellites."

"So, is that all you know?"

I hesitate. "No."

"What else is there?"

"Each lone gunman has a … a target."

Black Eyes does not reply. He fixes his sight on me and delivers me a narrow stare. Subject 277, on the nod of Black Eyes, gets up and leaves.

"Each gunman will, one by one, go to a designated, preplanned town or village and shoot a minimum of ten people," I say when the door clicks shut. "Then, after two days, the next gunman will strike and so on."

"How many locations are they planning for?"

"Two hundred ten in the first wave."

"And how many gunmen?"

I swallow, throat dry. "Twenty."

"That means they will kill two thousand one hundred people. Thankfully, not a high number."

Panic rises inside me. "The number will be higher. The intelligence on them suggests that each gunman will carry out shootings in a further two hundred towns in the second wave with twenty people killed per place. Which equals four thousand people killed, which, combined with the first wave figure, equates to a total of six thousand one hundred deaths."

"Okay, well, we'll leave it there for the moment. Thank you, Maria." He turns to leave.

I don't move, confused at his lack of action. "What do we now do to prevent this terrorist act from occurring?"

Black Eyes halts as, slowly, his head spins around until it almost appears as if it's facing the opposite way to his torso. I blink a few times. My sight returns to normal.

"They are planning more attacks," I say. "They are targeting purely villages and towns. These are places not normally selected by terrorist cells. These places have no protection or defenses. My conclusion is that to carry out this plan on such quiet, unusual geolocations would create maximum chaotic impact."

"And using lone gunmen to increase the fear factor," Black Eyes says, "means no one will know where they are shooting from or who is next."

I swallow. "Yes."

Black Eyes rests a hand on the edge of the console. His knuckles are white and his blood vessels line his skin in long bumps.

"I am very impressed, Maria, with your ability to focus on

the task. I know it is hard for you here—forgetting your friends, leaving what you know behind—I know how you feel. But let me tell you now that what you are doing is good work, important work, work that saves lives. I have seen enough of death in my time to know how saving a life feels. But this plot you think you have uncovered—I want you to forget it. It is merely a simulation exercise by another country's intelligence services, one we are fully aware of."

This does not make sense. I am unsure how to respond. "From the way the data was presented, it did not display itself as a simulation."

He inhales. "No more."

"But—"

"I said no more. Come."

And with that, he draws open the door and I am led out into the white glare of the corridor beyond. He checks his watch.

"Maria, it is lunch time. You will eat and will go to your next stage of training, at which there will be a new subject number instructing you. She is here now."

An officer strides over, gray fatigues, white T-shirt with SUBJECT 209 sewn on to the fabric. Her hair hangs in bob of mahogany and chocolate, skin clear and smooth. I look at her and freeze.

"Subject 209, this is Maria."

She nods to me. "I have heard you like knowing the detail of names, so mine is Abigail."

She waits for me to reply, but I do not move, do not want to show any sign of how I feel right now: unsure, panicked. Because I recognize her instantly.

"Subject 209," Black Eyes says, "will you please take 375 to the cafeteria—I hear they are doing a most wonderful chicken today."

"Yes, sir." She turns to me, but as she does, as she brushes slightly past me, I feel something odd happen, a small bump between us, barely detectable. "I will meet you at the end of lunch period at

1330 hours ready for instruction." She moves back and everything returns to as before.

Black Eyes checks his clipboard. He informs me of our next meeting time together, then with Subject 209 by his side, he turns to leave, and as he does, I track every single inch of the subject number's 162 centimeter frame as strange images in my brain begin to trickle in.

I stand still, in shock, as memories start to slap me in the face, and I don't know whether it's being hit by the lights of the corridor after the dark situation room, or seeing the face of Subject 209 just now, but recollections fly past me one after the other. They appear in my mind so quickly I have to steady myself to stand against the white wall. I recall a train station, snow, a dough-faced Project woman who killed an innocent family, a warning encoded in *1984* for us to flee, a CIA location in the Voronoi cover pattern, Chris, Patricia, gunfire at the hospital where … where Isabella may have been. It all floods back to me in one big bang.

I catch my breath, scan the area to check no one is watching me, then force myself back to recall the face of Subject Number 209, the one who looked at me in the hangar, as I realize now with total clarity that I know her. I know Subject 209.

She is the woman from the station in Switzerland who gave Patricia the Orwell book warning us to get off the train.

Conscious that I need to adhere to my schedule, I move to walk to the Subject area canteen, dazed, concerned, unsure what is happening, scared at the potential consequences. I reach the door of the dining room, slipping my hand into my pocket for my pass and feel something. Something that wasn't there until Subject 209 brushed by my side.

A small piece of notepaper.

Pulse pounding in my neck and wrist, I check the corridor. Empty. No personnel, no marching subject numbers. I glance to the surveillance cameras: all are faced at different angles and none of them singularly or conjoined, are beamed on the spot I now stand.

Where is this paper from? What does it contain? Do I take it out, completely against protocol, and look at its possible words? I should submit it. I should go to Black Eyes now and inform him of what the subject number has done.

And yet, I do none of that. Instead, for reasons I do not fully understand, my hand falls to my side and, slowly, my fingers slip into my pocket. I can feel the smooth slip of paper, the corner of its edge, and for a second I hesitate, debate again what to do. Then, I decide. My eyes automatically double-checking the cameras, I pull out the paper and, heart slamming against my rib cage, I read it.

You are in danger. The Project are not who they seem.
They are not here for the greater good.
Meet at room 17 at our scheduled training time.

CHAPTER 22

WEISSHORN HOSPITAL, LAKE GENEVA, SWITZERLAND
3 Hours and 17 Minutes to Project Reinitiation

Patricia flaps her arms against her torso and blows into cupped hands. "Doc, I'm so glad you didn't go in there."

I keep my eyes on the tablet in my hands. "Chris is in the building."

We are hidden by brambles. Snow all around us melts. It drips from the streams and branches, dew hanging in trinkets on the petals of the flowers that dance along the ground, necklaces of snowflakes linking each one from stem to stem, the bunting of Swiss springtime at the foot of the Alps.

So far Chris has not alerted any alarms, but I am nervous. The headache from before has gone, but in its place is a low throb at the base of my neck where my shoulders peek out, and when I inhale through my nose where the cartilage attaches to the ridge of my brow, a small pulsing throb appears and my nostrils feel on the verge of bleeding. I press my lips together and wait it out. For now, I will not tell Patricia.

Save for the birds in the trees and the faint trickle of a running mountain brook, all is quiet. I observe the hospital and try to picture what it would be like living there, being locked up for years; one year in prison for me was too much. My mind, for a moment, wanders to Papa, to him being in the cellar of Ines' Madrid apartment, leaving the photograph and the geolocation details. How scared must he have been? He knew so much about the Project and knew I was in danger, and he was killed for it. I swallow. The killings, all of them—Balthus, Harry, Ines, Ramon, Papa, and countless others who I myself have probably killed—sometimes the weight of deaths past becomes so much, it smothers life entirely.

"So what's the score with you and Chris then?"

Patricia's voice piercing the silence makes me jump. "What do you mean?"

"I mean, do you like him?"

I keep my eyes fixed on the tablet and consider my answer. "The verb *to like* is used to signal that we enjoy something. I enjoy Chris. Why are you asking me this?"

"Just chatting—it's good practice for you."

"Practice for what?"

She sighs. "D'you enjoy being with Chris?"

"Do you mean do I enjoy standing next to him?"

"Sort of."

"Yes. I ... I like standing next to him." I feel my cheeks flush, and I shuffle on my feet, my fingers tempted to stim and tap. I focus on the technology in front of me—at least that's something I can control.

I can feel Patricia's big blue eyes boring into me as I watch the entire expanse of the hospital grounds on the screen. I feel uneasy, odd at the thought of Chris, of how I feel about him, unfamiliar and strange as it is, and yet, at the same time, I like thinking about him, find myself at moments, caught unawares by his smell and his smile.

"It's nice to have someone you care about," Patricia says after a few seconds. "My family are, well, I don't think they care about me, and I'm ... I'm worried about my sister."

I am unsure how to respond. Here I am thinking that Patricia could be linked with the tracker when, in reality, it could be any one of us. I don't know Chris very well and sometimes my memory of my past actions has been so frazzled by the Versed given to me by the Project, my grip of the thread of what I have actually done is not always clear. Words, I decide, right now are the only life buoys I know will keep me afloat.

"To care," I say in the end, "means to attach importance to something, to look after, provide, feel concern and interest in something or someone."

Patricia closes her eyes for just a flicker of a second, then turns and pulls out a chocolate bar from her rucksack. She breaks it in two and holds out a portion to me. I take it, bite the block of cocoa, feel the sweetness melt in my mouth like syrup, and even though confusion and worry still whip round me, it makes me feel a little better.

"Good?"

"Yes," I say.

She smiles.

We finish the chocolate and I take out my notebook. I monitor the current status of the hospital and scouring at speed the perimeter for any snipers, I jot down the map points of Chris' current location and it makes me feel calm, the facts, figures, the glide of the pen on the paper, the smooth quality to it.

As Patricia watches, the tablet vibrates as a text comes in from Chris.

> *Hey Google. Security high in here. Can you get my location and find the trip wire alarm near me and disable it?*

I locate his position. Patricia sits right by me, watching everything I do.

"Is he okay?"

I move a fraction to the left. "I have to disable an alarm." I think back through the procedure of alarm disablement that I have learned from the Project and from Chris, all the points appearing in my head as if I were reading them on a piece of paper in front of me. I begin performing the procedure, fast and efficient, then type into the pad's keyboard.

No guards detected. Isolating alarm now. Deactivation will be complete in forty-five seconds.

My fingers fly over the keys so fast, I can barely see them as, ahead, a lone marmot scurries over, stops then burrows away under some leaves, disappearing in the white snow and earth.

"Is he where we need him to be?" Patricia asks.

"He is in zone two." I check the alarm capability, but something seems wrong, and as I analyze further, I begin to realize that what I am staring at on the map on the screen is not good.

"What are they?" Patricia asks, pointing to three moving black dots on the tablet.

"Guards."

I wait, expecting her to swear, to react or worry, but instead: nothing.

The guards are coming in quick and so I move fast. Running through the alarm again, assuming it will be deactivated any second, I work as per plan, but something is not right. "It has stopped processing."

"What d'you mean?"

But I am already texting Chris:

> *Three guards approximately thirty seconds away from you. Alarm deactivation has stalled.*

He replies:

> *WTF??!!*

I look to Patricia. "What do these initials mean? I do not recognize this code."

She squints at the screen. "Doc, it means *what the fuck.*"

"Oh."

The guards are twenty-five seconds away now. Why is the system Chris set up not functioning as it should? This is not routine. A text pings through.

Am out of sight, but need the alarm off NOW. Follow procedure.

> *Procedure followed but not working. Am switching to different system.*

NO TIME!!

> *There is time. Hide and wait.*

FFS!!

I look to Patricia.

A sigh. "It means *for fuck's sake.*"

I grab my notebook and move quickly. It's odd how the procedure Chris set up is stalling—it does not make sense. All the codes are in my head, but so many drugs have I been given by the Project over the years that sometimes they distill into my system and I forget and misplace the facts I want to recall. I switch to my notebook as back-up.

I flick to the page I need and, locating the details, switch back to the tablet and start the process. Despite the cold of the air that snaps around Lake Geneva, I feel sweaty with nerves, but I fix my focus on getting Chris in and out safely.

"Is he near the email source?" Patricia asks.

"I do not know yet. I have to try something." I type in the numbers I need, but it is a risk. The last time I tried this I was on an operation when I was in my twenties for the Project, but because they gave me Versed, the details of the operation are sketchy, and so when I use the coding now on the device in front of me, my brain is not entirely certain it's going to work.

Chris texts:

STATUS?

I check the map.

> *Guard twelve meters from your location. Remain out of the way. Fifteen seconds to go.*

And the alarm?

> *Await update.*

I work quickly, but it is hard. A pain near my shoulders is throbbing and each time I breathe, my nostrils feel as if they are about to burst.

Give me some good news here. I can hear the guards now!

"Doc," Patricia says, "you've gone really pale."

"My neck hurts."

"Bloody hell."

I work at speed. Ten seconds to go. My eyes fly to the screen where the guards are now and I picture Chris pressed behind a pillar, holding his breath as, in the very near distance of the tiled corridor, the guards walk, guards that, if our suspicions are correct, don't work for the hospital at all, but instead are ingrained deep into the organization of Project Callidus.

"Five seconds, Doc," Patricia says. "They're really close to him now."

Seven, two, twenty, and three. I input these, the final numbers from my notebook calculations, into the program on the tablet and, taking in a whiff of oxygen, hit enter.

"Three seconds."

I glance to Patricia, her teeth biting hard into her bottom lip, then look back to the screen at Chris' next message.

I have to move now or they'll find me!

Ping. The alarm deactivation noise sounds.

"It's done?" Patricia says, blinking, eyes wide.

I hold my breath. On the screen, I see Chris' dot slide out of the way toward the email source code room as, a mere two meters from him to the right, the three guards carry on by.

Wooooohooooooo!! Haha! Suckers!!

I read Chris' text then look to Patricia.

"It means—?"

"It means he's happy."

I sit back, wipe my forehead, relieved all is okay for now as we watch the dot of Chris' body move in what appears to be satisfyingly straight lines through the hospital on the screen for the next three minutes.

The air is now fully blue, a swimming pool in the sky, the sun a big yellow beach ball. The fir trees stagger in the daylight, the rustle of them a soothing sound after the worry of the alarm system, and when I watch the flowers on the ground, I see insects and flies and small worms coiling up then stretching out, daring to show themselves as the birds waltz above.

The text we are awaiting from Chris comes in after one more minute of calm breathing. I read the message in detail, unable to fully believe what it says.

Confirm that Project is the source of home sec email blackmail. Hacked the system and sent counter email as we agreed to end the blackmail cycle. Good news! She's already replied to say she will begin an investigation!!

I sit back, all my muscles suddenly pulsing, aching. I had not realized they had been so tense. Chris has done it. He has accessed the system.

"It is going to end," I say. "The investigation will mean the Project will cease and disband. They will be called to account for the illegal actions they have carried out." I blink, think of my papa, of Balthus, and my brother, Ramon. "They will answer for the deaths they have caused."

Patricia looks at me and I notice her complexion is even paler than normal, a plastic sheen of sweat on her skin. After a second, she swallows and slides over and, unfolding her hand, places her five fingers open next to mine. My eyes feel wet, warm and when I sniff, a small trickle of blood gathers on the rim of my nostril. I wipe it away,

"I'm right here for you, Doc. I always will be." And as her words come out, I feel guilt and confusion and happiness and worry all at the same time.

We sit there for ten, perhaps fifteen seconds, the nature of the Alps surrounding us, hiding us, all held in the loose warm arms of the Spring sun that ripples across the sharp bite of the frost, until another message pings through on the tablet from Chris inside the hospital.

I am here.

I pull myself up, wipe my eyes, text straight back.

Where?

The cursor winks on the screen. A white butterfly flapping in the air. One second, two. A twig peeking out through a snow mound. On the third second, Chris texts back with an update of the moment I have been waiting for.

I am outside door of Subject Number 21. I am outside Isabella's room.

CHAPTER 23

WEISSHORN HOSPITAL, LAKE GENEVA, SWITZERLAND

3 Hours and 7 Minutes to Project Reinitiation

Thoughts hit my brain fast, one after the other. My real mother. The fact that Chris is now, potentially, just meters from her. I text, but my fingers are shaking.

"Breathe, Doc. That's it. Breathe."

I do as Patricia says and, slowly, as my hands return to a steady normal, I manage to input the message to Chris.

What is your plan?

At first there is no answer and, even though Patricia inhales in steady, rhythmic patterns by my side, I begin to worry. From the sky, a black kite swoops down and plucks a mouse from the ground.

Finally, Chris replies.

I plan to enter her room.

Negative. Too risky.

The cursor blinks. Patricia runs a hand over her scalp. "Jesus, this is … this is nuts."

I look back to the screen. Chris is typing.

*Do you want to know if your mom is
here? I can check for you, I can see if
she is alive.*

This is it. This is the moment I've been waiting for and yet, now it is here, all I feel is worry, worry for Chris, for his safety, worry that everything we are doing is being tracked.

I text back. Patricia, watching me, has a frown fixed on her forehead. "I don't like this," she says. I don't reply.

I tell Chris:

Do it. Enter the room.

I hit enter and exhale. Sweat pools now in my armpits and behind my knees, but the frost in the air cuts through my clothing in a breeze that travels on the last waves of arctic tundra that whistle through the mountains. I shiver, clutch my coat to my chest, and, while I await Chris' next response, turn my attention to the electronic map. Alarms now disabled, I ensure that any activated triggers in the area where Chris hides are turned off, recalling when Chris had to do the same for me at the hidden Project facility in Hamburg, I make certain that in the control center of the hospital, to any onlooker observing the alarm system, it would simply appear at first glance that all is working as it should be. There is a lot in life we can be made to believe if it is packaged correctly.

"Is that him?" Patricia leans in as, on the screen, we see Chris' small black dot enter the Subject 21 room.

I watch, barely moving.

Finally, after three seconds, Chris sends a message.

Sorry: no sign of Isabella. Have
checked the first wall of the data
system and now all codes linking to
her subject number have been erased.
All of it. There's only one reason
they've done that: THEY KNOW WE
ARE HERE! I am getting out now! You
have to LEAVE!

I read his words, fear floods in.

They know we are here.

"Go," I say to Patricia. "Go!" We scramble fast, tumbling back into the bush then hauling ourselves out again. She helps me up, her soft fingers linking under mine as my head aches and my nose throbs where the blood desperately pushes from somewhere inside to rush out, and we run. Only when we finally reach a crop of tall trees that bow together in the middle providing a cave of cover, do we stop.

Patricia breathes hard. "D'you think they could be watching us?" She glances around, eyes darting everywhere, and I do the same, suddenly very aware of our exposure, of our close proximity to the hospital, but most of all, my mind is on Isabella. She is not there. No record now exists of her, no data is now available. Her life has been erased, simple, easy, as if irrelevant to the Project entirely, because, when it comes down to it, that's all we are now in this world of technology and power-hungry governments: numbers that can be eradicated with one click of a button. The sense of loss is so large, so unexpected that for a moment, I feel strange, as if all my life I've been asleep and I've just woken up now only to realize that all the people who matter to me are gone.

"We have to help get Chris out," I say, as I try to grab onto some kind of logic, pattern, protocol, and routine.

"I'm sorry about your mam," Patricia says.

"They knew we were here. How did they know?"

"I … the Project …" She jitters in and out until finally she exhales and shakes her head. "God only knows."

"God has nothing to do with it."

I watch her, her nails now at her mouth, teeth biting down on them. What does it mean? Is she cold or nervous? I take out the tablet, switch it on fast. There's another message.

A box, singular and green, blinks now on the screen.

SOS.

Immediately, I pull up the map, fingers flying frantically, at the same time ripping open my notebook.

Patricia looks. "SOS? Doc, what's happening?"

I ignore her, concentrate, then patch through to a line that gives us more security in communication, but when I try it, test it out, the signal is jammed. "This does not make sense."

I try again, link it all up once more, checking and rechecking with the instructions in my notebook, but still it does not work.

Another message comes in. I read it and go cold.

I think they know your actual location.

Patricia once again bleeds pale. She hugs her bag to her chest and whips her head left and right.

I go on autopilot and instantly scan the area. No guns, no officers, just an eerie quietness that drifts in a white mist of silence where, in the midst of it all, even the birds have fallen still. Clear for this moment, I next switch my eyes to the map. Chris is moving at speed. I try to disable the alarms as he goes—it is hard to keep up, but I do it. I stop them all from triggering and revealing his location, but, as I am about to deactivate the last and final section, the whole system dies.

Patricia leans in. "Doc? What's happening?" There is a crackle to her voice, a trace of a wobble.

The screen is now black, empty. I tap it once, twice, then over and over, but still it does not work and a deep feeling of dread rumbles toward me, an earthquake of fear. I lean back, hidden from the hospital by the trees, and rack my brain data, frantic to make any connection, anything that could help. "He was near the exit," I say, thinking aloud.

"Yeah, but where? Doc, we'd better go. They could be looking for us."

But I continue thinking. "He was at the rear of the building, the same place he entered at the side." I close my eyes, bring up a map of the internal hospital in my head and slot it next to one of the exterior area of the grounds. "There are cameras," I say, eyes still shut, the picture of it all in my mind as if I could touch it, "sensors and surveillance. Even though the tablet system is down, all of it should still be disabled. But the power on the screen over the course of the next three minutes—" And then it hits me. I turn to Patricia.

"How did they know to cut out power?" I say.

Patricia swallows. "What?"

"The power to the tablet, to it all—it cut at a precise time in proceedings. How did they know to cut the power?"

"I … I don't know, but … but Doc, let's get our things and go. Chris'll be here soon, I'm sure, and we can get out of here away from God knows who, and—"

There is a ferocious roar in the air. The fir trees thrash, the crocus petals are ripped from their stems and thrown to the snow. Birds scatter in huge dark swarms of panic, marmots duck under mounds of earth, and the pebbles and grains of dirt mix with the ice-cold snowflakes and whip our cheeks.

"What is happening?" Patricia shouts.

I look up but the noise is so loud, it is almost impossible, the air sounding as if it is being ripped in two by a thunderous apocalypse. We grab our bags and, I don't know how, but we manage to escape the frantic, see-sawing trees and stagger to a clearing where leaves and stones and blades of ice collide. I drag Patricia with me, the two of us running then falling, running then falling, as the thunder in the air grows louder and louder.

We stop by a thick tree trunk, cowering, the boom above turning into a rhythmic whir.

"Doc!"

"What?"

I look up to where Patricia is now staring and my heart slams against my rib cage so hard, I fear it will break out entirely.

For there, in the sky of blue pools and white wool-spun clouds, flies a black military helicopter and it is about to land ten meters in front of us.

CHAPTER 24

"Run!" I yell.

My palms are rammed hard over my ears as, to the right in a clearing by trees, the helicopter roars as it lands, firing off leaves and stones and dirt and worms in every direction, pelting the air with multicolored snow and debris and noise.

I spot the road, the one to the side where we came from. "This way!" I shout.

Crouching, we sprint as best we can. I count every step. I know how long it will take us to reach the road and if we do, there is a ditch there we can slide into and crawl along and escape. We keep running, feet stumbling every other second as just a few meters beyond the helicopter cements itself firmly on the ground in a clearing of grass where all flakes of snow have been blown away to nothing. But for the whole time in my head runs one question: how did they know?

We get to the road but the problem is that it exposes us, no fir trees for shelter, no bramble bushes to hide behind.

"Doc! What do we do now?"

Patricia is shaking. It feels as if one flick of a finger could snap her in two.

I look ahead. The helicopter door is opening, one foot then, two dropping down.

"Run!" I say. "Now, to the ditch."

Mouth hanging open, Patricia turns as the pair of us dash to the side and taking one huge jump, hit the edge of the road where the mud dips down into a wet, ice-filled ditch. We roll to a stop.

Patricia's teeth chatter. "Where ... where are they?"

My brain is firing in every direction as I try desperately to get a handle on what is happening. I cannot stop thinking of Chris. He is trapped out there somewhere or, worse, still imprisoned in the hospital where the Project could be, and the thought of it, I find, worries me immensely.

I ignore the stab of pain that shoots through my shoulder bone, and scan what I can of the area.

The helicopter blades have slowed now to a more listless dance in the air, but there is no one at first that I can see. The helicopter cabin empty, I switch to examining every inch of land I can to see what the danger is.

"It must be the Project," Patricia whispers, shaking. "What have we done?"

I try to focus on what I can observe, but Patricia's words filter through to my thought pattern. *What have we done?* We. Plural. More than one of us. What if the tracker being in our presence is the result of more than one person?

"We have to escape from here without being seen," I say.

"How?"

I slip out the tablet as silently as I can. There's no signal. That's odd. *What have we done?* "I require your cell phone."

Patricia immediately snaps still. "Why?"

"I require it in order to contact Chris."

For one second, she hesitates but then fumbles to her bag and passes me her cell. I start to use it then, for some reason stop. There is something unusual about the phone, and when I attempt to communicate with Chris, it fails. I hesitate, fear slowly spreading inside me. Is this the moment? Is this the moment now that, despite what Chris said, I actually mention the tracker and our worries about it?

"I am not totally certain why it is not functioning," I decide to say. "However I think there could be on it a ..."

I am cut off by a voice that booms down at us from the road. There is a man 172 centimeters in height, black military fatigues, bulletproof vest, machine gun across his chest, towering above us.

"Dr. Maria Martinez?" he calls. "This is the United Kingdom Secret Air Service. I need you to come with me."

DEEP COVER PROJECT FACILITY
Present Day

I file into the canteen hall with other subject numbers, collect my lunch and sit.

I chew on a forkful of food and take in my surroundings and think. While the zone is large, filled with people and plates, the noise is muffled. Walls thick as cotton wool shelter the perimeter where soft-booted feet shuffle on a brushed tiled floor and above our heads from a high, insulated ceiling hang gentle low lights that cast paint smear colors of yellow and orange across the plastic faces of the quiet subject numbers that move by. No one looks at each other, no small talk is made. The note from Subject 209 sits heavy in my pocket.

The lunchtime food we are served is bland. White breasts of chicken smothered in a saliva foam lie anemic on the plate next to insipid string beans limp and washed up on the side, with a preweighed amount of pebble potatoes, boiled and laid neatly in a line. None of the foods touch one another—all order, routine, regulation fully adhered to and monitored.

I eat. All the while, I keep my eyes down, my mind consumed

with the note in my pocket, with the battle in my head of what to do. Do I perform as it asks? Do I go to room 17? But it is out of routine, against protocol and, above all, it is risky. The woman who wrote it did so for a reason, but what is that? She was Kurt's girlfriend. His real name was Daniel and I know he worked for MI5 initially then switched to the Project full time because his brother was killed in Afghanistan, but what about her? Why is she here now? Is she like me, with Asperger's? Is she too being conditioned? Why would she say the Project are not who they say they are? So many questions fly around my head and threaten to overwhelm me, that I have to focus on my plate, count every item on it then recount until, finally, the panic surge subsides and my brain once more can think in a calm manner.

I spear a vegetable, slotting it into my mouth, chewing five times before swallowing and drinking water. I keep to my routine. Five chews, then water, followed by five more grindings of teeth on the next mouthful; if I am being watched, I cannot break my regulation pattern.

Abigail. Her name, the woman's. It means father's daughter. I think about the word, *father*, what it truly means, but all I know is that while you can have a biological link to someone and share their DNA, until you really get to know them, that link may as well be made of chains, chains that can be uncoupled so each person drifts far away from the other, never able to speak to the other or understand who that person really, truly is.

I finish my meal and check the clock. Soon it will be the time the woman stated in the note for us to meet. I scan the room and try hard not to stim, not to tap my leg or hum. Lines of subject numbers are sitting in regulation Project attire: black combats, black T-shirts, overhung with slates of gray, sleeveless, thick cotton jackets. Some talk—numbers, code breaking and such—others simply sit, motionless at times, staring straight ahead, only every twelve or thirteen seconds feeding themselves. All of them so young, and me, the eldest. I shiver. Nothing feels quite right.

I touch my pocket and think of the woman's face. Clear skin, nut-brown shoulder-cut hair, muscles taught and trained. I think of the memory of the Orwell book that contained the warning, the one from the train from Zürich. She alerted us to the Project awaiting us at our next station stop, so is that a good thing, that she helped us? Is she on my side or is this simply another lie, another game by the Project to test my loyalty to them?

I watch the subjects, their ease of movement, the way in which their conversation hinges on logic and mathematical certainty, and I find it comforts me. No nuances or hidden messages for us to misinterpret—the only hidden message we have is code, and that's one we can crack.

Clinging onto the comfortable safety of routine and regulation, I decide then to ignore the note, indeed to report the woman to Black Eyes, when my food, as I eat it, arranges itself on the plate to resemble a diagram and my mind slips to something that alters the course of my thoughts: the Voronoi diagram.

My brain immediately goes to the book again, *1984*, to how Patricia dropped it when we saw the police, and to all that has happened since that moment. Pip, pip, pip, one after the other, the pictures of what occurred at Lake Geneva start to roll across my brain in a movie reel of a show that, until now, I had not fully recalled. Chris trapped in the hospital; the helicopter and the chaos and the deletion of all records that Isabella Bidarte ever existed. I sit straight up, the room swaying a little from the recollections, aware that I may be acting odd. For some reason, I think to the last time I had my injection of Typhernol.

Careful not to draw any attention to myself, I remember, for the first time in a while, the image of Patricia lying beaten on the floor of a room within these very Project walls. Why? Why did they beat her up? The thought starts to move slowly in my head then faster and faster, a Wurlitzer of questioning. She is the enemy, that is what Black Eyes has said of her, but, really, truly, why? Could this woman, this Subject 209, tell me more, enlighten me on what I should do? Friendship, closeness, Patricia's five fingers of kindness that calmed me when I was distressed. The thoughts come to me and tap me on the head, reminding me, somehow, that I am not yet done with the people in my life, and again I find myself asking the question: *why?*

I touch my pocket where the note sticks to the inside fabric. What harm could it do to simply ask some questions, to hear what this woman has to say? If it is a test, then I will handle everything correctly, and if she is a traitor, I will inform. The course to take here is simple.

Isn't it?

I scan the area to plan my next steps. The only way I can get to room 17 is if I break routine, but that will be difficult. Every day here, our timetable is set, marching, as we do from place to place inside the cave of the Project facility, mostly glued to computers and laptops and acres and acres of detailed data. It is hard. I check each subject number for any faces familiar to me as the woman was, but nothing registers. No one speaks, no one looks up. If I am to get to room 17 without being detected, I will have to be quiet and quick.

After four more minutes of eating, drinking, and silence have passed, a low siren sounds to indicate the end of lunch. Along with the other subject numbers, I gather my plate, cup, and utensils and place them in neat rows on the gray plastic tray, stand, and file into the line ahead to place them in their slot. It is then that I see her, Subject 209, two meters ahead and leaning against the corner of the wall where the serving area juts in as a jetty to the main room. I stare. One second, two, three pass until, joining the line of subjects beside her, number 209 files out and exits by the door.

I step forward, one foot deliberately in front of the other, careful not to be too quick as to cause alert and, as discreetly as I can, brush against the wall were the woman had stood. There is something there. I look around, heart smacking hard and check the surveillance camera trajectories then, cautious, I risk a glance to the wall.

There is a message in Morse code. Simple, short dashes and dots are etched into the plaster, tiny, barely detectable, made with what must have been a fork. Fast, I read it, translate the code to words and, just in time, suppress the gasp that threatens to sneak past my lips as I interpret what it says: *Trust me.*

My back snaps straight, conscious that my hands have adopted a slight shake, my brow puckering with tiny beads of sweat. Without allowing myself to think anymore, without convincing myself to do otherwise, I move, disappearing into the swell of subjects, then I take an unregulated turn to the left corner and along a corridor with white walls and pink, peppered low lights.

Pushing back a sudden flash image in my head of Patricia's bound and broken body, mixed with the image of one lone gunman and multiple towns and villages, I hustle forward, head up, shoulders back, feet striding forward, strong, purposeful.

Toward room 17.

CHAPTER 25

"Ma'am, you're not safe here. We need to get you out."

Patricia and I blink upward at the SAS solider who towers above us and blocks out the light. My eyes dart to my surroundings, to the mud and the ice and for a second, I feel as if I could burrow deep down inside the earth right into its core and never again come back out.

"How can we trust you?" I shout, the helicopter blades beyond still whipping a light wind in the air and sending tendrils of frost spinning in tiny droplets of ice into the skin on our hands and faces.

"Ma'am, we have direct orders from the home secretary of the United Kingdom to get you to a safe place immediately." He ducks a little under a sudden loud blast of noise from the helicopter engine. "I have been instructed to tell you that an organization named the Project are here and are aware of your location. If you and your friend do not come with me and my colleagues, you cannot be protected."

I look to the man, to Patricia, to the leaves that spin in a tornado above our heads. Noise, chaos, panic, and fear, each of them banging against my skull, loud and violent.

"Doc!" Patricia shouts. "We have to move. They will protect us!"

I am acutely aware of the danger I am in, only I don't know who the main threat is.

"I can protect myself!" I yell, but before I can get out on my own, I find I am being lifted from the ditch, the thick, brown hands of the man in hammocks under my armpits as he hoists me up and over.

"Get off me!" I shout. "Get off me!"

I keep yelling, my whole body desperately attempting to recoil at his touch, at his foul metallic smell mixed with aircraft oil and dirt.

I hear Patricia explain to the man about me, one to one, and I tumble forward into the road, gravel scraping on my cheekbone, as I topple down, the man letting me go, my head hunched into my knees as my lungs try to refill themselves and my brain attempts to recalibrate after the assault to my senses. I wonder if she speaks that way to him, if she tells him about me because she knows him.

There is the helicopter engine roar, winds slicing through my skin, shouts, knives of leaves in the air, and at first I cannot see Patricia, but then I spot her five meters away. She seems to be talking with a different SAS officer, his frame dressed head to toe in black, a little further away where the helicopter sits.

What does it mean? Under the fire of sound, I watch them, curious. They are talking a lot, Patricia animated, hands flying outward, and I try to decode her body actions and language, but even though my head works hard, none of it means anything to me, and so instead I pull myself up, check my rucksack is not ripped, and search inside to feel for the safety of my notebook and of the old photograph of me and Isabella, and the one of my papa. Satisfied they are all present and correct, I look to the solider who pulled me out and yell out my words.

"Tell me again why you are here!"

He repeats almost word for word what he said just moments earlier.

"And what does the home secretary want with me?"

"Ma'am, I just need you to come with us. We need to return with you to London."

At this point, Patricia hurries over, ducking under the whir of the nearby helicopter blades. Her five fingers spread out on her thigh and even though I want to go to her and fan out my fingers, too, something stops me. What—fear? Doubt?

Patricia halts, looks to the SAS man then to me, cups her hands around her mouth, "Doc," she calls, "they just want you to come in!"

"Come in where?"

"Doc, I've spoken to the solider—the home secretary's asked for you personally."

"I do not understand. Asked for me personally?"

"She wants to see you."

Prickles run up and down my skin. Why do I feel lost? A boat drifting from its moorings? "Why does she want to see me?"

A beat. "It's something to do with Balthus and … Isabella."

No. No, not her. "Is … is she safe?"

"I don't know." A tornado of leaves thrashes past in a roar of noise, scrambling any coherent thought in my head. "Doc, they aren't sure yet what's going on, but … it's best we go with them," More leaves, engine blasts, flying snow, and spinning vegetation debris. "We don't know how near the Project is."

Uncertainty, a lack of pattern to the events, losing Chris, the noise and chaos and utter fear, not knowing what or who to believe. I don't like it, find it hard to process and I start to stamp my feet. At first it's just mild, but then as the rhythmic movement takes hold, I stomp faster and faster, big thumps of my boot prints in the snow.

Patricia watches me, but says nothing as ahead, the SAS officers wait, checking their watches, guns held tight across their bulletproof chests scanning the area.

"Ma'am," the first soldier calls to me now, cutting across the air of ice that hangs heavy. "We have detected an imminent danger. We need you to come with us. Now."

I cease stamping, glance to the blare of the helicopter, look at Patricia.

"Ma'am?"

"What about Chris?" I say, ignoring the officer.

"Ma'am!"

I turn, irritated. "What?"

"Get down!"

Gunfire rips out from the right side of the clearing. We roll out, diving by a small wooden fence decorated in confetti of snow.

The soldiers fire their weapons and I wince, hiding from the noise until the officer who pulled me up gets shot in the shoulder. He cries out, rolling halfway back down toward the road. I look at him, at Patricia, at the air suddenly filled with gray smoke and charred leaves, and, without thinking, with subliminal Project training kicking in, I fling myself to the soldier grab his gun and open fire.

"Sniper at ninety degrees left," I shout to the others as, near the ground, Patricia crawls, head down, through the dirt toward the injured man.

I shoot fast and hard, not recalling any time that I have been trained in this weapon or even used it before, yet still my fingers and my brain register instinctively what to do.

"Doc!" Patricia yells. "There's one to the left!"

I spot an armed figure on the top of the hospital roof. I shoot, aim straight at their head and watch half in horror, half in strange satisfaction, at the anonymous body wavering then toppling backward into the bowels of the hospital building. I scour the area for Chris, frantic to see him somewhere, anywhere, but all that's visible are leaves and smoke and the stench of bullets and gunpowder.

"Ma'am, let's go!" a soldier yells.

Before I can object, I find myself running toward the helicopter, stopping to help the injured officer, hauling him up toward us, another officer running over, as, to the left, the helicopter engine revs.

"What is his status?" the soldier shouts above the roar.

"Shattered shoulder blade." I do a fast assessment, check for blood loss and extent of injury. "Give me your belt!"

"What?"

"I need your belt!"

He unloops what I need and, moving fast, cowering in the wind that now whips back up, lashing great big scars into the calm of the early morning, I secure the leather up and around the limb to prevent any further blood loss. Satisfied all is okay, I allow the patient to be led to the helicopter, and turn to Patricia.

I look at the helicopter, then back to the area of trees near the hospital where Chris should be. "We cannot leave him."

She ducks as the blades rotate faster. "We have to go! They're shooting at us. It's going to be okay." She shouts louder. "It's … it's going to all be over."

I hesitate—what does she mean? How is it going to be all over? I glance back, search again for Chris, battling against the onslaught of feelings in my head as I sense Patricia close by me amid the noise and chaos, and I feel confusion, anger and sadness all at the same time. Is the home secretary there to help me, like Patricia says? Can Harriet Alexander really help finally eliminate the Project, after all this time has passed, after all these deaths—family, friends, subject numbers?

"Ma'am," the soldier calls, "we have to leave!"

I breathe in. Trust, friendship, a sense of who we really are. I glance to see Patricia's five fingers hover on her lily-white skin, her warm smile, and think back to when I first met her at Goldmouth Prison, how kind she was to me, how gentle. My friend, my first true friend. How could I think anything less of her when nothing is certain, when nothing in this mad world is ever as it seems except her. She took a risk by associating herself with me; now it's time for me to return the favor.

"We need to check for tracking bugs," the soldier yells to us once we clamber aboard the helicopter. "We need all mobile phone and electronic devices."

Patricia shifts back in her seat. "W-why?"

"Routine check, ma'am. This is a high security situation."

I hand over my phone, plus Chris' tablet. When Patricia passes across her cell, her hands are shaking.

Aided by a colleague, the soldier begins to dismantle the items. Patricia is jigging her leg. I watch it in the roar of the helicopter blades and engine, her bony knee jutting up and down. Does she need to use the bathroom? Does she have a muscle spasm? Or is she stimming, as I do, to ease the pressure of some internal anxiety? I continue to observe her, curious, concerned, as the soldiers pull everything apart, craning my neck every other second to see through the window for any sign of Chris, when one of the soldiers snaps up his head.

"Sir?" he says. "I think we've got something here."

Everything feels as if it is standing still. The air falls cold, the howl of the helicopter fades, the sweat of the soldiers, the engine oil and closed-in tin can space, the lights and switches and controls, the too-tough leather—all of it evaporates away as my eyes lock on what has been discovered in Patricia's phone: small, black, barely visible, but still clear and real and utterly devastating: a tracker. A single black transmitter tracker of a make that I recognize immediately.

Hands shaking, Patricia so still she seems a waxwork model of herself, I rip out my notebook and tear to a page where a sketch sits from my deepest drugged memories. Frightened now, I force my eyes to look to the device on the page, until finally, I lift my sight to Patricia.

"It is made by the Project," I hear my voice say. I keep my vision locked on Patricia. "It's made by Project Callidus."

CHAPTER 26

LAKE GENEVA, SWITZERLAND

2 Hours and 51 Minutes to Project Reinitiation

The officer turns over the tracker in his fingers. "It has a code number." He shows it to me. "Do you know it?"

"Doc, please! I can ... I can explain."

But as she tries to talk, she is stopped by the officers as they each sit by her side, door slammed shut, the helicopter rises, engine ripping and thundering into the sky. A single tear rolls down Patricia's cheek. "Doc, I can explain. It's not what it seems."

I feel a black mist dropping a cloak over me as I check the tracker code and tear at my notebook, flipping the pages fast. When I find what I need, I am trembling so much, it is hard to speak.

"This is an activation code," I say, a sharp crack across my voice. "It ..." I scan the pages, but the words blur. "It is ... it is a Project code that links straight to the cell and is a number that can only begin tracing its target when it is ..."

Patricia is crying. "Doc ..."

"... when it is directly activated by the owner of the phone. The phone owner controls"—I catch my breath—"controls the tracker." I close the notebook, my movements frozen. I slot the book back into my bag and, inch by inch, raise my head—my whole body feels numb. "It was you." Scratchy throat, a heavy chest. "You had your phone. You were using it. I … I saw you. That was when … that was when you must have been activating the tracker."

"Doc, I didn't … I didn't know what was going on, Doc. I didn't know they would do this!"

"It was a tracker that could only be activated by you!"

Tears in waterfalls down her face. "There has to be a better way than this. There … there has to be."

"No," I say. I shake my head over and over, begin to pound my hand into my leg. "No. No, no, no, no!"

Patricia goes to speak again but a soldier grabs her arm, demanding silence from her for the entire flight. I turn away, destabilized, not knowing what to say, unable to cry or react or yell. I smash my fist over and over into my thigh struggling with the fireball of emotions burning inside me. I blink at the window where the wind whips past the graying sky outside, stare at the white and green windblown ground below, hurt and numb and confused, until, just there I see a solitary figure sprint out, sudden, fast, arms waving over and over.

"Chris!"

I bolt forward. "Stop! Stop! That is my friend down there! Stop!"

But the helicopter ascends among the white, frozen snowcaps of the Alps and pulls away into the ice-blue sky where nothing else sits but one wisp of cotton-white cloud and lone blackbird dancing in the air to its own private tune.

DEEP COVER PROJECT FACILITY
Present Day

Room 17 is only three meters ahead of me but there is a problem. I cannot be seen.

Two officers are standing outside the room. They are not guarding the area, but instead are talking, discussing a problem with an algorithm and its dynamics. Each are leaning on their sides against the wall, facing one another, locked in what appears intense conversation. They haven't seen me.

I slip behind a white pillar and think. The Project makes it very clear that any traitors or deserters will be thoroughly cut from the Callidus family, no one from inside the covert program or facility ever acknowledging the deserter's existence. Subject 209, if she's to be believed, is a traitor, betraying the Project by implying that they're not who they seem to be, and yet, for some reason—maybe it's the increasing memories that keep appearing, the recollections of recent events that I keep remembering—what she says feels real to me, a warning signal somewhere inside me urging me to listen to what she may have to say. I shift from one foot to the other and tap out the Morse code message from the wall. My scar throbs where my finger hits my thumb.

Each corridor in the warren of areas crisscrossing the Project is equipped with close-quarter cameras that track the entire zone. They are small, barely visible black dots and when I observe them now and count them, seven are instantly recognizable in the immediate proximity. I inhale. I am, as far as I am aware, the only Subject who has seen these devices up close, know what they can do, how small and invisible they can be, the cameras skilled in tracking and recording all events without being detected. The last one I saw was fashioned into a house spider. These, however, here at this facility are different, smaller and potentially more complicated, dust specs of black that can easily be dismissed as simply dirt. I regard them, count up to ten and back down again, then begin.

The trajectory of the viewpoints is what matters. If I am to arrive in room 17 without being seen, then mathematics is the key. It takes me less than thirty seconds in the end to arrive at the ideal route to get to the room, undetected by the cameras, and while even to me, the speed at which my brain can currently work surprises me, there is one more real, less digital problem: the officers.

They are tall, each of them with short, blond hair, wispy at the edges, treble clefs of curls licking the napes of their necks. I check my watch. Three minutes until I am to be in that room if the note is to be believed, but if the men are there, if they show no sign of exiting the area, even though I know an invisible route off-camera between here and the door, then there is only one way to get into the room: I have to wait and watch for Subject 209 to come.

But it doesn't happen. The intelligence officers do not leave and the woman does not show up. I check the time. Two more minutes have passed and yet no one appears. The seconds tick by, counting up to the hour, to the time on the note. My pulse raises, pumping blood so hard around my body that I can feel my chest vibrate at the force of my heart beating against the cavity wall. I am scared. And yet, I am unsure why. The image of Patricia, bound, bloody, floats in my head. I squeeze shut my eyes, try to remember what I can from before I arrived here and get small fragments: a helicopter, the device in Patricia's phone, Chris alone on the ground surrounded by towering mountains of snow and ice. Her betrayal. Is that true, that she is the enemy, my enemy? Do people deceive someone so they can make good? Or is truth a whisper on the wind that can be blown away?

People in the Project facility move on time, a clockwork machine of military precision. Concern floods me. Have I made an error? Is this note a test I am to fail? If so, what are the consequences?

I turn. I smooth the crease in my shirt, calculate the trajectory of my steps back so I can slip away unnoticed to my regular, routine station when, without warning, a gloved hand is slapped to my mouth.

I am dragged away out of sight.

SECURE LOCATION, WHITEHALL, LONDON
0 Hours and 29 Minutes to Project Reinitiation

I am shown out of a black car with shaded windows into an underground parking lot with armed guards at the entrance. A damp blanket of air throws itself on me and I pull at my sleeves, count under my breath, and ensure I make eye contact with no one.

Patricia is dragged to the side and made to halt. I cannot bear to watch. The air has a chill to it, a cold sting, but not of snow and sun as in the Alps where the atmosphere was fresh and clean. Here the sky that peeks through is thick and gray, and the air smells of damp concrete after a rainstorm.

"Dr. Martinez," a man says, greeting me now as the vehicle that transported us from a nearby private airstrip pulls away. "We're so glad you could join us. The home secretary is waiting for you. This way, please."

"Doc!"

I feel a sharp slap of sadness, of hurt and confusion as I look at Patricia. She is being held with wrists cuffed by an officer dressed in a black combat jacket with a gray sweater and no tie. I waver. Throughout the flight, Patricia proclaimed over and over again her innocence until ordered by the soldiers to be quiet, but since then the tracker has been through a sophisticated surveillance analysis system and, without a doubt, the device that was inside Patricia's cell phone belongs to the Project and her fingerprints were discovered on it, the activation of it triggered from her and her alone. I have checked and rechecked it myself, and the intelligence analysts who dissected the device also confirmed that it is not a piece of apparatus that exists within MI5. I have been assured that MI5 currently does not know of my whereabouts in the UK on order of the home secretary.

"Dr. Martinez," the man urges, "we have to go I'm afraid."

But Patricia cries out again. I tell the officer to stand aside, to permit me to speak to Patricia without being overwhelmed by any new bodily scents or proximity to strangers. A shaft of cold air whips around me.

"Doc, I'm so sorry."

"What are you sorry for?"

Her eyes are red and swollen from almost constant crying, and I find I have the greatest urge to reach out and touch her face, but something holds me back. What? Uncertainty? Or worse? Shame?

"I'm sorry I put us in danger," she says after a moment.

I drop my head as the words tumble from her mouth, because, in truth, I am so tired with it all now, so very near the end. Tears spring in my eyes, trespassing across my cheeks. "You have been lying to me."

"No."

"Yes! Yes. The evidence is there." I wipe my face, feeling dizzy, lost. I am a feather in the wind, a petal broken from its stem. "You said you were my friend."

"I am!"

It's too much for me to process. I close my eyes and try to shut it all out. For a long time throughout my life, I have been on my own, yet when I met Patricia, I thought I'd found someone I could trust, finally someone who accepted me for being me, but life isn't always that easy, is it? Life is hard. Life smacks you in the face, kicks you down and just when you are getting up, it kicks you again, harder, over and over, until your face is in the dirt. Only the strong rise once more, time and time again, the determined, those for whom the drive inside propels them forward when all around them stumble and crawl. But how long can you keep picking yourself back up when there's no hope of the kicking ever stopping? At what point do you say "enough to it all" and give in to the inevitable?

"I have to go," I say.

"Doc, no, no, don't do it. You can't trust them."

That's when I see red, confused at my friend and yet, for the first time in a while, thinking with total clarity. "You told me to come here. Do you remember? It was on the train. All along you told me to come here and to see Balthus' wife. You said it was the correct thing to do, and now you are saying I cannot trust them. Who can

I not trust? MI5? The Project? The CIA? You?" I move in. "You?"

"Doc …"

"The truth is none of us can trust anyone. That is what you have now shown me with your deception. That is what I now know. You had the tracker. Your fingerprints were on it. Your activation. The code was linked to it. No one else had your phone."

"Chris did!" she cries. "Chris had my phone!"

"Stop!" I yell.

My voice echoes around the deserted parking garage as the tears roll down Patricia's face, and I feel a stab of anger inside me mixed with guilt, with doubt, love, and with utter, desperate confusion.

"They all died," I say after a moment, my voice low, my whole body feeling suddenly drained of energy, as if I have been walking through a desert with no water for a very long time and now I am on my knees. "They all died because of me. I have an opportunity to make that better. The email worked. Chris confirmed it at Weisshorn."

"But Doc, we don't know he's safe. And … what if it was him? What … what if Chris planted the tracker. I'm telling you—he had my phone."

"I, too, had your phone," I say, but even as I speak, a seed of doubt springs up in my mind.

"He had access to my phone if he wanted it," Patricia says now, quicker, more urgent. "And he's a hacker, for God's sake. He went to prison."

"All three of us have been to prison."

The man from before hovers nearby. Patricia falls silent, spits out a mixture of snot and tears, the fluids landing on the ground, staining the light-gray concrete a cloud of black. I think of Chris stranded back in the Alps. Could he have done something without me knowing? He was in prison when Balthus was governor—how well did Balthus really know him? My brain flicks through every picture it has taken of him, every sentence recorded, every scene documented. But then I think of the tavern—Patricia had her cell phone in the Swiss tavern when she went to the bar.

After a moment, I look up, every muscle in my body drained. "It has been you all along." The words limp out of me. "I do not know how I did not see it before."

"Doc, no. It's not what you think. I've only ever been helping you."

"You used your phone when you were not supposed to."

"I … I was texting my sister!"

"Texting your sister does not compute."

"Oh, Doc, please," Patricia says. She stands there, stiff for a moment, until, finally, her shoulders fall. "My sister isn't well," she says after a few seconds. The air hangs around us, heavy, damp. "She has cancer now, just like my mam … just like mam did."

"Cancer? So you were texting your sister, why—to check on her?"

"Yeah." She lifts her head back up, gulps. "She says she's only got three weeks or so to live. I … I contacted her on … on Facebook. My family—they left a message." Tears stain her cheeks and when I look at her hands, her fingers are scrunched into tight balls. Upset, sad—are these the emotions my friend is feeling right now? I am tired. I am too tired to determine what it all means.

"What type of cancer does your sister have?"

"Huh? Oh, er, breast. She has breast cancer."

Alarm bells. "What stage?"

"What?"

I move in. The armed man moves with me. "What stage of breast cancer does she have?"

"Oh, um, stage one, I think."

I remain now very still as bit by bit, the lie that Patricia has woven begins to unravel. "Her diagnosis and prognosis do not match. You texted her when we agreed we would not do that due to security. You have used Facebook to contact family. You … you do not even like your family. The book at the train station was given to you by a woman who works for the Project. And it is a possibility that you left the book on the ground at Lake Geneva so the Project could know where we had been."

"No!"

"You never told me about your sister. People share things, other people. You like to talk. Yet you did not talk about this."

"I didn't want to … It was something I could deal with alone."

"Lies. Lies, lies. You do not like your family." I rub my scalp. "All along you have wanted me alone, away from Chris. You did not want me to go into that hospital, but why? So the Project could find me out in the open? Only they did not get their chance and now all the connections make sense."

"Doc, Doc, stop it. Stop it, please." She smears snot from her face. "I haven't … You're making links, Doc, and I get that, I do—it's just the way your brain works—but they're links that aren't connected. They're assumptions, and … and you don't like assumptions, Doc. Can't you see that? I didn't put the tracker into my phone. I have nothing to do with it."

But my brain fires out from my mouth exactly what it thinks, no social filter available, my feelings hurt, scorched, red hot from flames. "You texted. You were on Facebook." I start to reel off the facts, precise, logical. "You said yourself your sister does not like you. You killed your mother. That is why they do not like you, your family, because you killed their mother."

Tears flow freely down Patricia's cheeks, cuffed hands unable to wipe them away. "Doc, stop it. You're being mean now. You know I … You know I didn't kill my mam."

"You did." The urge to state the exact situation is strong and I don't know how to cloak the details any other way as other people do, dressing the truth in lies to save feelings. Anger washes right through me. "It was euthanasia, but it is still a killing. You served time in prison for it."

"Yeah," she sobs, "next to you. And that's why we're friends, because we understand each other."

She tries to step toward me, but the officer holds her back. "No." She shakes her head over and over. "No. No. Doc, you can't do this to me." She heaves in a gulp of oxygen. "Balthus—Balthus was married to the home secretary, Doc. *Married.* He put you in touch with Chris—ask … ask yourself why."

I slap my head a little. Facts. I need to stay with facts. Data. Control. "Balthus was … was a good man."

"I know, but, Doc, I'm not lying!"

"Yes, you are," slides in a new voice.

A woman dressed in a tailored navy skirt suit with a cream blouse of cotton thread and silk, strides into the courtyard just ahead of the car park where a large black door now hangs half open to a stone and metal bunker inside. She strides over to us, heels clicking on concrete and straight away I smell rose, musk, juniper, and sharp red berries. Her freckled face is instantly recognizable, not from someone I have met in person, but have seen through the confines of a screen in data beamed between one country and another.

She extends her hand, long, French manicured fingers of translucent skin, skin that shines in the low-level light of the bulbs above, her hair the color of flames.

"Hello, Ms. Martinez. I'm Harriet Alexander, the UK home secretary. So pleased to finally meet you."

CHAPTER 27

SECURE LOCATION, WHITEHALL, LONDON

0 Hours and 23 Minutes to Project Reinitiation

Harriet Alexander stands in front of us, just as we saw her on the tablet screen in the Swiss tavern.

I look at her outstretched hand, but do not take it, instead trying hard, in this closed-in space, to recall how to be socially polite. "Hello. My official title is 'doctor,' not 'Ms.' Your name Harriet means 'ruler of the home.' It is a Teutonic name."

She smiles with perfect straight white teeth. No eye creases. "Of course. Of course. *Doctor*—do forgive me." She swivels around to Patricia. "And this is Patricia O'Hanlon, isn't it?" Each word, when she speaks, sounds like plush velvet, like thick cream over a rich, dense dessert.

Patricia bites her lip but says nothing. The officer steps forward and grips her arm.

Ms. Alexander turns to me. "You met this woman in prison, Maria—may I call you Maria?"

"That is my name."

A short nod. "Thank you. Am I right in believing that you met Ms. O'Hanlon in the prison my husband ... ran?"

"Yes."

She drops her stare to Patricia. "It is wrong to deceive, Ms.

O'Hanlon—you are aware of that?"

"What?"

"You know what I mean." Harriet Alexander nods to an aide in a gray suit and tie who has appeared at her side. He hands her a pink cardboard file and she opens it.

"You said to Ms. ... to Dr. Martinez that you were from a large family and that you murdered your mother as an act of kindness, is that correct?"

"What is this? Doc?"

But I say nothing. Confusion seeps through me, conflict. I am torn between the face of my friend, between Chris, Balthus, and the truth, set on proving the decades of lies by people close to me, by governments who were supposed to protect its citizens and uphold its most sacred principles. My throat feels dry and the garage ceiling is low, the air damp against my skin. It's all too close and I don't like it, it aggravates me, clouds my cognitive thought. I tap my finger very slightly on my thigh.

"You see, Ms. O'Hanlon," the home secretary continues, "you are a liar."

"No!" She shakes her head, the officer still holding her. "No!"

I open my mouth to respond, then hesitate as ahead a close protection guard with a blue pin in his lapel touches his ear, a small breeze whistling along the cold concrete causing his jacket to flap up; a handle of a gun rests by his hip.

The home secretary turns to me. "We have been able to run a thorough check on this woman, Dr. Martinez—Maria. She is not who she says she is." She shakes her head. "I'm so sorry you have to find out like this. But you see, I ... found letters from ... from Balthus." She performs a tiny gulp then nods to her aide, and he produces from a file three small A5 pages scribed with green ink.

"We have uncovered these." She pinches the pages with her porcelain fingers. "Balthus ... he wrote about you when, well, it must have been when you were at your home in Salamanca."

An alert inside me fires. "How do you know about my villa in Salamanca?"

"Oh, forgive me. Yes, of course. Please, do not be alarmed—I know you have been through so much. Since your email with the files on this Project Callidus organization, the investigation has already begun."

"It has?" Elation, hope spring up inside. "It has begun?" I want to turn to Patricia and whoop, look at Chris and watch him grin and call me Google, but then I realize that can't happen now. That everything has changed. I blink at the damp, thick concrete and feel a strange weight inside me, a boulder in my stomach.

Harriet Alexander tips her head now with just one slight angle of her face. "I think you'll agree with me, Maria, when I say the investigation is of huge importance to the nation, to … to me. But of course, we had to know whom we were dealing with. We had to know all about you and so we accessed … well, we accessed highly secure data and the process of investigation into the entire Project network has begun."

"Doc, don't listen to her."

My eye flits to Patricia as I wrestle with my thoughts. "This is what you wanted. You wanted me here. You wanted me to be with the government, for an investigation to begin. Why should I now not listen to her?"

"Because … because I thought we could trust her, but Doc, look at me." She tries to hold her arms up, but the officer restrains her. "They have hold of me, literally, and they are telling lies about me. Loads of lies! What I told you about me, about my family— Doc, it's all true. And now they are trying to twist it all. Why am I the only one that can see that she's a lying fucking bitch!"

The officer yanks Patricia tighter; the government aide whips up his head. Along the low ceiling of the car park, a small, brown bird flies in, trapped, then flitters away searching for an exit.

Harriet Alexander regards Patricia for a second, then, turning to me, inhales one, neat breath. "He talked about you a lot, you know, Balthus, in his notes that we found. Of course, he never said to me where you were or indeed *who* you really were." She stops, wipes an eye with her fifth finger. "I'm sorry. I'm just learning of your ... relationship to my husband. It is still all new. But of course now"—she clears her throat—"now he's dead."

I shift on my feet, unsure what to say. "When dealing with grief it is important to express your emotions in a productive and tangible way."

She gives the tiniest of sniffs then smiles, but still there are no eye creases. "He said you were one of a kind." She consults the letters. "Where is it ...? Ah, yes, here." She points to the page with a manicured fingernail. "He said he was worried about you because of your relationship with Miss O'Hanlon. Because, and I quote"—she reads straight from the page—"'because Patricia O'Hanlon didn't kill her mother with kindness, but murdered her brutally to gain an inheritance that wasn't hers.'" She looks up, still quoting. "'And I suspect Ms. O'Hanlon has been working for the Project all along.'"

"No!" Patricia yells, and pushes the guard away, but he grabs her, shoves her to the ground. "That money was from my nana! She left it to pay for college! Doc, don't believe this shit!"

The home secretary ignores her and stares straight at me. "Maria, Balthus mentioned a letter you received from your stepmother, Ines, when you were in Goldmouth."

I try to think, scramble my normally fast functioning brain. "Yes. I ..."

"Who read it?"

"Pardon?"

"Who read the letter?"

I look to Patricia with her face to the floor, the air around me feeling cold, the world I know collapsing in on itself. "You did."

Patricia raises her face to mine. I feel so sad. I feel so lost, so back to the beginning when I was totally on my own.

"You read the letter from Ines," I say, numb. "But it was—"

"It was in Spanish," Harriet Alexander says. She turns to Patricia. "Balthus always wondered about you, about that letter."

"No. Doc, this is wrong."

"You read it, but Ines wrote in Spanish. How did you understand it?"

"I picked it up! I learnt stuff from the old woman I used to look after in the homes before I was banged up. And … and me mam loved Spanish. I must have …" She searches the ground. "I must have picked some up from her. Doc, please!"

"So from that," the home secretary says, "you can read a full letter?"

"Yes." A shake of the head. "Sort of. Just the gist." She looks to me. "Doc, you have to believe me!"

"But they found the tracker, didn't they?" Harriet Alexander continues. "A Project tracker. Maria herself confirmed it. And Maria, how do you think they found you in Montserrat? Think." She steps nearer in. "How do you think the Project officer you killed on the Geneva-bound train managed to intercept your email with the incriminating files?"

"How do you know I was in Montserrat?" I say. "How do you know about the train? You cannot …" I stop as the answer forms: the investigation.

Harriet exhales. "We are already unearthing all the details of your activities on the run up to now. Our security services have worked fast to lock down all the data we can find."

I rub my head, tap my foot. It's too much. It's all too much.

"Maria? Maria, you do understand that the Project found you through Ms. O'Hanlon, don't you? And how was that possible? Because she was working with the Project right from when you were at Goldmouth Prison." She holds up the letters. "And all along, Balthus suspected her. It was all a set-up." She pauses. "She was never really your friend."

"The tracker," I say to myself.

"Pardon?"

"The tracker allocated to Patricia only." I raise my eyes to my friend, to the woman I thought I could trust. "I had the code in my notebook … my notebook." I look around for my rucksack. "Where is my bag? I want my bag." I feel odd, woozy. An officer hands the bag to me and I clutch it to my chest, rip open the zipper, pull out my pad. "I … You … It says … here. In here, it says what the code you have on your phone means. I remembered it, that's what I do … They drugged me, but, but I remembered it." My breathing becomes rapid.

"Doc?" Patricia says as her shoulders are hauled up by a guard. "Doc, it's okay, Doc. You're just panicking. Breathe more steady. That's it."

I find myself listening to her, to my friend, then realize with a flash of rage that she isn't that at all. "Why?" I hear myself say. "Why? I … You speak Spanish …"

"No, I don't. I just … I can just understand a few words, like I said—to get the gist."

"No. No, no, no." I beat my head a little with the heel of my palm. Exhaustion, fear, chaos, confusion. They all fire heavy rounds of shelling in my mind, mortar fire slamming thick and hard. Bang, bang, bang. I grip my skull, the confusion and despair and sadness too much to take. Bang, bang, bang.

"Doc?"

"Maria?"

I drop my hands, jerk up my head at the sound of Harriet Alexander's voice.

"Maria, I've just had this information patched through to me. It's from our security services team."

She hands me a computer tablet. "This … this says …"

"It confirms that Patricia O'Hanlon controlled the tracker." She glances to Patricia then to me. "It says she's the source. There is a file link."

I gulp and, with shaking fingers, press on the link. "I … How can they be certain? What proof do I have?"

She steps forward, points. "There."

I read. Confirmation that the code I had has been traced back to the Project. It all flashes in front of me. Details of all their facilities, of Scotland, of Hamburg, how the code links to the access data that patches the phone GPS directly to Project control via one thing, one person: Patricia. I stumble a little as I then flick through surveillance image after surveillance image of Patricia with her cell, using it. I look at the times, the dates, cross-reference them in my head with where we were exactly during that period, what we were doing.

My eyes sting. "You … We … No phones," I manage to say. "We said we would not use our phones. They were for …" I slip away, caught by an image of Chris and I in the booth as Patricia stands at the bar in the Swiss tavern. "You had them follow us."

Patricia cries. "No. No …"

"You allowed surveillance on us."

"No, that's them … I mean her, I mean MI5. I said no!"

Harrier Alexander frowns. "You said no to what? And how would we do that, MI5? We had no access to you nor any need to gain access."

"Because … because you wanted Maria killed. Doc, tell them."

"We are the government of the United Kingdom," the home secretary says. "I have not sanctioned any killing nor know of one, and as Ms. Martinez knows from these surveillance images before her, we have intercepted them from the Project she has helped reveal to us!"

I stare at the photographs on the screen, at the tens of images before me of places and situations we have only recently been in, swiping to a file that confirms again through linked codes that the only way a tracker could have been activated was through direct and deliberate actions from Patricia.

"You … you have been with the Project all along."

"Please, Doc …"

"You said you wanted to help me."

"I do. Being here is"—she shakes her head—"*was* the right thing to do."

"The pictures," I say, pacing. "The images and the surveillance. The need to get me to the UK, the tracker and the activation of it, the ability to read Spanish, the way you appeared in my cell … Were you … were you my handler?"

"Doc, stop. You don't know what you're saying."

"I've had handlers all my life, and I did not know they were with the Project. You are another one of those." It all makes sense now, connects, computes. "It … it was all a plan. Balthus even suspected it."

"Then why didn't he tell you?"

"Balthus would have kept it to himself," the home secretary says. "He was like that. With Maria as"—she falters, swallows a little—"I'm sorry. With Maria as his daughter, he would have done all he could to solve the problem himself. Before he died, he told me he was trying to … trying to solve something." She pauses. "He would have found a way. And with the letters"—a brief flicker of eyelids closing—"he did."

"That's a load of bullshit!" Patricia shouts. She spins her gaze to me, drops her voice. "Doc, I never meant to hurt you."

"What?"

"No. I mean—"

"You said you never meant to hurt me."

"I mean … I mean I always wanted you to be safe. None of this … none of this was ever supposed to happen."

"That sounds very much like a confession," Harriet Alexander says.

"Why?" I say to Patricia.

"Doc, I didn't want to—"

"A confession. That means admitting to something."

"Yes, but—"

"All the facts add up."

"I've never ever wanted you to get hurt, Doc, through any of this. You have to believe me."

"The files," I say. "The photographs, the evidence trail. They are all facts and data."

"Data can lie."

"Humans can lie!" I yell. I stand, catching my breath, chest heaving. An empty crisp packet blows in the breeze.

"Maria?" the home secretary says. "You deal in facts. You deal in information and figures. Well, I'm afraid the information we have is undeniable, no gray areas, just black and white. Right and wrong. Patricia O'Hanlon is—has been all along—working for the Project."

I slap my hands to my ears, not wanting to process her words. The reality is there, I know it is, but I can't face it. My world, my world of data and logic. It's what protects me—and it's what tears me apart. I try to resist it, attempt to fit the information into a different hole, but no matter how hard I try, I realize Harriet Alexander is right: the facts, the data, and the irrefutable information exist. My brain knows that it all adds up to only one conclusion and when it does, when I grab hold of myself and shove my face forward to blink at the hard, cold reality, everything inside me detonates.

"Why?" I shout.

Before I know it, before I can ask myself what I am doing or why, I sprint so fast, no one has time to stop me as I thrust my hands around Patricia's neck, squeeze her lily-white skin tight between my fingers, tears rolling down my face, as her hands cuffed, are unable to pull away.

"Doc! P-please …"

People shout, but still I grip the neck of my former friend. "You were with them! You were with the Project all along! I have seen the evidence! The tracker links to the code, which can only be set by you! You!" I wobble. "I thought you were my friend!" Tears run down my cheeks. "I thought you were my friend."

I squeeze again and her body falls limp and an officer finally drags me away, my torso bent double as I slump to the concrete. I cry out so loud that I stop myself with the sheer decibel of the sound, the wave of my rage going out to sea, replaced now by a long shore of emptiness, so vast and wide I fear it there will never be an end as I curl up into a ball and hide and moan.

The officer is crouching over Patricia's unmoving, limp frame on the hard concrete.

I unfold my body slowly and blink away the tears. "P-Patricia?"

"Dr. Martinez," I hear the home secretary say. "We must go."

It's then Patricia coughs, spluttering into the air, and despite my anger, I find myself relieved, exhausted. The officer helps Patricia up and the urge for me to be a doctor, to fix and mend is so strong, I have to wrap my hands around my chest, rocking, my brain spiraling out of control from Patricia. The scent of her talcum-powder skin still lingers on my palms from where my hands were locked around her neck.

Patricia is taken away. She shouts for me the whole time and it is only when I drag myself up and look at her that I see her five fingers held up out high above the grip of the handcuffs, breaking through the officer's clutch and damp air with their soft, padded tips.

"Maria?"

I tear my gaze away, turn to the home secretary.

"There is a security situation," she says. "We need to go right now."

I stagger to a stand, and sway across the concrete in a haze as I am lead away. The muffled cries of Patricia's voice yelling out her nickname for me over and over echo in the gray damp air.

CHAPTER 28

DEEP COVER PROJECT FACILITY

Present Day

The door slams shut and the hand slips away.

I stumble to a halt, gasping in air, ready to slash into the neck of whoever had hold of me. There's a light, soft and yellow, blinking on the ceiling. I squint, ready to attack, to defend myself.

"What is happening?" I say. "Who is there?" My sight adjusts and before me emerges the sight of five computers, all linked to a stand-alone server. I investigate a little more and realize that the devices are not connected to any outside system. This is highly unusual. Cautiously, I observe some more. The room is small, six meters by six meters. Two soft leather chairs are angled to the side, and by the computers stand rows upon rows of bound books, leather spines with gold embossed writing, and on the consoles that rest near wooden shelves, lights of blue, green, yellow, and pink glow, gentle and soft where a filing cabinet made of metal and plastic rests. I feel the beat of my own breath in the air, acutely aware that someone else is here, but my eyes are locked on the unusual sight of the filing cabinet and the bookshelf. Everything in the Project is computerized, no books normally kept, and only people like Black Eyes and the situation room supervisors have access to any traditional paper data sources. It is how we live our lives today, online, exposed for all to see, privacy just an indulgently naive word.

"This is room 17," a voice suddenly says.

I jump and look to the source. In front of me stands Subject 209. Abigail. Daniel's girlfriend. I press myself into the wall, hands ready to fight. "Why did you drag me in here against my will?"

She remains where she is and holds her hands up in the air. "I'm on your side."

"We are all with the Project," I say. "We are all on the same side. Yet it was you who gave Patricia the book at the station warning us. Why?"

"So you remember me?"

I clock the door—I can be there within two seconds. My hands are able to break this woman's neck.

"You brought coffee when I was in the room with Kurt," I say now, bargaining for time. "His real name was Daniel. He was working for the Project, but before that—"

"Before that he was with MI5."

She appears as if she is about to say something else when her head drops. I don't know what to do. Is she sad? Is she going to hurt me? Knowing the answer to neither, I aim for facts.

"Why did you send me the note?"

She looks up, wipes her cheeks dry. "I used to be with Daniel in MI5 and then, when the NSA Prism scandal blew up and they threatened to pull the plug on the Project, I went entirely over to the Project, thinking they were going to protect people."

"You are—were—Daniel's girlfriend," I say.

"Yes."

"Daniel tried to kill Balthus …" I stop as I say his name, a scratch on my voice, a pain. "Your boyfriend wanted to take me against my will to the Project."

"And yet here you are anyway. They got to you. They always get to us, eventually."

It throws me. Because she is right. I am here. All that time I fought it, battled against being part of the Project machine, and yet I am in their group now, part of their secret system. A memory floats into my mind, something about Patricia and the home secretary of the United Kingdom, Balthus' wife. I shake my head. The whisper of thought blows away.

"Why are you here?" I say.

"To help you."

"Why?"

"Because what they have created here"—her shoulders drop—"it's not what we signed up for, me and Daniel. He wouldn't have wanted it to turn into this. They are doing things—things that ..." She stops, inhales. "When I heard Daniel had been killed, I was mad as hell. I went straight to the Project, to Dr. Carr, and said I'd get you, track you for them. And I did. At the monastery, the abbey in Montserrat. But then ..." She trails off, her eyes drifting to a huge black screen plastered to the wall.

"Daniel had a brother, killed in Afghanistan," she says now. "He told you about that, didn't he?"

The memories are all there of the therapy after prison. Piercing, painful. Deceitful. "Yes."

"That would make sense. He wanted to get you on our side then. God, he'd laugh if he saw you now, knee-deep in the Project's shit. And it is shit, because they made him into nothing."

I inch just a little to the left. "I do not understand what you mean."

"They wiped him from the database. According to their files, Daniel never existed. He was just a number they could delete. In the end, who he was didn't matter, I mean, they just didn't care. I don't matter to them, you don't, none of us do. All that matters to Callidus is getting what they want."

"We are all numbers that can be deleted. That is the modern computer age."

"Yeah, and that's okay, is it? To allow that to happen?" She coughs and when her hand draws away, I notice tiny specs of blood on the padded flesh of her palms.

"We're not robots," she says now, wiping her hands then striding to a keyboard on the right side of a console that sits near the filing cabinet.

Feeling unsure, unsteady, I try to hold on to facts. "What is this room used for?"

"This?" She glances round. "This is where they keep information they don't want anyone to see. This," she says, floating out her arms, "is room 17—information ground zero."

I follow her sightline. The old books, the cabinet, the lack of main server. Something is not right. "How do you have access to this place?"

She inhales. "Because I have the highest clearance level."

Nerves shoot through me. It is a test after all? She must be part of the Project organization seeing if I can handle this type of situation and I am failing.

"I have to go." I start to stride to the door, but a buzzer sounds, loud and piercing. My hands slap to my ears as I endure the noise. When it ends after seven seconds, my limbs feel drained, my mind heavy.

"Why did you do that?" I say, gasping for oxygen.

"Because you can't go. I need your help. This Project has to end. What's the phrase they use?"

I say nothing. It is clear what I now have to do: this woman is against the Project. "I have to report you."

She laughs, but there are no creases on her skin, instead her eyes are downturned, her shoulders weighted. "Go on then, report me. I've got nothing left to lose anyway."

I hesitate, my gaze flipping between the door and this woman whose eyes never light up. There is a feather-like quality about the way she moves, a delicate, eggshell film to her limbs and skin.

"You are coughing up blood," I say after a moment, the air

cold, the distant sound of boots on tiles marching somewhere in the building. "You are not well."

She leans back on a desk made of white Formica. "I have stomach cancer."

I say nothing. I want to ask for data, reel off a series of in-depth medical questions, but something tells me that right now, I need to be quiet.

"I was tested on, just like you. I don't have Asperger's or anything, but when I started out at MI5 and worked with the Project, they asked for volunteers, so I said yes. Daniel told me not to, but I thought, why not? They know what they're doing, right? The service cares for us, cares for the people who work for it." She laughs, but not light or lemony, this is a deep, chalk scratch of a laugh, a rough slice of tree bark. "They said the drugs were to help the brain, to help people focus and work fast." She looks straight at me. "To help people like you."

I stay close to the door. "I know of the Project's conditioning program. These drugs are to help us be better, perform better. They are giving me Typhernol now to help me remain calm. To ensure—"

"These drugs are killing you."

The air, the breath from my lungs, the flash of lights on the computers to the side—it all halts. "You are lying."

"My God, I wish I were. The blood, the stuff I'm coughing up? That's the cancer the drugs they gave me years back caused. I know you found a file in Hamburg about drugs they were giving your mother, Ines Villanueva."

I grip the edge of the table. "She was my adopted mother."

"Yeah, well, that piece of work who was selling you and your adopted dad down the river for drugs to stop her cancer, she was the only one they worked on. After that, they began to have the opposite effect."

My brain begins to make connections. "You did not have cancer before the medicine?"

"No. The drugs gave it to me. And now I'm going to die because of them—and so will you."

"No. No, you are wrong."

The woman turns and, walking to the filing cabinet, opens the top drawer. I watch, my heart racing, torn between truth and pretend, between what to believe and what to ignore.

Opening a blue file, Subject Number 209 locates a sheet of paper with black ink on neat lines. "It's ironic that, given that the Project watches everyone and tracks what they do online—and was nearly closed down because of the NSA Prism scandal—they choose to keep their most confidential and secret documents on paper so they can't be hacked."

My nerves rising, I watch now as the woman brings up a file marked Subject 375.

"Here you are."

She slides across a document that contains everything about me since I was born. It is extensive. I track it and each time I take in a word and a detail, my heart rate rises and a worm of worry grows in my stomach. "Why are you showing me the data?"

"Because of this."

She flips the document to the last page. "You've noticed, right, that you are the oldest around here?"

I swallow. The worm of worry burrows into me deep now. "Yes."

"Well, this is why."

I read now page upon page of analytical detail about me and my medical state: heart rates, drugs administered, oxygen level tests, dexterity conditioning, IQ levels, mathematical ability, speed, and accuracy. It is only when I get to the end that my sight become milky and vomit swells in my throat. "I could die before I am thirty-four?"

"You are the oldest here," Abigail says, "because you are the only person the conditioning testing—and drugs—has not killed so far. Everyone before you—everyone—has died. Including this woman."

She hands me a photograph now and immediately I recognize

the face. "It is his wife." My voice shakes as I struggle with what is happening.

"Dr. Carr's wife. You know her?"

"No, I …" I stop, blink. "I … I saw her in my mind when I was in the sensory chamber."

"That place? Oh, Jesus. Don't tell me—Dr. Carr told you that you had to forget all your friends and that the Project are your family now?"

I nod, numb.

"And let me guess, he told you your mind had made up what you saw in the chamber, right?"

I look at the words on the document. "I have been changing," I say now, more to myself.

"How?"

"Headaches. Nose bleeds."

"Performing tasks faster?"

"Yes."

She sighs. "God, they've really done it with you, haven't they?"

"Done what?"

"With you, the training's worked, the conditioning on you. This Dr. Carr, he set up the whole Project with his wife back in the seventies after their daughter was killed in Tehran in an attack."

I think back to the sensory chamber, to the memory, and the discussion between Black Eyes and his wife. "She died, too."

"Yep. And looks like it's driven him forward ever since. I found files, accessed stuff they thought was safe, but I managed to get in. They are trying to use you, Maria, don't you see that? And this is just the tip of the iceberg."

Iceberg. Why is she saying iceberg? I stand back, hazy, confused, sick. Will I die before I am thirty-four? "I am thirty-three. It … it is my birthday in two days' time."

She lets out a breath, long, slow. "Look, I don't know what'll happen before then, but they're watching you. All the changes going on with you, the nosebleeds and stuff. If you get past thirty-four, it means the conditioning has worked, and they'll want to know why. You'll never get out of here."

I look at the four walls, at the lock on the door. How long has there been a lock on my life? I think then of the train journey, of Chris, of the eye on his computer screen in Montserrat and how we found the ticking clock: it was counting down not only to my birthday, but to the day I may die.

"How … how long do you have left to live?"

She pauses. "One month now, maybe two?" She exhales, long, heavy. "I don't know."

We both stare at the file, at the books and the lights and the black screen by the keyboards. I trace with a solitary finger the details about me on the paper of ink and offline data. My birthday, my age, what I have seen, all connected to a number, one number, Subject 375—a number that, at one touch of a button, can be made to disappear forever.

I look at this woman, this subject number who says she wants my help. But do I need hers? Is this what my life has been leading up to? To die now for the Project? For the greater good?

"You said you accessed information the Project thought was safe," I say now. "Classified Callidus information that is highly protected. How did you hack into it?"

"Because I had someone help. Someone you know."

"Who?"

She smiles now, and this time, small creases fan in thin lines from her eyes. "Chris. Chris Johnson."

CHAPTER 29

SECURE LOCATION, WHITEHALL, LONDON

0 Hours and 18 Minutes to Project Reinitiation

We are led to a room of mahogany and birch. The door is shut behind us and I notice one small window on the wall. Instantly, I recognize the space from the video feed Chris hacked into on his tablet in Switzerland, yet now I am here, what dominates my mind is not my surroundings, but Patricia and her betrayal.

"Patricia was working for the Project," I murmur aloud, oblivious to the stare Harriet Alexander throws me, not knowing at all what it could ever mean.

She pours me a glass of ice water and instructs me to drink. I do so, the liquid cold down my throat, awakening my brain to where I am, creating an alertness, but one that is tinged with a sadness and confusion I cannot place.

"Why don't you sit down?"

I lower myself into a chair made of wood and brown cloth and see on the table a computer and next to it a picture of the home secretary and Balthus. Immediately, I reach forward and pick up the frame, staring at the image of the man who was my real father.

Harriet Alexander observes me. She reclines in a high-backed leather chair that smells of fruit pastels and she lets out a small mew.

"It's a shame when we don't get to spend time with the people that really matter to us."

Uncertain what she means, I keep my sight set on the picture. Balthus' strong jaw, tall height, straight shoulders, deep tan, and dark hair. Basque, like me. Like Isabella. I take out my notebook and pen, record the photograph in a fast sketch, then lay it next to the grainy picture of my birth mother.

The home secretary blinks at the images, then, clearing her throat, looks up. "I am sorry you had to find out this way about your friend, about Ms. O'Hanlon."

I give the photograph one more gaze then return it to the exact spot from where I took it. I feel numb, a boat lost at sea about to capsize, hull flooding with water that has nowhere to go but down. "Everyone lies," I say after a second, my mind set on Patricia.

She sighs. "I'm afraid they do."

A phone sounds and she picks it up. I allow my eyes a search of the room. There are no bookshelves, no files, just a desk and a small window, two chairs, a television mounted to the wall, and a door. No nameplate adorns the table, no other images sit in frames by the computer, just a keyboard, screen, and phone in an atmosphere thick with dry, musk-perfumed air.

Finishing her conversation, the home secretary slots in a breath then looks straight to me. "We have a very serious situation." Taking a slim, black remote control from a drawer on the desk, she directs it at the television screen, and a breaking news report from a fast-speaking reporter comes to life.

"… approximately thirty minutes ago, a bomb was detonated in the Southbank Centre area of London. Initial reports are suggesting up to three hundred people could have been killed so far with many more injured. There was no warning and no details as of yet as to who is responsible for what is already being called one of the worst terrorist attacks on British soil. The prime minister will be calling an emergency COBRA session within the next hour, before which we should expect a statement. As you can see the entire Southbank Centre has been shattered ..."

Harriet Alexander hits the mute button and the news reporter's mouth continues to move as, behind her, the now-obliterated Southbank arts and music building lies unrecognizable in blasted shards of white rubble on a blood-splattered ground.

"It's appalling," she says, "appalling."

I look again to the screen then to her. "You are the home secretary of the United Kingdom. You should be at the COBRA meeting."

She nods, murmuring agreement. "I shall be there soon." She pulls her keyboard forward and taps out some numbers, the sound clicking in my head and clashing with fresh, raw memories of Patricia and her screams at being dragged away, of her betrayal, all of it merging with news of the bombing and the visceral images on the television screen.

"Maria," Ms. Alexander says now. "I have something very important I need to talk to you about. This Project Callidus—tell me: how well do you know it?"

"I have been part of the Project since my birth."

She glances to the screen where the reporter is now interviewing blood-soaked people as, along the bottom, a bulletin feed reads, "ISIS attacks UK."

"So you'll know," she says, "that Cr—Callidus fights to prevent big attacks such as this."

For some reason, I feel wary, cautious, but I cannot place why. "Project Callidus works to protect nations, using intelligence services to create a safer world. MI5, though, no longer works with the Project as the Project was supposed to cease existence after the NSA scandal, however, the Project carried on without MI5's support. And now you have begun an investigation to end it."

She regards me as a knock sounds at the door and the aide from earlier enters, presents a file to the home secretary, then leaves. Ms. Alexander reads the data then looks to me.

"We have an election coming soon, were you aware of that?"

"No."

She leans forward. "Many countries have elections due—the USA, Spain. And now a terrorist attack in the middle of it all. It makes everyone very … fearful."

I do not respond. On the TV, a woman with dark blood scratches on her face is crying.

"Maria, what would you say to … helping us?"

"What with?"

She angles her head to the screen. "To preventing this type of thing from happening again, this mass murder from overseas terrorists."

I sit up, eager at the news that at least something good can come out of my bad experience. "I am trained. I can assist your government. I can be a witness against the Project in the investigation you have underway."

She taps the table in front of her then looks up. Her face, before soft, features arranged in a mild smile, is now oddly frozen, fixed. I shift in my seat.

"Maria, there is no investigation."

"Yes—there is an investigation. You said you have started it."

She inhales, and when she does, her neat suit jacket shifts up her shoulders. "There never was going to be one."

A red flush hits my face. "That is incorrect. You said there was one. There is an investigation."

"There is no investigation."

I think about this, confused, worried. "We sent you the email. The Project has been blackmailing you. How can you not investigate an organization that is blackmailing you and your government?"

She pauses. A ripple of rain taps at the tiny window. "Because there was no blackmail."

"Yes, there was," I say fast, my head feeling packed in, crammed to the brim. "We hacked into the Weisshorn hospital system and found the entire trail."

She dances her fingers on the table then, opening a file in front of her, slides an open page to me. "Is this the trail you located?"

I read it. Names, numbers, facts, and codes. "Yes, but ..." I stop. When she said Callidus just before—I realize she had begun to say another word, then stopped.

"We have very good computer analysts here, Maria. Almost as good as you, but not quite."

"I do not understand."

"Maria, we knew this terrorist plot threat was high."

I speak slowly, as if going too fast would detonate everything. "The news report said there was no warning."

"Yes, well, we have to handle the press as best we can. Handle the ... information feed to the public."

"That is called lying."

"Maria, as you said, everyone lies."

I look at her, at the TV, at the desk and door. "If you were not being blackmailed, then where was the data coming from?"

She exhales. "Us."

I make myself look at her, look at the television screen, but it all merges into one wall of color. Nothing is making any sense.

"We needed you back, you see, Maria. So we set it all up. The blackmail trail, the codes. We knew you'd try and see if the Project was looking for you, so, naturally, it made sense to create some injustice for you and your friends to want to ... remedy. And we knew you'd want to see your mother, so the link to Weisshorn seemed the right course of action to take."

I am shell-shocked. How did this get past me? How did I walk into this? "You ... pretended you were being blackmailed and because we found the trail, it triggered a trace on our geolocation," I say, the logical part of my brain working faster than my emotional one.

"I think that's how they phrased it to me, yes. Look, I'm sorry it's had to happen this way, but we really do need you, and we had to be sure that you could still do what the Project trained you to do. Yes, we know you had help from your American computer friend, but, Maria, the Project has confirmed that you're still very much operational."

It hits me then like a punch to the face. The Project. Harriet Alexander is working with the Project. Which means the UK government is on their side, too. "Cranes," I say, feeling numb, dazed, "before when you said Callidus you initially made the sound 'Cr ...' What were you going to say?"

But she doesn't reply, instead shifts in her seat, her fingers drumming the table.

"Project Callidus has the nickname 'Cranes,' which means peace. Only people affiliated with the Project know of it. Which means you have known of the Project for a significant amount of time."

She exhales a measured breath. "Maria, to think I didn't know of it would be naive. Of course I knew. Not, granted, for a long time, but enough to know of its ... value. Particularly at a time like this." She looks to the television.

I work it through in my head despite my distress, fast and hard as, before me, Harriet Alexander sits and watches. "You had people tracing me," I say, voice low, slotting it all together.

"Yes. It had to be done, I'm afraid."

"You sent someone after us on the train from Zurich, the dough woman."

"I don't know every single operational detail, but yes, I believe there was an officer trailing you."

"Was Patricia part of it? Part of the Project's trace?"

But her sight is distracted by a moving image on the television. "Sorry, one moment." She points the remote control, turns up the volume. The reporter is talking about the body count.

"It's now been confirmed that three hundred thirty-five people have died as a result of the blast. The area is in complete lockdown and nearby hospitals are struggling with the sheer volume of patients. Calls are going out to people for blood donations and ...”

Harriet Alexander turns back. She breathes in, smooths down her lapels and, waiting for one second, looks straight to me. “Maria,” she says, “we need you to return to the Project.”

“No.”

“It has to be the case. I’m so sorry.”

But my head shakes, fear ripples through me. “No. Project Callidus is not a good organization. They kill and lie and they have controlled my whole life. You have to investigate them.” I can feel my senses firing, my stimming increasing, my leg tapping as my brain spirals at the thought of the investigation not happening, of the deceit that has happened.

“I cannot go back.” I stand, pace. “The Project killed Balthus, they killed my papa. You have to stop them. We sent you the files. You have seen what they do. The way they operate is wrong, immoral, and unjust. Do not believe whatever it is they have been telling you.”

She gestures to the television. “And you think what terrorists are doing is right?” She waits for a moment, her slim green eyes on me. “I know it was Ines who killed Balthus,” she says now.

I halt, turn. “What?”

She slots back a stray hair. “I know all about what happened at Ines’ house. I know she shot Balthus and your brother. I know you killed Ines. I know your brother killed your adoptive father, Alarico.”

At hearing his name, at hearing what she has to say, I stop, my hand slapping out to the wall of wood and plaster. “How ... how do you know this? I only told you that the Project was involved in killing Balthus. No detail was given in the email.”

“Maria, when will you wake up and see that, when it comes to security, governments know everything.”

"What do you—"

"What do I mean? Is that what you were going to say? What do I mean?" The veins spring out on her neck as her voice rises. "I mean we have known for a long time of the existence of the Project, Maria. The UK government, the US government, even the Spanish government—we are all involved. There—do you understand that now?"

I feel as if I've been hit by a bat to the head. The Basque people, the ones on the file who died. "Did ... did the Spanish government supply Basque people to be tested by the Project?"

"They were all former ETA members, convicts, yes, supplied by the Spanish government. People with no one who would really care if they disappeared." She sighs. "I know this all sounds harsh, but Maria, you must understand that this is what we have to do as leaders, as governments—make the tough decisions, carry out the terrible things others don't want to do, things we have to do on behalf of our electorate in order to protect them. To protect us all."

I lean back on the wall now as the whole picture forms. The Basque subject numbers and their original test origins were all ETA terrorism convicts. Somehow I find the chair and sit in it, although I don't know how much time passes, just seconds, probably, but each one feels like an hour.

"Ines, my adoptive mother, was a prosecutor of ETA terrorists," I say in a daze, my mind drawing the inevitable conclusion. "She was the Minister for Justice. Did she supply the convict names to the Project?"

"I believe so."

"And so my papa was killed because he found out that Ines was supplying ETA convicts to the Project ..."

My sight blurred, I look to the television, to where now the Prime Minister is talking to the screen, a frown on his brow, deep circles under his eyes. I blink back tears, a deep lump in my throat forming. It hits me in waves, all of it crashing up and over my mind. Who tells the truth? Does everyone hide behind a cloak to mask their real selves? "Does he know about the Project?" I say after a moment, gesturing to the screen.

"The prime minister? Now he does, yes. As does the US president. We all have security at heart you see, and it's never been needed more than now, which is why, Maria, to cull the Project's work, now we all know about it, at such a vital time would not make sense."

Her words: *now we all know.* They all know about the Project, about the lie and the testing, yet they want it to continue. And why? Terrorists will carry on murdering, I alone can't stop them, and meanwhile, everyone will continue to spout a mantra of words that mean nothing, words that, with one press of a button, can be instantly transformed to sound like something more convenient. I stand. "I want to leave."

"Maria …"

"I want to leave. Now. Restart the investigation into Project Callidus and let me go. I will not work with them again. You said you would investigate. You have to stay true to that commitment."

Harriet Alexander rises. "Maria, I'm afraid I can't do that. Believe me, please, when I say this: working with the Project—it is the right thing to do for the safety of our country."

But I have decided I am leaving and that is that. I go to the door but it is locked, so I bang at it, set about unbolting it when a buzzer, low, growling, sounds and the door flies open. Quickly I am pushed back as two men and one woman in gray suits, each with a button pin, pile in. They wrestle me forward, grip me tight, cuffing my wrists, and I panic, thrash my head, arms, torso, the metal scent of their skin punctures the air, their arms banging into me, brushing against the scar on my thumb, sending a bolt of pain searing through to my chest.

"Let me go!"

Harriet Alexander walks over from her desk, holding the document from the aide in her hand.

"Balthus thought I didn't know about his little fling with that woman that led to you, but he, like you, thought there were things that could be kept secret." She whips in a breath, momentarily glances to the photograph on her desk, then dabbing one cheek, she clears her throat. "There is an election coming up and we need to have order. But to get order, we first need chaos. And while terrorists think a big bomb in a city will do it, we know that all it takes to create what we need is one lone gunman." She leans in and I flinch. "A single match can launch a thousand fires."

Then she nods to the officers and they start to drag me away.

"No!" I shout. "No!"

"The Project needs you, Maria," she says now. "We need you. I promise you, you will see. It will all make sense to you. We need to take you to their black site facility in Scotland now."

And as the officers pull me from the room to take me back to the Project, on the television screen that hangs on the wall the camera lens pans to the chaotic bombed sight of the Southbank building lying in broken steel and rubble where bodies lie torn and strewn in deep, charred pools of their own blood.

CHAPTER 30

BLACK SITE PROJECT FACILITY, SCOTLAND

Present Day

I stare at an image of Chris on the small screen of a cell phone propped up on the table.

"Google! You're okay!"

At first, I do not speak. I am frightened. Still not 100 percent sure if this is a test or not. I gaze at the face of a friend who, it feels, I have not seen in a long time.

"Where are you?" I hear my voice say.

"Not far from where you are now in Scotland."

"This is a black site. There is no map for it."

"In this day and age, there's always a map. And besides, I had to find you." He pauses. "I had to find you and Patricia."

At the sound of her name spoken in Chris' stretched-out drawl, flashes of memories fly back and forth, faces of the people and the places I have known, the images fuzzy and blurred. Chris being here, near; Patricia being held by the Project. The thought of it destabilizes me and what is happening hits me. Whether it's unexpectedly seeing Chris' familiar face or hearing the words that Subject 209 has to say, it seems to be jolting me out of what feels has been a long, dormant time, as if I have been sleepwalking these past few weeks and I'm only now waking up.

Abigail looks to me. "Are you okay?"

I blink at the screen where Chris' solid frame sits. "How did you arrive here from the Alps?"

"Hitchhiked to stay low. You know me"—he grins—"the relaxed type." He pauses and his grin drops. "It's so good to see you."

I track the contours of his face and have the strongest propulsion to reach out and touch it, to have him here, next to me, not to hold him or him to hold me, but to at least smell him, his skin, see his hair flop into his sunken eyes. Until this moment, I hadn't realized just how much I miss him.

"How did you find me?" I say now, choking back a dry throat.

"Through me."

I turn now and look to Abigail. She is resting by the bookshelf, clutching her chest, struggling to breathe. I go to her immediately.

"You need to sit down."

"No."

"Sit."

She does as I say, her body sliding to the chair and, as I aid her, I feel her rib cage and realize how slight she is, how underweight.

"I'll be okay in a minute."

"Does this happen often?"

She nods. "Too much, now."

I check her pulse on her wrist and feel the heat of her forehead and realize that I didn't even hesitate at touching her. It's been what feels like a long time since I have worked as a doctor, but the need inside me to treat and mend must still be strong.

"How did you contact Chris?" I say, checking her pulse once more.

"Is it okay?"

"Hmmm?" I count. "Oh, yes." I drop her wrist.

"You'd all been tracked." She coughs, rubbing her arm. "That's how I knew who Chris was and that he'd been left behind in Switzerland. That's how I found him."

"They were tracing us all along," Chris says.

As the words sink in, in a slow-motion movie reel of a movement that gets quicker and quicker, pictures start to flash in my mind one after the other. Memories return fast, click, click, click, images of events that have not long happened, of Patricia and her betrayal and the tracker found in her phone, her gentle lilting voice screaming for me in the concrete parking garage. Of the home secretary and her perfume and the office with the TV and the tiny window, of her words about Balthus, about her knowing that Ines killed him, about her knowledge, in depth, of everything that happened that day. Of the officers bursting into the room and how she said I would be taken to the Project black site facility in Scotland, of what she said about the emails from … click, click, click … until, instead of being blurred and far away, the memories become vivid, real, and clear and, finally, I recall every single aspect of what happened up until now.

"The UK government was behind the blackmail messages," I say fast, breathless at the speed at which the memories have hurled themselves at me, wanting to be remembered, all the information finally coming to me. I tell Chris about all of it, about the whole setup and how the home secretary and Spain and the USA are involved, about the messages, the deceit of it all, how she is now part of the Project, about Abigail and what she has told me. And what the countdown clock Chris found really means amidst it all.

"What? Jesus fucking Christ! Are you sure? You mean, that clock thing we found could count to your … to your death? Oh, my God."

As Chris swears into the phone, calling world governments liars and scumbags, and calling the Project evil motherfuckers, I look to Abigail.

"Why could I not initially recall everything that happened just before I came here?"

"You're being given Typhernol."

"But that should not affect memory. Dr. Carr said that is a drug to help keep me calm. Versed was the drug that made me forget. That is the one they have used since I was young."

"And you believe everything Dr. Carr says?"

I think about this. "Y ... yes." But even as the word tumbles out, I am doubting it.

Abigail looks at me with downturned eyes. "Maria, they're trialing Typhernol now. And that's what's messing with your head, making you forget, making you ... easy to manipulate. They want you to forget what happened before so you will do what they want you to do."

The reality seeps in as I realize the Project has been giving me something to make me forget key information in order to mold me into the person they want me to be: obedient, pliable. If that's the case, if my mind has been used, bent to someone else's will then who, really, am I?

"When was the last time you were given an injection?" Abigail says now.

"Two ... two days ago."

"Well, it should be out of your system soon."

She coughs up more blood and I find a tissue on a shelf and hand it to her, fingers shaking a little at the news, my brain processing the entire time. Black Eyes lied to me. He lied to me about Typhernol, he lied to me about what I saw in the sensory chamber. So, if he lied about that, what else was he lying about?

I turn to Chris. "Can you access the system here?"

"Huh? Oh, yeah, but there's a wall stopping me from remotely finding where you are specifically. Why? What do you need?"

I stay motionless for a moment, bring up the floating memories of the time in the home secretary's office, of the words she spoke. "There was a bomb ... in ... in London at the ..." I think, wait for it to come, tick, tick. "At the Southbank Centre."

"Yeah, it was massive. It killed over five hundred people or something like that."

Taking to Chris must be helping, as the memory comes faster now, fully formed. "When … when I was in the home secretary's office, she talked about requiring chaos to create order, then she said that it only takes one gunman to kill many. She mentioned this in the context of upcoming political elections in the UK, the USA, and Spain."

Abigail sits up. "There's some intel about a lone gunman that involves the UK."

I look to her. "You have seen that data, too?"

"It was when you were in the situation room with Dr. Carr. It came through on the feed to go to you and I wasn't supposed to look at it, so I didn't because it was too risky, but then when you'd gone, just before I saw you with Dr. Carr in the corridor, I managed to sneak a look at what you'd deciphered and saw it. Thing is, it reminded me of something."

"Of what?"

"I'm not sure, but I've seen chatter before on this that seems to keep slipping under the radar. The Project keeps letting it pass by."

"Dr. Carr said it was just a simulation."

She shakes her head. "Nope. No way. From all the data I've seen, this thing seems real."

"Then why would he lie?"

Chris' line crackles. "Anything I can do to help?"

Abigail swivels her chair to the keyboard. "This system here isn't connected, but, Chris, let me see if I can set up some sort of worm you can catch." She taps a device. "If you're stopped from accessing the facility here each time by the wall, maybe the worm'll help you pull through and burrow in under it into the geolocation system so at least you'll know exactly where we are … just in case."

"Cool. And the surveillance?"

"I'll see what I can do. It might take a while though."

As Abigail's fingers speed across the keyboard in front of her, I shake my head, struggling to comprehend what suddenly, unexpectedly, seems to be unfolding in front of me. It's all come on so quick. Only three hours ago, I was fully signed up to the Project, to what they meant, what they stood for, and how they act. But now? Now I am discovering that, just like everything else, it is all a lie.

"I need to sit down."

I shift to the second chair and check the time; soon I will need to be at my next appointment to avoid any suspicion.

Abigail leans in. "I know this is hard," she says, "hearing all this, hearing what I had to say. You don't know who you are in here—I didn't after a while, even though I'd put myself inside Callidus to find out what the hell they were really doing. They do a number on everyone, the Project does. They're experts at getting everyone to think their way, to believe that what they're doing is for the greater good, but I'm telling you it's not. I mean, look at what they did to your friend, setting her up like that."

I freeze. "What did you say?"

She pauses. "I ... I thought you knew, you know because you mentioned the trace thing the home secretary talked about."

"Knew what?" Chris says, his deep eyes now wide in the cell screen.

"Oh shit." Abigail rubs her head, coughs once, and looks to me. "The Project got Patricia's sister to say she had cancer so Patricia would worry and contact her."

I go cold, a line of ice sliding down my spine.

"How do you know this?" Chris says.

"Because they roped me in to set it up, create the Facebook trace, all of it." She turns to me. "I'm so sorry. I tried not to be part of it, but they ordered me to. If I kept refusing, it would've looked suspicious."

My whole body feels paralyzed and when I speak, my mouth doesn't seem like it's mine. "What ... what happened?"

Abigail swallows. "The Project knew that Patricia's sister hated Patricia for killing their mother—"

"It was euthanasia," Chris says. His voice is a hush, a brushed breeze of his normal zippy self. "It was euthanasia."

"Sorry." She clears her throat. "We, um, we got her sister to … to, um, lie and say she only had three weeks left to live. They wanted it to sound like … to sound like Patricia was making things up."

Chris' head drops. "Oh, Jesus Christ."

Abigail looks between him and me, continues. I feel as if the floor has opened up beneath me. "The Project was watching Patricia's sister's Facebook page and realized Patricia was monitoring it, checking her status update, that kind of thing, spending a long time looking at old family photos. They wanted you back with them, Maria, but were struggling, so that's when they got the idea to get the sister to post the message about her fake cancer."

Chris shakes his head. "But then everyone who friended her page would think she had cancer."

"No. They mocked up the page and created a coded link to it so only Patricia could see it, and the Project told the sister they were Interpol and searching for Patricia, saying she'd committed a serious crime or something, and, of course, Patricia's sister, hating Patricia, happily agreed to help track her down, go along with the fake Facebook bait."

My hands tremble, body shakes. "Who"—I stop, swallow—"who planted the tracker on her cell?"

Abigail lets out a long breath. "The woman on the train."

"Jesus," Chris says, "the old woman who killed that family?"

I stare into the room and everything in front of me blurs. The woman I killed.

Abigail looks to me, a soft orange light glowing from the console behind her. "The officer on the train was from the Project, yes. Look, I'm so, so sorry, but Maria, this is what they do, the Project. They got you to believe that it was your friend all along who was betraying your trust. Got you to think it was her who had the tracker, led you to them."

"I thought she dropped the book you gave her on purpose, to show the Project where we'd been," I say, but to myself, my eyes down, tears threatening to spill over and break away. "I even … I even told her that. I called her a liar."

"It was all the Project. They knew how you'd react so they set it all up to lead … to lead you back to them."

"So the blackmail messages," Chris says now, "the ones the home secretary received—or so we thought—that was all a—"

"A setup, yes." Abigail nods, mouth downward, lines crinkling on her forehead. "It was all created to make it appear that Patricia was the mole."

"Fucking hell." Chris throws something. "Fucking bastards."

Tears stream down my cheeks now, stinging my skin, falling past my neck to the bones on my shoulders underneath my Project-issued shirt. I feel dazed, as if my head has been hit by the heaviest hammer, the hardest blow. "Patricia is … is not with the Project?" I say, the shock gradually beginning to take hold. "She was never my handler in prison or sent there by the Project or MI5 or any other group?"

Abigail shakes her head. "No. No, she's exactly who she's always said she is. Everything she told you in prison, about her family, about who she really is, what she's done—it's all true."

I listen to her words, each one piercing me and, as the pain of the reality hits, my mind turns to ask the one question I have been dreading, the one that makes my stomach fold in on itself. "Is she … Is Patricia the enemy?"

Abigail coughs, blood flakes streaking her skin. When she sits back and inhales, the orange light still pulses behind her as she says the words my heart was dreading to hear. "No." She wipes her mouth. "Patricia is definitely not the enemy."

The words slam into me, *bam!* And I stand, cannot take it or bear it or deal with it. I pace, Abigail watching me, leaning forward, one hand stretched out toward me, but I ignore it, ignore her as she asks if I'm okay as I pace and pace and pace, all the time moaning slightly, then more, tapping my leg then shoulder then head until I reach the bookcase and, halting, spread out my ten fingers to it, leaning on it, lungs burning, as in my mind a picture of Patricia emerges, her beautiful long-limbed body, beaten on the ground, beaten by the Project for what? For the biggest deceit? For me? To get me to do what? Kill? Maim? Lie for them?

"What have I done?" I say quietly then louder and louder. "What have I done?"

"Take a breath ..."

"No," I say aloud, as what has happened fires in bullet rounds in my brain. Bang, bang. "No, no." Bang, bang, bang. "No." Bang. "NO! I hurt her! I hurt my friend!"

"Google?" Chris says, but again, I do not respond, and I hear him say to Abigail to bring the phone nearer so he can speak to me, but his voice seems distant, as if in another room, another world and I am here, trapped forever in my own never-ending nightmare.

"Maria?" Chris' voice is nearer now, Abigail close to my side, but I can smell her, a nauseous scent of antiseptic and blood, and it hits my brain, congeals in there with all the other thoughts and with the lights in the room and the computers and the filing cabinet containing the details no one wants the world to see, all of it spinning round and round and round.

"I need you to breathe," Chris says, reciting the words he has heard Patricia say to me, and for a moment it works, and I become calmer, but then the orange light behind Abigail pulses faster and the whole thing spirals again, Patricia's beaten body floating once more into my consciousness.

"Talk to me. Talk, for God's sake."

"I thought she was lying to me ..."

"Good. Good that's it."

I breathe hard. "I thought ... I thought she was working for the Project."

"That's because they made you believe that. They all lied. It's not your fault."

"No! No, she was not ... She was my friend ... I should have known ... I should have trusted her."

I rip my hands from the shelf, smear the tears from my cheeks and eyes. "They lie, they all fucking lie all the time, all of them. Governments, leaders—all of them. And for what?" I stalk now, almost toppling over Abigail, nearly knocking the phone from her thin hand. "For themselves! Because they think ... they think they are doing the correct thing, think that the decisions they are making are the right ones, but they are not and the end result is people die. People ... people die and get hurt and they ruin lives because they do not care! They just do not fucking care! And now I am one of them and I believed Patricia was the enemy. I believed everything they told me, let them drug me and let my mind forget and now my first ever friend is being held by the Project. And"—I pause, heave in a great bucket of breath—"and I helped put her there!"

Everything now merges into one, and despite Chris shouting out to breathe and Abigail pleading for me to sit down, I run over to the shelves, stop, chest heaving, staring at all the books, cases and cases of information that means what? Nothing. Nothing when, with one flick of a button or one lick of a flame, it can be gone in seconds. Forever.

"Aaaaaaargh!"

I throw myself forward and begin tearing all the books from the casing. They all topple over, each and every one tumbling to the ground, leather and binding broken, bent spines. I pull at them, tear and scream until I finally stop, gulping in air, body bent double, my head dropped, eyes rammed shut.

I am exhausted, distraught, not moving for one second, two, three. Everything is still, quiet, save the brush of Abigail's breathing, the rustle of Chris on the cell phone wherever he may be, as in my head, it all comes up and out, all the images of everyone in my life. Of Balthus and Ramon, of Ines and Harry, and of my beautiful papa, all of them standing there inside my mind, and I cry out, not a scream, but a deep, guttural moan of love and loss and pain and all that it's caused me my whole life. Of priests dead, of nuns lying, of Kurt—real name Daniel—and his corpse on the street, bullet in his brain, of Dr. Andersson from MI5 pretending to be a doctor to help me then trying to kill me at my villa, and, oh, my precious villa, my idyllic, calm Salamanca. Of running. Of being at Montserrat abbey with monks and the abbot shot just helping us, and me then letting the Project take me to Hamburg. Of the officer I killed there, strangled with my bare hands. Of Raven and the files that told me about the other subject numbers, of the cancer drugs for Ines. Of Chris, of him walking into my life and making it better. And of Patricia, who has been who she has always been—calm, loyal, kind, caring—lying somewhere in this facility at the mercy of the Project. "Google?" Chris says now, voice hushed, steady. "I need to know you're okay."

Slowly I open my eyes and the strange sight of the ransacked room swims before me as I register what's in my line of vision. "They … they are empty."

Abigail watches me now as I stumble back and take in the view of the books that lie strewn on the floor, but, instead of pages inside them, there is nothing but space. "They … they are just boxes. Empty boxes."

I pick one up, turn it in my hands, run my fingertip along the gold binding. I hold it, this empty vessel that should be full and feel the weight of the thirty decades of my life bearing down on me, the clock ticking on the time I have left.

"We have to find Patricia," I say, something in my brain finally clicking into a logical, methodical place, my heart tired, a blank void opening wide somewhere inside me at what I now know. I look up now to Abigail.

"I can help," she says. "I've got nothing to lose."

She stands near me, holding out the cell phone as we blink down together at the books, at the shelves and the empty spaces. Chris' voice breaks the silence.

"Er, guys?" he says. "I think we have a problem." He squints forward. "There's … there's something trying to get through on the screen behind you."

We turn. The orange light that was glowing before is now pulsing wildly.

Abigail squints at it. "Oh shit."

I move forward. "Why is the light …?" But I stop, because now on the screen in front of us, an image is transmitting, live into the room and what I see on it makes me shriek, makes Abigail cry out, causes Chris to shout, "No!"

There, on the monitor in front of us, is Patricia with a gun to her head.

And holding it, looking up to the camera, is Black Eyes.

CHAPTER 31

BLACK SITE PROJECT FACILITY, SCOTLAND

Present Day

"Let her go," I yell at the screen, striding forward. "Let her go!"

Abigail pulls me back, but, jumping at the unexpected touch, I yank my arm away and round on her.

"How did he know I was here? Was it you? Was it?"

"Don't say another word!" She shakes her head, scanning the console. "He doesn't know we're here. He only has hold of the computer feed line. They're trying to track our location. They must be picking up some sensory movement somewhere, but it's being blocked. Room 17's transmission feed must have an output wall around it."

"Maria, I want to talk to you," Black Eyes says, his voice slicing into the room, a blade against my skin. I freeze, every hair on my body rising. I want to run, not away from him, but this time at him, at the Project, at every single fucking one of them.

I stalk to the screen. "Is this microphone working?"

Abigail checks it then nods as, reaching for the phone where Chris still is, she pulls it to her ear and begins feverishly tapping on a keyboard.

"Let Patricia go," I say to Black Eyes. "I know everything now. I know you set her up so we would think she was the one who led you to us. I know the UK home secretary is involved, the US, Spain. I know all your secrets."

"Doc?"

"Patricia!"

I spin closer to the screen and scan every inch of my friend's beaten body as she struggles to speak. Bruises now track her skin alongside welts of old wounds, and on her head where her scalp is bare and her hair shaven, long lacerations circle her skull from her brow to her ears.

"She is not the enemy," I say now, fast, urgent. "You have to let her go. You have misunderstood why she is here. I have misunderstood why she is here."

Black Eyes stares at the camera, the gun lowering a little and for a second, it seems as if he might let go of it entirely, but then he inhales a sharp lick of breath, his chest protruding, the spindle of his knuckles twisting around the handle of the revolver so his skin pulls tight and white over each and every translucent bone.

"Maria, I am very, very worried for your well-being."

He lifts his head and in his eyes I think I see tears. I step forward, mesmerized, as if in a trance, the image of this man I have feared for so much of my life suddenly looking older, more lined, a sag to his skin where his cheeks droop, a weight to the lids of his eyes.

"I know about your wife," I say now, unsure why the words want to come out, yet somehow understanding that it is the right thing to do. Beside me, Abigail continues to tap on the keyboard, the cell now by her fingers, simultaneously texting Chris and working on a complex code. Specks of red blood lie in pinpricks on her lips.

"I know that she set up the Project decades ago. I know that what I witnessed in the sensory chamber was real, not a hallucination. The drugs were tested on her. Your daughter died."

"Maria, stop whatever it is you think you are doing."

Patricia flops a little and he pulls her back up. I jump, desperate to get to her, yet, for one of the few times in my life, I hesitate, not knowing quite what the next step should be. I reach my fingers to her image on the screen. My friend. My first friend. I'm sorry, I want to say. I am so, so sorry.

"You mean a lot to me, Maria," Black Eyes says now. "I know you may not believe that, and I wouldn't blame you for, quite frankly, hating me, but believe me when I say that I am on your side."

"You lied to me."

He sighs. "Yes. Yes, that is true, but Maria, everyone lies. I did it with good reason, with you at the heart of my interests."

The phrase, *everyone lies*—it casts a line in my mind to the home secretary, to the things she told me about in London.

"Harriet Alexander knows all about the Project," I say, rapidly, no time to rethink. "The Project was supposed to have separated from MI5 and the UK government was not supposed to know anything about it. That is what I was always taught in training when I was young and when I was growing up, that Callidus was secret, covert, and performed better that way."

He nods. "Again, yes, this is all true, as for a long time, governments were indeed unaware of our existence. But Maria, the world changes, needs change, as do critical situations, and that therefore alters our actions. And we are forced to lie. You know this happens."

"It should not." My sight flips to Patricia; her eyelids are drooping. Fear billows.

"But it does happen," he says. "Neurotypical people lie over two hundred times a day. Two hundred, Maria."

"Many of these are white lies. Twenty-five percent of lies are told for the sake of someone else."

"Yes, which is precisely my point. We like to help others, it is what we do as a species—deceive. It's called survival."

"It is not what I do."

"It isn't? Are you certain of that?"

Patricia's head and neck hang a little to the right, the butt of the gun resting on her ear.

Abigail leans over to me. "Keep him talking," she whispers,

angling herself so she cannot be seen on the camera. "We're just seeing if we can locate which room they're in and if there's anything Chris can do remotely to help."

Black Eyes' Scottish lilt floats into the room. "You didn't tell Patricia about your headaches and their severity, did you, Maria?"

My mind tracks back through the memories I have which have not been blurred by the Typhernol.

"You see," he continues, "by not telling her, by omitting the facts, you are, indeed, lying. And you have been deceiving yourself, Maria."

"No."

"Now your memories are returning, you believe you have been forced here, but, if you think about it, is that really the case?" He exhales, long, heavy—nostrils billowing in two sails from his nose, flapping up then falling again. "You came here of your own will."

"I did not."

"Really? Think about it." He tilts the gun to Patricia's skull and she whimpers. My heart nearly collapses right there and then. "You accepted what we said about your friend, about her being the enemy, but Maria, if you think about it, she is. She is stopping you from being who you are."

My eyes flit to Abigail; she mouths, "Keep him talking," except chitchat has never been my strong point. I try facts.

"I am a person who is thirty-three years old and who may not live to their thirty-fourth birthday."

"Ah," he says, "so you know about that."

My vision flicks to Abigail, to her fingers on the keyboard. "I have seen the file that details the drugs and conditioning," I say to Black Eyes. "I have seen the file that says I am the longest-surviving subject number. I have seen the subject numbers at the Project facility here—they are all younger than me."

For a moment, Black Eyes does not respond. His fingers fall loose on the gun handle leaving a tiny escape gap, and when I look at Patricia, I will her to take the chance, to slide away and run, but instead her body remains limp, the bones of her chest barely moving at all. Tears once more threaten to erupt from my sockets.

"You are the one who the conditioning has truly worked on," he says finally, his eyes rising, yet his shoulders still down, weighted. "I ... we ..." He stops, looking at Patricia then back to the camera, exhaling into the cold, clinical air. I grind my teeth, petrified at what he might do to my friend. To my side Abigail shows me a text from Chris that just reads: *breathe*.

"My own daughter was so young," he says after a moment. "So young to die. And at the hands of monsters." A tear, solitary, barely visible, slips down his face. He wipes it away. "That memory you had in the sensory chamber, Maria, yes—that was all true. You must have ... you must have recalled it from when you were very young."

"Your wife founded the Project," I say.

He smiles now for the first time since he appeared on the screen, small lines fanning out on his worn, pinched face. "My beautiful wife. She was so clever, so sharp. I owe everything to her—we all do."

Abigail motions for me to talk more, pointing to her watch, but it is hard and I am so worried for Patricia. I hook on, instead, to connections, let my brain run with the data.

"Your daughter died and you began the Project," I say.

"Yes." He doesn't look up, instead hangs his eyes low, gun in his grip. "My wife knew it would all get worse—terrorism, the rise of such groups, the growth of the use of computers, although even she couldn't have predicted the extent to which the cyberworld has developed. She was already working for the intelligence services when I met her."

"She had the drugs tested on her."

"Yes." He sighs. "Yes." Again he smiles, tiny fanned eye creases. "She developed the drugs herself, originally, did you know that? Exceptional biochemist." He pauses. "But she got to see you. She got to see you before she died and somehow, she knew you could be it, the test child. Your blood type, straight from Balthus and Isabella."

My heart nearly stops. "You know the name of my real mother."

"Oh, Maria—I know everything."

"Was … was she ever at Weisshorn Hospital in Lake Geneva?"

"Yes. For a time."

"Where is she now?"

He does not answer.

"Where is she now?"

He holds me with one stare. "You know I cannot reveal operational details unless you have clearance."

I try to breathe steadily, think fast now as, before me on the screen, Black Eyes pulls Patricia hard and brings her to him. She lets out a small shriek, but then it fades as quick as it came, a child's balloon of a cry floating out of view in the sky.

My brain panicking, Abigail gets my attention. "We've found something on this lone gunman thing," she whispers.

Trying to connect what the link could be, I turn back to the screen to see that Black Eyes has beckoned two officers into the room and is instructing them to hold Patricia under the arms.

I instantly fly forward, fear filling every part of me. "Let her go!"

"Maria, I'm sorry, but I can't do that, not if you're going to stay where you are."

I turn to Abigail. "Do they still not know our location?"

She shakes her head. "Chris managed to patch through a few minutes ago after he caught the worm I sent out. It's blocking our geolocation just for the moment, but it won't hold much longer."

I turn back to the screen ready to fight with facts, but before I can speak, Black Eyes is stepping aside as, in front of him, Patricia is hauled up, her legs buckling underneath her weight, feet splaying at awkward, unnatural angles, and when her head finally rises, her eyes, her beautiful blue eyes are rimmed with red lines and bloodshot veins that crackle across her eyeballs.

My hands slap to the screen as Black Eyes raises his revolver and looks straight into the camera lens.

"Do not hurt her," I say, fear and guilt imploding inside me. "She is my friend."

"I do not want to do this, Maria. I do not want to upset you—you are like a daughter to me. I have known you for a long time—you feel part of me, mine, as if I have raised you. But …" He pauses, exhales. "But you need to come out now from wherever you are. Do you think I didn't know Abigail would try and speak to you? Why do you think I introduced the two of you?"

Abigail jerks her head up, eyes wide.

"I have weeded out the dissidents," Black Eyes continues, "and you know all the truth, all of it, so now when you come to me, you can do it with your eyes and exceptional mind fully open and informed, be ready to work toward the greater good."

I keep my sight locked on the screen. "I will not come to you."

"Think about it. You are changing, aren't you?"

My hands open and close, faster and faster, stimming out the worry as his words hit me.

"The headaches, the nosebleeds," he says, "the skills you already possess getting faster, even more intelligent. How long has this been going on for now? Two years? It was happening when you were in prison, wasn't it? We have it on file, we have the evidence."

My mouth doesn't move. Panic fills my entire body as the reality of what he is saying enters.

"You see, Maria, I can help you, the Project can help you. We are your family. Order and routine are your friend. And right now, you are coming up to your thirty-fourth birthday and we don't know what will happen to you, which way it will go. Life balances on a knife edge and whether we get cut depends on how we hold the handle."

I step back a little as, by my side, Abigail looks to me, whispering, "Don't listen to him," then, frowning she goes to where the empty books lay strewn on the floor and, crouching down, one by one, starts peeling off the inside covers.

"I cannot be part of the Project," I say to Black Eyes, my fingers opening and closing. "Too many people have died."

Black Eyes emits a sigh and, with one nod of his head to the officers beyond, raises his gun. "Then, Maria, if you do not come to me, I'm afraid we have no use for your friend here anymore."

"No!" I yell as in front of me, it happens. The revolver, raising an inch at a time on the end of Black Eye's arm, swings into the air, aiming to shoot, the officers hoisting Patricia up, ready, just another target shot in the field. "Do not kill her!"

"Got it!" Abigail says, rushing forward thrusting out a fist full of paper-thin, transparent A5 sheets at me. "Microfiche," she whispers, catching her breath. "The whole thing they're planning was hidden in the boxes all along on millimeter-thin slices of microfiche! They weren't just empty books—they contained top secret data."

"What?" I read the microfiche, look to Abigail. "This was all in the books?"

She nods frantically. "Yes."

I fling myself toward the screen. "Wait!"

Black Eyes turns, gun suspended in the air, Patricia's head flopping to her chest.

"I know you are planning a lone gunman terrorist plot," I say, fast, urgent. "I know that the plan involves multiple governments, and that the plan is being carried out in order to help governments secure electoral results."

I stop, pulse racing around my body as, on the screen, Black Eyes stares in to the lens. Time passes, one second, two, and my throat runs dry, Chris appearing now on the cell phone screen on the table watching, his sight following me. The officers holding Patricia wait until, finally, Black Eyes nods to them and they let her go, her body tumbling to the floor, splaying in a jumble of limbs and blood.

My whole body floods with relief at the sight, at the last second reprieve, but I don't get too elated because now Black Eyes is facing the screen and, weapon slightly down, he speaks straight to me.

"Tell me what you know."

CHAPTER 32

BLACK SITE PROJECT FACILITY, SCOTLAND
Present Day

I talk fast, not wanting to lose my chance, my sight locked onto Patricia and her broken body next to the two Project officers.

"We know what you are planning."

"And what is that?"

"You and the British, American, and Spanish governments are simultaneously planning to launch a terrorist attack on a series of smaller towns and villages across Europe."

Black Eyes laughs, a creep, a vine of ivy that curls over the air, suffocating it. "Oh, Maria, I knew you'd find it."

Why do I feel fearful when I have uncovered what the Project is planning?

I flip through the microfiche, read it and as I do, it dawns on me. The reason why he may be laughing, the reason why he is not concerned.

Because if I know all about his plan, he knows I've found the microfiche. I turn to Abigail. "He knows where we are."

Her head drops. "The microfiche. Oh fuck. Of course—the only place it and the details of the plan exist is here."

"In room 17," I say to myself.

"Is that Abigail? Subject Number 209?" Black Eyes says now. "Can I hear your voice?"

"Fuck you."

"Room 17," he says. "It's a great place, isn't it? A place where we can keep our most delicate of information."

"Information you don't want online," Abigail says, "so no one will find it. And yet here you are, working with the secret services and the governments and the NSA, snooping into everyone's online data, yet when it comes to your own secrets, you'd like to keep them private, thanks very much. Welcome to modern democracy, people."

"Oh, the irony, yes?" Black Eyes says. "How are you feeling these days, Abigail? I hear you are not very well. By the way, we don't work with the NSA."

She raises her middle finger at the screen and turns away, grabbing the cell phone to connect with Chris.

Fear ballooning inside me now, I look to Black Eyes, grasping the facts. "I identified this plan in the situation room, but you said it was just a simulation. I knew a group was organizing it, but they were not using electronic data." I look to the microfiche, to the torn-up book boxes. "Now I know why."

"Maria, this is not easy, but leaders make difficult decisions that the public doesn't want to make or even know about. To achieve our plan we couldn't risk it being found, risk it being hacked."

"You have trained me to hack."

"Yes, and it's all for the greater good, Maria. Remember your conditioning."

A cold shiver slices into me as I recall the details of the data I saw in the situation room. "Twenty lone gunmen across Europe means, combined, you will kill two thousand one hundred people. That is what you are planning to carry out. And there are more attacks scheduled on the data, too."

Black Eyes glances to Patricia then back to the lens. The gun hangs in his frozen fingers.

"Maria, you have to understand something: when we began the

Project it was to gain some control, prevent attacks like the one …
like the one that killed my daughter." He stops, inhales, a wetness
to his eyes. "Maria, believe me when I say it is essential for stability
and peace that this plan goes ahead."

Abigail comes from the phone and whispers. "They'll be
here soon. They know where we are." Then she turns back to her
keyboard, hands shaking.

My eyes drift to Patricia. Her chest is shallow in breath now,
and though the screen is slightly pixelated, it is clear that, without
immediate medical intervention, she hasn't much time left.

I look at Black Eyes, a steel forming inside me now, thick, strong.
I have to save my friend. "Your plan is that each gunman will carry
out shootings in a further two hundred towns in the second wave with
twenty people killed per location. Which equals four thousand people
killed, which, combined with the first wave figure, equates to a total
of six thousand one hundred deaths." I reel off the facts almost word
for word from the discussion in the situation room. "You are planning
to do this—you—the Project, and international governments. Why?"

From the corner of my eye, I see Abigail copying every single
microfiche with her cell phone then sending them on a proxy link
to Chris.

"We thought, when we began the Project, that simply by
fighting terrorism we could prevent it, slow it down, but of course,
that never happens. It was naive of us, silly. And then you came
along and the conditioning began to work and we knew we could
make a difference. But still, in the back of our minds was control.
You know all about control, I know you do, Maria, you need it, too.
You need it to stop a meltdown."

Waves of uncertainty wash over me as I watch Black Eyes speak,
watch Patricia wither, the officers hovering nearby just waiting for
the order to act. I need to get her out.

"What you have found in room 17 is data, planning, times and
locations, people and numbers."

I glance to Abigail; she is furiously texting all the remaining data she can.

"The control is the key here, you see, Maria," he continues, his eyes for the first time lighting up, no tears. "If we initiate a lone gunman attack around Europe, it creates fear—no one knows where the gunman will strike next. And, of course, with fear, we have control. And with control we have order. Think about it. Often, the public disagree when politicians and armies want to invade a country in order to protect their own, yet, as soon as an attack occurs on their own soil, public opinion changes—people then, we find, accept a government's invasion of another country more freely, even demand it. And what does that do? That then allows us to do our job, fight the terrorism on soil and in cyberspace and create peace." He pauses, exhales. "Our nickname—Cranes—represents peace, after all, and it has been in the plan all along, the lone gunman campaign, it was just a matter of timing as to when we implemented it. We needed the right governments on board at the right electoral times to boost support—and we needed you."

The horror of what he is saying hits me. "You and state governments are planning to attack innocent people to create fear so they can get the vote results they require."

"Don't be so horrified. It has happened for centuries. A bit of fearmongering to get the outcome you require, to gain order. We are all signed up to the mantra that to gain order, you need to create chaos."

"You … you got me to kill for you, for what? For political gain? For personal power?"

"For peace, Maria. For peace."

My mind slams thought after thought through my head as I digest the reality of what Black Eyes is saying. I look at Patricia's beaten body, think of what she has done for me, how she has been nothing but kind, nothing but loyal and understanding. Nothing but peaceful. And how did I repay her? By immediately believing that she was against me. Is that what happens in life? One too many bad things occur and so we assume that from there on in, all else will fail? Is that really the right way to live? Separately? Fearing each other? Continually suspicious?

"How do I fit into all of this?" I say now.

"You have the skills, Maria. You have the skills to help, on one hand to keep terrorist groups at bay, yet on the other hand help us track what people do so we can keep control, keep the order that a civilized society so desperately needs to thrive." He pauses. "We need you so no more sons and daughters will die for no reason."

"They will die if nations are prepared to kill its own citizens for the greater good."

"But it is, ultimately, the right course of action to take if it means that millions more people *live* as a result."

"No," I say, an anger building inside me. "When dictatorships kill their citizens, western nations bomb them and justify it under NATO rules. Who will bomb you?"

"We are not in a dictatorship, Maria."

To my side, Abigail slides over to me. "We've got it all. The microfiche data has been sent to Chris."

I turn back, heart rate rising at the news, pleased that we have the proof of their plan backed up, yet, at the same time concerned. Patricia is still in trouble. I look to her, thinking: if Chris has the data, then he can use it, he will have it and can tell people. Which means my choice now of what to do, is clear.

"I will join you," I say. "I will join the Project."

Abigail's head jerks up. "What?" She thrusts the phone to me with a text from Chris that reads:

Google! No!

"Why?"

I pause. "I have nothing left."

"We are your only family."

My heart races as I lie. "Yes," I say. "Yes."

Black Eyes immediately smiles. It is warm, one with creases, the same one he had when he thought of his daughter. "Maria, I am delighted you have seen sense—it is the right decision. It is, really, the main reason we wanted to keep Patricia here like this—so we could use her to help you see sense whenever it may have been required. Friends will go, we find, a long way for one another—and I am your friend, your family. I'm so glad this has worked out. My officers shall be with you soon and—"

"There is one condition."

He stops. "What?"

"You let Patricia go. You get her to a safe place where her injuries can be tended. And you will leave her alone."

Black Eyes remains unmoving as the words I have spoken hang in the air. I feel scared, unsure, yet all of that, as I look now at Patricia, falls to the side as, slowly, her hand moves a little and one by one, her fingers spread out into our mutual star shape.

Tears trickle past my eyes now as I watch her, elated, yet concerned, my own fingers moving to the same shape connected by an invisible thread that can never be cut, reaching out to my friend who has always been there for me, even when I have not been there for her. The bond of friendship, once made, once forged in events of past, present, and future, can never be broken.

"Okay," Black Eyes says, nodding to the officers. "We can do that. Patricia will be released."

A breath billows from my lungs, relief washing over me.

Abigail shakes her head. "Do you realize what you've just done?"

I look to her and nod, my body and mind exhausted. "It has to be done." Taking the cell phone, I text Chris.

Patricia will be set free.

I heard. You're crazy, but I get why
you've done it. What's the plan?

I glance to the computer screen—Patricia is being helped to stand.

> *You have the microfiche*
> *data?*

Yes. You thinking it needs to get to
a wider audience? Published on the
internet, to journalists?

> *Yes, but not yet. I need to*
> *see Patricia safe first.*

There's a one second delay in his reply, two.

Abigail turns to me. "Shit, I'm picking up some activity further down the next corridor—I think they're on their way to get you."

I swallow, nerves building, as I look now at Patricia standing, just about, on her feet, an officer having to assist her.

Chris finally texts back.

Might be able to track your location in
the black site facility there now as have
the hacker worm from Abigail. Will
do what I can to help. Sit tight and be
safe until we get you all out, together.
I miss you, Google.

I read his message and, despite the stress and the fear, I catch myself smiling. Abigail takes the cell when I hand it to her and immediately rips out the SIM, smashing it under her boot into tiny unusable, untraceable shards.

"What will you do now?" I ask.

"I don't know." She pauses, the distant sound of boots growing louder by the second in the cold air. "I don't want to end up in interrogation. I have a pill."

I try to think what to say, think what Patricia would do, and so I raise my hands and hold out my five fingers. Abigail blinks at me, smiling, small tear drops slipping out on her worn cheeks.

"Thank you," I say.

A knock on the door sounds loud, quick. Abigail inhales, sharp, and her eyes go wide. "It's okay," she says to me, watching me wince, sight locked on the door as a voice shouts my name from outside. "I know where your notebook and rucksack are," she says now, fast.

"You do?"

One bang on the door.

She swallows. "Hospital wing. There's a small cupboard with a keypad lock, simple number combination. Belongs to Black Eyes. The code is two-seven-zero-four. That's where it is."

The number. I recognize it. "That is the date of my birthday."

Another bang.

"You won't stay here, will you?" she says.

"I need to know my friend is okay." Bang. "I have to know that she is—"

The door smashes open and five officers in black spill in, reeking of gunpowder and oil, grabbing Abigail straight away as she kicks and thrashes. They pull out a needle, stab her in the thigh with it, and I watch in horror as she fights then goes limp and is dragged away.

My eyes follow her feet around the corner as, on the screen in the room, Black Eyes calls my name.

"Maria?"

I turn, trying to count to stay calm, three remaining officers guarding the door. One, two, three, four …

"Can you see me?" he asks.

Five. I make myself turn to the screen, I watch now as Black Eyes stands five meters from Patricia who, I am relieved to see has been given a chair and is already being tended to by a physician. "Yes," I manage to say. "I can see you."

"Good, because, Maria, you mean so much to me. And when people mean a lot to us, we often find we have to do things for that person for their own good, even if, at the time, it might not feel that way to them."

I swallow, uncertain why he is saying this, but relieved my friend is all right. "Yes."

"Which is why I need to make sure that your commitment to the Project is one hundred percent solid."

I hesitate, don't reply.

"Because you see," he continues, "when I said everyone lies …"

My heart races. "Yes?"

"I meant it."

The attending physician steps out of the way and, raising his gun, Black Eyes shoots Patricia dead in the head.

CHAPTER 33

BLACK SITE PROJECT FACILITY, SCOTLAND
Present Day

"No! No, no, no, noooooo!"

The officers try to grab me, but I throw them off, arms and legs punching and kicking out as on the screen, Patricia's body lies on the floor, one solitary red hole in her clear, milky, pale forehead, a pool of her blood staining the clinical white tiles of the room where she was held.

I slam myself forward, grabbing at the computer where my friend's image lies, as if doing that will save her. "Wake up! Wake up!"

I yell, shout, fly my fists as tears rip down my face and cheeks, staining every part of me as the officers grip my wrists tight, but I kick them off, hard, bolting for the door.

I get to the open corridor, darting my head left and right, disorientated, blinded by the wetness that floods my eyes and brain and mouth. "Patricia!" I shout. "Patricia!"

I run, the officers chasing me, and I try to think straight, figure out where she could be, picture the space from the screen, get the map of the facility in my head. I take a right, sprinting now, faster than anyone can catch me as I slam through doors, past subject numbers, knocking them over, surging forward. I skid to the situation room, an alarm now blaring above my head, but it is not loud enough to drown out the distress and pain inside me. My friend. She is my friend. No one can hurt her, no one. She is mine. Mine. Mine. Mine.

My fingers moving fast, I somehow input the code on the door and slam into the vast hangar of computers and people in the situation room. Everyone stares. They look up from their work and watch as I streak into the area, shouting out Patricia's name, yelling for her over and over again.

I stop, heaving in great swathes of breath as 120 pairs of eye blink at me and, as I see them, it hits me: they won't be here for much longer.

"You're all going to die!" I yell. "They are killing you! The Project is giving you drugs that will kill you! You are just a number to them! A fucking number!"

The officers burst in now and I run fast toward a deep blue door the color of the ocean on the very far right side, brushing past the shoulders and backs of subject numbers who are now whispering, and I hear the word Typhernol mentioned in a ripple of rising chatter.

The blue door, when I skid to it, is locked. There is a keypad but I don't know the code, my brain so wired and distraught, I can't think straight to decipher it. The officers are rounding on me now and so, fast, I spot a subject with a gun at his side and, before he can even react or speak, I grab the weapon, point it at him and tell him to open the door.

He hesitates, glancing to the officers.

"Input the code—now!" I shout.

His hand shakes as he moves forward and I grab him, hooking my arm around his neck, shoving the barrel into his skull.

The officers, three of them, move in, but, while they have guns, what bothers me more is the needle that is gripped in the hand of the one to the left.

"Stay back or I'll shoot him!"

They stop, eyes darting between each other.

I instruct the subject number I'm holding to tap in the code and he does so, but it does not work.

"Do it again!" I yell.

"I … it … it needs my thumbprint, too."

I hesitate, checking the door then seeing he is correct, I twist him around and, grabbing his wrist, shove his thumb to the door. It clicks. Quickly, I return my arm to his neck, slam him in front of me as armor, then point the gun again to his head.

"No one moves," I say, inching back. When I glance into the room behind me, I see it is the same one Black Eyes was in on the screen in room 17.

One of the officers moves a foot. "Stay back!"

He halts, and ramming the subject number once in the ribs then slamming the butt of the gun into the back of his head so he collapses out of the way, I dart into the room and lock the door.

I catch my breath and turn. It is dark. The lights that were on before on the screen in the room are low, but I can see enough to put one foot in front of the other. One step, two. The heat is high and sweat springs out all over my body.

"Patricia!" I call into the void, but all that comes back is the echo of my own voice.

Black Eyes could be anywhere in here and my training, distant, comes straight back to me now as I scan the room, check all areas, slowly, carefully, gun out and ready at all times.

"She is dead."

I jump at the sound as, from behind the shadows to the right where a small table sits, Black Eyes appears.

He looks frail, his pinched face more pale than normal and when he inhales, blue veins spike out on his neck and brow, and his hands rise and fall in a branch formation of twigs and leaves of bones.

"It's over now, Maria, your past. It's over."

I point the gun at him. "Stay back."

He halts, resting a finger on the edge of a narrow red chair.

"You lied to me," I say. "You killed her." Tears tumble down my cheeks. "You said you would let her go."

"I'm sorry."

"Sorry? Sorry? You are not sorry!" I wipe my face, still holding the revolver straight out. "You only care about power! You and all the fucking governments. Harriet Alexander is the home secretary of the United Kingdom. Her job is homeland security and yet she believes killing her own people is justified!"

He exhales. "It is a necessary evil."

As I hear that—*evil*—Chris' words come to me, the ones he muttered on the phone when we were in room 17. "The Project are evil motherfuckers," I say, spitting the phrase out at him. I point the gun toward the red chair. "Sit."

He does as I say, staggering a little then lowering himself down.

"I need to have all the codes to this facility, including the location and code to Isabella Bidarte," I say now, thinking fast.

He shakes his head. "I'm afraid that isn't possible."

"You are lying."

He sighs. "I'm not."

"You are!" I shout. He falls silent, my voice bouncing off the concrete walls.

He regards me. He crosses one leg over the other and drops his shoulders. "Aren't you tired?"

"What?"

"Tired—you must be so tired running away all the time, my dearest Maria. Running away from who you really are."

"I know who I am."

"Do you?"

I go to speak, then hesitate. Isabella, Balthus, Ines, Ramon, and Papa. All the faces of the people I knew appear in my mind, each one of them smiling with eye creases. I shake my head, wipe them away, refocus, hold the gun tight. "I want the codes. I want to know where Isabella is being held."

"I can get them, the codes, but I have to make a phone call."

"No phone calls. You will have them with you. I know Project protocol."

He smiles. "I am so proud to regard you as like a daughter to me. It's been … nice to act like a father to you, Maria."

Anger surges up. "You are not my father!" I stride straight to him and ram the gun to his thin skull. "Where is Isabella Bidarte?"

"I don't—"

I shove the gun harder. "Where. Is. She?"

"Room 720. The … the hospital wing."

I hold the gun by my side, move back, and he exhales hard, heavy, his whole torso dropping.

I watch him and a hatred forms inside me, years and years of trauma and abuse rising to the surface. "I am not your fucking daughter," I say, words seeping out like venom.

He nods, wiping his mouth, sitting back up. "True—you are not, but …" he coughs, "but you must admit, Maria, we have known each other for a long time, and with that, don't you think, there comes a certain bond?"

I don't know what he means but as I start to demand the codes, something catches my eye. I look to it, unsure at first, the air darker, but then, as I inch forward, I see it: the bare sole of a long, milk-pale foot.

"P-Patricia?"

Black Eyes glances to where I am staring, but doesn't say anything.

"Patricia?" I move faster now as an ankle comes into view, a leg, a hip until finally, limb by limb, the whole body appears.

"Patricia!"

I drop to my knees, gun toppling to the floor, and grab her under the arms. "Oh, my friend! My friend!"

I smear away the blood from her eyes, her beautiful blue eyes, open but not seeing anything, her brain no longer working, her brain that made her who she was—loyal, kind, caring, and above all understanding. She loved me. Patricia loved me.

"Help her!" I cry. "We have to help her! I need medical supplies now!"

I haul her up to me, hugging her into my chest, the faint scent of her still there, of talcum powder, of warm baths, and washed linen. I breathe it in, tears slamming down my face in heavy waterfalls. "I am sorry!" I sob. "I am so, so sorry!"

I hold her to me, her neck flopping into my shoulder, her long spaghetti arms sinking to the side as I think of all the times she has been there for me, from when I first met her at Goldmouth Prison, when she tried to kill herself, when she helped me understand people and their words and hidden meanings.

"Wake up!" I say, shaking her. "Wake up!" But even as the words come out, I know they will never come true.

Her arm hangs by me and I take it now, blinking back the tears, sight blurred as I hold up it up, saying her name over and over as, spreading out my fingers, I put her five to mine, our palms touching for the very last time, the tips of her skin still tinged with warmth.

I don't see Black Eyes walk over. I hold my friend tight and I don't see Black Eyes picking up the gun I'd thrown to the floor. I don't see the officers enter or the medicine vial in the hand of the one to the right who gives it to Black Eyes.

And when Black Eyes comes over to me and crouches down, I don't feel the needle pierce my skin and puncture my thigh.

All I see, as the room sways and my sight begins to fade, is, for the last time, the face of my friend.

My first ever, my first true friend.

CHAPTER 34

BLACK SITE PROJECT FACILITY, SCOTLAND

Present Day

I wake up strapped to a hospital bed in a white room with no windows.

I blink, glance down, head groggy as I take in the bleary sight of my body. I am dressed in a gown, cornflower blue, tiny dots all over it in regular diamond constellation patterns and when I turn to the side, there is a low, sustained beep that indicates all my physical outputs are being monitored and recorded. I try to see more, but my vision goes hazy and the room sways.

I go to move but a pain shoots through me up from my groin and into my stomach as, on my arm where the flesh of my bicep lies, I see the words that Black Eyes scratched into me in Hamburg with the nib of a fountain pen: *I am Basque.*

"Who is there?" I say, my voice croaking as I lift my head now, limbs heavy. The pain in my groin fires again and this time it is so severe, it knocks me back, and I flop to the bed, drenched in sweat.

"Try not to move."

I go rigid. Black Eyes is in the room. He scuttles in from a door that slides to the right and I start to shake. My hands, arms, legs, chest ripple, yet even though I am scared, trapped, the tremble I feel is not because of my mind, it feels more physical, more medical.

"What have you done to me?"

Black Eyes steps to my side and, checking my heart rate on the monitor, turns. He scans my body, every inch of me, circling my legs and stomach.

"Do you feel hot?" he asks.

"I said, what have you done to me?"

He stops, looks straight at me, the darkness of his eyes seeming heavier somehow as, stretching out the branch of his arm, he clatters his fingers to my brow. I go rigid at his touch, at the sandpaper of his skin, at the tobacco and garlic stench of his breath that has haunted my nightmares for three decades.

"We have taken some of your eggs."

He moves back a little, reading a file that sits on a small metal table to the side. I replay his words in my head, yet each time I repeat them, they still seem unreal.

"You took my …" I stop, swallow. "You took my eggs?"

"Yes. For tests."

"I … I … What?" The horror of what he said hits me and I try to get up, but nothing works well and I flop back and cry out.

"Shhh. There's no need to worry. You'll see. This is all just routine."

I glance around, frantic, my brain attempting to grasp onto something, anything, that will give me an anchor to the present, but nothing comes up.

He inhales. "Maria? Maria? Do you know what day it is?"

I don't reply, I thrash my head, desperate to escape.

"I'll tell you: it is the twenty-eighth of May."

I halt, compute the date, mind still fuzzy, then, slowly, realize the significance. "I am now … thirty-four years old."

He smiles. "Yes. It is truly marvelous news, isn't it? You are okay, Maria, my dear. It has worked after all these years of knowing each other—the test child program has worked!"

"I … I will live?"

"Yes. Your blood results are coming back normal. It seems the drugs haven't harmed you, rather, they have improved you. You're in the tiny percentage that the conditioning has worked on, we're unsure why, and will run more tests, but it's amazing. I didn't dare believe it would happen, but it has!"

His words, as he says them, sink in, triggering something in the back of my mind that flickers—a question, a frightening conclusion. If the conditioning has worked on me, the Project will want to keep me here. They will never let me leave.

Black Eyes keeps smiling but all I feel inside is horror as, inch by inch, I look down and, my vision now fully returning, see metal stirrups on either side of me with my legs hanging in them.

"What have you done to me?" I immediately begin to slam my legs. "Let me out!"

"Shhh. Shhh, it's okay. You'll make it worse if you move."

I wriggle my feet, yell out, but it does no good. Black Eyes jots down a note on a file then looks to me, his head tilted to the side.

"Why have you got me in stirrups?"

"Our doctors have given you a full examination and its seems the day-to-day routine drugs on you have also been working."

"I know about the Typhernol," I spit. "Take my legs out of these."

"Yes, well, Typhernol has worked, that and other drugs."

I fall still, a lick of fear whipping across me. "W-what other drugs?"

"Hmmm? Oh, hormone drugs, to make you ovulate. We wanted to test your eggs, you see, to find out why the conditioning has worked on you specifically. If we can re-create what you have achieved, understand the DNA of what makes your brain work, then ..."—he exhales—"we'll know how to help the world. We'll be able to keep up the greater good."

A panic rushes over me as I listen to what he says. Eggs. DNA. The greater good. "You cannot do this!"

"It's okay. We can. I know it seems a bit extreme, but it really is a standard process, analyzing your eggs. The plans are still all in place. The governments are now fully signed up to our strategy of chaos and order. We are all working as one now, for the greater good. Everyone on the same side." He pats my hand. "To save lives, Maria—that's what you and I are here for. You are a doctor, you know what it is to save a life."

"Your plan is not saving lives—it is killing them."

He nods. "Yes, well, perhaps, to a very tiny extent, but either way, when we issue you again with Typhernol, you won't remember this conversation and, as far as you'll be concerned, the Project will be your only friend."

He checks his file once more and leaves, and the air swamps around me. His words fly around my head and as I think of them, I slam my legs again, try to break out of the stirrups, but no matter how hard I bang my ankles against the metal, it does no good.

I flop back, exhaustion washing over me in waves as the reality of my situation strikes. Abigail is no longer here. Chris knows where the Project black site facility is, but even then, he will not know where I am and won't be able to get past security. I may be alive, I may have reached thirty-four years of age, but when I think of my future, it feels as if I am already dead.

I slide in and out of consciousness for the next hour. Black Eyes returns to check on me, as does a doctor, probing between my legs, my body unable to escape. They take notes, swabs, record data, but no injection is given, no medicine is administered, but then, as the hour tips into the next, the door opens and Black Eyes returns with a nurse by his side dressed in a white tunic and trousers.

"Maria," Black Eyes says, "it's time."

I immediately hunch back, press my body as hard as I can into the belly of the bed. "Time for what?"

"We have checked you thoroughly now," he says as, one by one, he unstraps my legs, "and we think we have everything we need."

My ankles drop to the mattress, the skin and bones throbbing, but I can't rub them because my wrists are still tied to the frame.

"I want to get out."

"I know, I know you do." He unhooks the monitor and I instantly worry. If he is doing this, he is following protocol—protocol that is set out as a routine to follow before administering Typhernol.

The nurse moves forward and I start to panic. "Get away!"

"Maria, it's okay," Black Eyes says. "We're family and family don't hurt each other."

"Yes, they fucking do!"

The nurse is closer now and I feel hot and no matter how much I will some strength and fight to come, nothing arrives. What do I do? Which way do I turn? I am tired, so tired. The nurse is nearer again and my mind goes to all the people I have ever known in my life, and I want to see them all again so badly, just once, see the face of my papa, my kind, sweet, strong papa, of Balthus and Patricia, and Ramon and Harry, Harry who helped me get acquitted for the murder of the priest yet then was murdered himself.

The nurse is by me now, and I plead with her not to do it, not to put the needle into my blood and make me forget, because I want to remember. I so desperately want to remember all the faces of the people I loved, how they smelled, recall their hair strands and color, the way they moved, what they said, how many times they tried to help me. I want to remember it all.

"Stop, please," I say, and Black Eyes comes to my side and watches me as the nurse prepares the vial.

"It's okay. It's going to be okay."

And he wipes my hair from my brow and I can't stop him because my hands are tied, and so I thrash my head away from him and he removes his palm, but he remains close as the needle hovers in the air, and all I can think of now, as a numbness of resignation flows over me, is that I was so near. I was so near to having a normal life, to having what I always craved. I had friends. For a while, I finally had friends.

"Ready?" Black Eyes asks the nurse.

She nods, the needle lowering and I watch it, tears flowing freely, mind exhausted, my eyes closing.

There is a vast crack of gunfire in the air.

My eyes fly open to see the nurse collapsing as a red circle stains her white tunic, her torso falling onto the bed then tumbling to a dead slump on the floor, the needle clattering from her hand and rolling away under a metal cabinet.

Black Eyes crouches, scurries to a wall where a small panic button sits, but before he can hit it, he is shot in the chest and he drops to the floor.

I suck in air, over and over, watching it all, fear peaking now as the door flies open and the shooter slams fully into sight.

"A-Abigail?"

I blink in shock as Abigail now runs to me, unstraps my wrists and hauls me up from the bed. "You okay?"

I gaze around at the floor, wobbling at the movement. The nurse is dead, but Black Eyes is still breathing. "How … how did you find me? I thought you were dead."

"Here, put this on."

She flings me a set of clothes and I shove them on, muscles weak, wincing as the combats go over my legs.

"I've taken down the guards and disabled the surveillance system and the alarm alerts so no one can track you."

I nod, the speed at which everything is happening making my brain shake. I draw in a deep breath, try to stay steady.

"Chris knows you are on your way."

"On my way? What does this mean?"

"That you're getting out of the Project."

I stop, take in what she is saying, the words hard for me to comprehend. "Why are you helping me?"

She exhales. "Because this is all fucked up. And besides"—she shrugs—"I'm dying, so what have I got to lose? Get out there, use the microfiche texts and nail the bastards."

Black Eyes groans on the floor; Abigail watches him. "Let's move."

We tiptoe, my legs shaking, along a corridor that leads to the cupboard where Abigail said my bag was and when I open it, inputting the code from memory, just as she said, it is there. I grab it, smell the fabric, its woody scent, the tiny slice of familiarity it offers helping my brain stay calm enough to think straight.

"Chris says there's a cell phone inside," Abigail says quickly. "He said he's managed to link to it."

Willing some strength into my fingers, I rip open the bag, find the cell, switch it on. Straight away is a text from Chris that simply says:

Hello, Google. Let's get you out.

A tear rolls down my cheek, my hands, as I read the message, fumbling, finding the photograph of Isabella with me in her arms, my papa's writing fading on the back, a lump swelling in my throat as I look at it and, searching in my bag again, find the second photograph, the one I saved from my Salamancan villa, of Papa and I. Next, quickly, carefully securing the images safely away, I search for my notebook and, when I find it, I drag it out and immediately flip to the page I want. I stop, trace my fingers on the words: Patricia and the meaning of her name—*noble woman.*

"I'm sorry about your friend," Abigail says.

I wipe my eyes, read again what I wrote so long ago in prison, then, looking to Abigail, say the words I know Patricia would have taught me to respond with. "I am sorry Daniel died."

A shout sounds from somewhere in the far distance and, grabbing the bag and belongings, we run.

"Okay, so there's not much time," Abigail says, running,

struggling for breath, "but now your phone's switched on, Chris'll be able to track you." She pauses, coughs, smears away some blood. "He's through the firewall and they don't know he's in their system. He's been able to disable all alerts, but that'll last, I reckon for only, what? Fifteen? Twenty minutes, tops? But if you get out now you should be fine."

I stop. "No."

"What?" She slows to a halt, chest hauling in oxygen. "We need to move."

"I cannot go yet. I cannot leave her here."

"Leave who?"

"Isabella. My mother."

Abigail hesitates. She wipes away some more blood from her lips, glances up and down the corridor, then, checking her watch, she nods. "Which room is she in?"

Muscle mass returning now, I start running, the map of the entire facility clear in my head for the final time. "Room 720. This way."

CHAPTER 35

BLACK SITE PROJECT FACILITY, SCOTLAND
Present Day

We arrive at the room and watch as an officer stands nearby. We can't, with the officer's current position, get past. We need help.

Abigail immediately gives me a small gun, checking her own and checking her cell. "Let's see how much Chris can help."

She taps her phone and I look at mine and message Chris our location, but he has already texted.

I heard about Patricia ☹

I blink at the symbol he has put down and I think it means he is sad but am unsure. Swallowing and glancing down the corridor to check all is clear, I message him back.

I am sorry, too.

I pause, swallow, then recommence.

There is an officer outside Isabella's room. We require assistance.

He replies immediately.

On it. The guard has a cell phone.
Have accessed it and he should be
gone in three, two, one …

I look up. The officer's phone bleeps. He scans the cell screen then, raising his head, strides the opposite way to us down a corridor that leads to the situation room.

"Whoa," Abigail says. "Chris is good."

I text him.

Abigail says you are good.

I am ☺

We creep down the walkway until we reach the door. I stop, look around, then set my eyes on the number: 720.

"This the right room?"

"Yes," I say. "This is the one Black Eyes told me about when I had the gun at his head." I keep my sight on the door, blue, made of metal and wood, no other markings, no other words or numbers adorning it.

I place my hand at the door, fully expecting it to be locked but it's not, instead, the handle simply clicks open. I look to Abigail, worried.

"I texted Chris the room number. He unlocked it," she says.

Concern subsiding, I rapidly try to call up in my mind the image of Isabella that we saw, of her older, more lined and worn self.

I hesitate, suddenly feeling uncertain, doubting whether what I am doing is right, whether it will be good for me at all.

"Are you going in?" Abigail says.

"She is my real mother."

"Yes."

"How do I know whether meeting her is the correct thing to do?"

She sighs. "Sometimes, we don't know if what we're doing is going to be the right thing or not. But that's the thing about the future—it's unpredictable. You've just got to go with what you feel is right, what you think, for you, is good."

"But what if it is not good for you, but good for the other person?"

"Then that's called being selfless." She smiles then coughs and, from my rucksack, I find a cotton handkerchief and hand it to her.

"Thanks." She wipes her mouth and scans the corridor. "You'd better go in—we haven't much time left. I'll wait here. Be quick, yeah?"

I nod and, linking my fingers around the handle, I go in.

The light inside the small room is low and orange. I step one foot in, two, test the air. "Hello?"

A low moan comes back, guttural, but faint. The room smells of medical bandages, antiseptic, and emollient cream, and to my right is a lamp, small and black. I switch it on and immediately see a bed in the center. Sitting on it, with her back to me, is a woman in a floral gown and light blue, crepe-paper trousers.

"H-hello?"

Nerves rising, hands tapping my thigh, I inch around the bed where the large metal frame arcs over the end and links to the mattress and legs below.

The woman, as I come nearer, looks up at me and my breathing almost ceases. It is Isabella. Her hair is speckled with more gray, her skin wrinkled and more sallow, her chin smaller, her body thinner, more bony, but when I scan her and compare what I see in front of me with the image in my brain, there is no mistaking it—it is her. It is my mother.

"Isabella?" I say, her name when I speak it aloud seeming odd, alien.

She lifts her eyes and at first, they do not move but then, as she scans me once, twice, three times, her hand raises and a shriek escapes her lips.

"M … Maria?"

"You know my name. Do you … do you know who I am?"

She seems as if, for a second, she is going to tumble off the bed, but then she pulls herself up, staggers to a small wooden cabinet by the far frame where a small glass vase of woodland flowers rests. She opens the cabinet and, reaching inside, takes something out then turns to me.

"This is you," she says in a broken Spanish accent.

I look down to what is in her hand and stumble a little to the side as I see there, in her hand, is the picture of her holding me as a baby. The same one I have.

Blinking, swallowing, fighting back the tears, I zip open my bag and pull out my photograph and hold it to hers.

She points a finger at it, scratches and welts lining her delicate skin. "You and me." She smiles and there are so many creases by her eyes I cannot even begin to count them.

"How …" There is a lump in my throat and I cough it back, start again. "How do you have this same photograph?"

"Alarico gave it to me."

"Papa," I say, the tears falling at last.

She nods. "He was a good man."

I look again to the image, turn mine and see the writing on the back, think of Balthus and how he loved this woman next to me all those years ago, and how he turned to Ines, thinking she would help them both. So many questions fly around my head that I almost start to moan out loud at the overwhelming sensation of them, but then I think of Patricia and smell my rucksack, see my notebook and its pages peeking out from the zipper, and my brain manages to settle, to focus on what needs to next be done.

"How did you know what I looked like now?"

"Dr. Carr showed me … he showed me pictures, but …" She hangs her head. "I'm sorry, it's been so long since I've spoken to someone else."

"Dr. Carr showed you pictures of me—why?"

"He said he didn't want me to miss my daughter as much as he missed his." She falters. "I can only imagine what they have done to you … what they have made you do."

There is a faint knock on the door and Abigail's head peers in. "It's time to go." She pauses. "Are we … all coming?"

A smile breaks out on Isabella's face.

Isabella finds it difficult to move. Her feet shuffling, we struggle along the corridor, checking for officers and dodging out of the way when a large group of subject numbers strides through one walkway toward the canteen.

"I … I know they kept you," Isabella says when we come to a stop near the main side exit that Chris has disabled for a few minutes only. "I know Ines lied to … to Balthus."

I look to her. "She lied to everyone."

Isabella taps my hand, her fingertips warm, soft petals, and I find myself not flinching, instead oddly comforted by her gentle touch. "I'm so sorry," she says.

"Why?"

"For leaving you."

"But you have found me again."

She smiles, eyes downturned but lines spreading out on her skin. "I have."

"Stop!"

I turn to Abigail and see three officers striding up ahead. I hold my gun, push Isabella behind me. "They may be walking past here. We should go now."

She shakes her head. "No. That could reveal our position. Let's wait. They might be going to the canteen."

We wait, my finger tapping the handle of the gun with nerves as the officers move in a different direction to where we are standing.

Abigail billows out a breath. "Phew. That was—"

A gunshot fires in the air, hitting Abigail in the shoulder. She cries out and I instinctively start to go to her when she's hit again, this time in the chest.

Boots sound far away then nearer as I freeze, unmoving, my eyes locked on Abigail, Isabella crouching behind me.

"Go," Abigail croaks as blood seeps on the fabric over her chest, red lines trickling from her mouth.

"I have to help you."

"No." She coughs; the boots sound nearer now. "I'm dying anyway. I've got nothing to lose, remember?"

I hesitate, scan her wounds. "You are losing blood fast."

"It's okay." She coughs again and this time her eyelids ripple. "You only have five minutes left. Chris is ... Chris is waiting for you. Outside here is ... is moorland. Get to the edge of it. There's a clear way through ... through this door."

More boots, more shouts now, too.

I look at Abigail, glance to Isabella.

"Go," Abigail says. "Go!"

An alarm from somewhere sounds and, blinking at Abigail one more time, I reach for her gun and, taking it, pause. "Thank you."

"Go."

As the alarm blares louder, I grip Isabella's wrist and dart down a small walkway in a restricted zone. I stop, text Chris, who uses the message as a trigger to release the door remotely.

> *You have one minute to get out. The far gate is open for sixty seconds only.*

I shove the cell in my pocket and, drawing in a breath, haul open the door.

Night air hits me and the smell of it, for a second, shocks my brain as I realize that I cannot recall the last time I was outside since being at the black site. I can smell heather, peat, the heady scent of mud and grass when it has just rained.

Shots sound from inside the building and, even though it is dark, I can see the perimeter fence. I start to run, but Isabella lags behind.

I turn to her. "We have to go."

She catches her breath. "I … I can't run. I haven't moved like this for over ten years. You go, get away from here."

I hesitate, think of the little time left. Then running to Isabella, I link my hands under my shoulders and hoisting her up, gasps billowing from her, I saddle her on my shoulders. Checking I have all my belongings, my gun and my cell, I run with her on my back until we are through the perimeter fence and out of the Project compound entirely and I don't stop. I stumble in the heather, I trip on the moor, but each time I get back up, secure Isabella on my back, run and run and run, until, finally on the edge of the moor, just as Abigail said he would be, I see a light and a car and the familiar shape of a man stood next to it.

I sprint hard, get to the vehicle and slide Isabella from my back and stare now at this man, mud streaking my face as I take in his sunken eyes, his floppy hair, the familiar scent of his baked bread skin.

"Oh, my God, Google, I cannot tell you how glad I am to see you."

He rushes to us, helping, his eyes with me the whole time and, sliding Isabella into the car, I watch and I stand there, drooped, drained, scared and it all hits me, all of it, everything that has happened and even though I know the Project is just a few hundred meters away and we have to go, the fact that he is here, someone familiar, a friend, one of my true friends, helping me, accepting me, as Chris pulls out of the car, ensuring Isabella is safe, for a reason I don't understand and don't want to analyze, I grab his arm, so relived he is here, twist him around to me, and, putting my face to his, I kiss him.

CHAPTER 36

SCOTTISH BORDERS, UK

We drive to a parking lot one hundred kilometers away from the Project site and stop.

It is late, the night black and heavy, a warmth to the air where a southern wind is trying to get through the atmosphere. Isabella is asleep in the back of the car, Chris having gently laid a blanket over her to keep her warm.

Engine off, he turns to me now and scans me from head to toe. "Are you hurt?"

"I have some scratches and bruising, and I hurt ... inside."

He lets out a breath and for a moment I think he is going to speak when, from his eyes, tears suddenly spill.

I am unsure what to do. "Why are you crying?"

He wipes his face. "Oh God, I'm sorry, it's just that ..." He billows out a breath and I have a strange urge to reach forward and stroke his cheek. "It's just that I thought ... I thought I'd lost you."

"But you did not. You found out where I was."

He smiles, crinkled creases forming and for a moment, we don't speak and the only sounds that float in the air are the gentle rasp of Isabella's breath and the distant sound of a sheep bleating in a field.

"Did you see Patricia die?" Chris says after a moment.

I close my eyes, images of the bullet going into my friend's skull, her milk-bottle skin, of her beaten body toppling to the ground replaying in my mind. "Yes. I saw her … I saw her die."

I feel Chris' fingers close to mine, feel the warmth of his skin touching my hand and I don't pull away. Instead we simply sit there, the two of us, the smooth belly of his palm resting on top of mine, five fingers spread out in a star.

One minute must pass, two, three, both of us resting, hands together until, opening my eyes, I turn to Chris.

He looks at me, moves his hand. "You ready to get going again?"

I nod.

We drive for fifty more kilometers until the sun begins to rise and the daily commute on the roads begins. We dip off and away from the main routes, not wanting to be spotted, and park by a woodshed café and get some take-out breakfast of bagels and black coffee.

There is a shop next to the café, and Chris brings from it some simple medical supplies, which I use to tend to Isabella. The welts and scars are slightly infected, but once I treat them and clean them and bandage them up, I feel better, and when she smiles at me and thanks me, a warmth inside flows up, and I breathe a little easier.

When Isabella is again resting, Chris and I open up his tablet and devices and bring up all the data we have.

He clicks on the microfiche files patched through from Abigail and scans them. "It was good of her to send these."

"Yes."

We look at them and I think of what she did for me. The data is full and complete, detailing each element of the lone gunman plan Black Eyes said was due to be put in place.

"Jeez," Chris says, "it all implicates Harriet Alexander, the head of the CIA—everyone. They're all in on it."

He taps his device and begins to transfer the documents. "I was thinking we could expose the Project with this but, to be honest, I'm worried it won't be enough. I don't have all the files we had before, the one from Hamburg, and without it, it could just look like another conspiracy theory."

"Why do you not have the files?"

"When we sent it to the home secretary's email, it threw a worm in my files and automatically erased everything, all the back-up, the lot." He exhales. "They could see us coming."

"And if we have the Hamburg files, you think it could really work?"

He nods. "Hell, yeah. I have that many contacts, we could fire it everywhere, viruses, and newspapers, TV, Twitter—the lot."

I think about this. "Do you have a knife?"

"What?"

"Do you have a knife?"

He frowns at me then, leaning to the glove box, he pulls out a small Swiss Army knife and hands it to me.

Taking it, I put the point of the blade to my thumb and start to slice open the skin. It stings.

"Holy shit! What the …? What the fuck are you doing?"

I cut into my thumb, a sharp pain shooting down my arm, but I ignore it, ignore the blood that immediately trickles from the wound until, ten seconds later, I set down the knife and pull from under the flap of skin now hanging loose, a tiny black computer chip.

Chris' mouth hangs open. "Is that …?"

"It is a chip containing all the files you and I downloaded from the Project detailing all the data and information on their entire activities."

"Holy crap!" He squints at it, rakes his hands through his hair. "When … when did you put in … in your … in your thumb?"

"When we were at the airport in Madrid. I carried out the small procedure in the toilets there, at the sink. I wanted to be sure we wouldn't ever lose the data we had."

He laughs, light, a dance of a child's feet on the sand, his lips smiling, infectious and I cannot help but smile, too. He cups my face in his hands and, staring at me, still smiling, he kisses me on the lips. It is warm, soft, and I don't want to pull away.

Eventually, Chris sits back, shaking his head. "You're amazing."

He takes the chip from me and I wince.

"Ooh, sorry! Are you okay? Do you want me to put a bandage on that?"

"No. I can do it myself."

I take the first aid kit, patch up my thumb as Chris gets busy downloading all the data I had hidden for so long, and prepares to send it out into the world.

In the back seat, Isabella yawns and wakes up. She blinks at us and smiles, her skin wrinkling around her mouth and eyes.

"Hola," she says.

"Hola."

"Is everything okay?"

I look to Chris, to his laptop and the computer chip, look to the microfiche data revealing the lone gunman plans, look to Chris' hands, how they can spread in a star shape for me, just like Patricia did. I have my friends. I have my memories. I finally know who I am.

"Everything is okay," I say. "Everything is okay."

EPILOGUE

MARIA'S VILLA, SALAMANCAN MOUNTAINS, SPAIN
Two Months Later

I return from my morning run and stretch outside. I throw my arms up high in the air as, along the perimeter of the villa, the sun beats down in the early morning heat where the cypress trees drift in a lazy breeze and the sky fills with the pungent perfume of the orange and lemon tree groves beyond. Olives hang in small green baubles from the stubs of olive tree rows that line the far area of the grounds, and in the distance, a murmuration of starlings swings in a large black pendulum in the sky.

I breathe in, close my eyes, and, kicking off my trainers, feel the scorched grass underneath my feet, and let my body slide through a series of yoga movements. Up and over my body goes, my mind focusing on my breath, on the fluid movement of my limbs, bending, reaching, stretching as my mouth chants aloud the words I have now spoken each day since we all arrived here.

"I am Dr. Maria Martinez. I am free. I am not a member of the Project. I am free to be who I am. I am free to be me."

I recite the words over and over, feeling the ground beneath me, the movement of the earth, the gentle click and brush of the animals and insects. Four, five minutes pass as I repeat the process until, slowly opening my eyes, I stretch one more time, then, counting the twenty-four steps back into the villa, I enter the kitchen.

I open the cupboard and take out one of three white coffee cups that sit next to three plates, three bowls, and three wine glasses. Shutting the cupboard, I turn to the coffee pot and, filling my cup with the black, hot liquid, I pad into the lounge area.

Chris sits on a crate with his laptop open, feet bare, body brown, his shorts black, his T-shirt blue. He looks up to me when I enter and smiles, and I see the now-familiar creases fan out from his deep, sunken eyes.

"Hey, Google. Good run?"

I nod. "Is that the news story?"

"Yep."

I drag another crate next to him at just the precise angle and watch the newsreel that plays now on the screen, and when I see the face appear, I hold my cup midair and do not move.

"Hey," Chris says. "Breathe."

"It is Black Eyes."

"Yes."

Chris touches just one of my fingers, his way of reassuring me as now, and he turns up the volume and the newscaster's voice springs into the room.

"… in what people are calling the world's biggest cover-up, a major investigation has begun today into the corruption and potential murder that has been happening right at the heart of governments around the world. Today, Dr. Samuel Carr will give evidence for an organization known as Project Callidus, in a trial that is set to last for months. Dr. Carr, who is currently being held without bail, is at the center of an alleged plot to carry out terrorist attacks on European soil and already, the UK home secretary, Harriet Alexander, has been arrested along with other key figures from both the US and Spanish governments and secret services. Dr. Carr and associates of the Project, MI5, and the CIA have been implicated in what can only be described as an immoral program that used people with Asperger's syndrome, including illegal drug testing. At the center of the program is this woman, Dr. Maria Martinez, who was acquitted of the murder of a Catholic priest one year ago. Dr. Martinez, innocent in all of this, has been asked to give evidence, but has so far declined to speak …"

Chris hits the mute button and turns to me. "Are you sure you don't want to give evidence?"

"No." I look now at Black Eyes' face as he goes to trial and feel a shiver run down me, despite the warmth and the sun. "It is done now. I will let the system deal with him."

"Okay."

I sip my coffee. "Okay."

Once we finish our drinks, I take a shower, write in my notebook about the trial and, glancing to the piano, I walk my fingers on the keys and stop as my eyes rest on a series of photographs that sit in small wooden frames made by Chris. I see the photograph of my papa, him smiling big and wide and warm at the camera; of Ramon when we were little playing in the pool, one of us eating churros, chocolate on our faces. Another has an image of Chris and I, a selfie, he called it, taken on his phone, and the other is the one of Balthus, tan showing, teeth glowing, and it stands next to the old worn picture of Isabella with me swaddled in her arms as a baby.

But the final frame I linger on a little longer until Chris calls to me that they are ready: the picture of Patricia.

I gaze at her milky face, long limbs, swan neck one more time then, feeling a heaviness inside me, a weight, a hole that will never be quite filled, I walk outside to the end of the garden where the two people I know stand.

Chris and Isabella.

Isabella's wounds now healed, and the sun having warmed her skin, she seems brighter, more alive, her gray hair flowing long and free, her bare feet peeking out from a white cotton skirt that billows in the morning breeze.

She smiles at me. "Are you ready, *mi hija?*"

I nod, look to Chris, see five fingers on his thigh and, one by one, we kneel on the ground. Taking in turn a candle each, we strike a match and light the wicks and small orange flames flicker in the air.

Turning, we place each candle against small wooden boards that sit in flowers in the soil, each carved by Chris in smooth curves and angles, and on each board, there is a name.

Harry.

Ramon.

Balthus.

Papa.

Patricia.

Leaning forward, I feel the brush of the Salamancan sun on my cheeks as I take my candle and set it down by Patricia's name, Chris and Isabella placing their candles down too, until each memorial is joined together.

I kneel in the long grass that sways now in the warm wind and I look at the names on the wood. One minute passes, two, no words spoken, as the birds flying in the air, the sun glowing down on the hills around us, we slowly rise to a stand, Chris taking my hand in his.

And as we turn, the three of us together heading back to the villa, in the soft beat of the gentle morning where the cicadas click and the citrus trees spritz their fresh, fragrant aroma, the candle flames flicker and dance in the breeze, keeping alive the memories of the family and friends I will never, ever forget.

ACKNOWLEDGMENTS

I am fortunate that there are so many people to thank. Thanks, first off, to the amazing, dynamic team at Blackstone Publishing, and to my eagle-eyed editor, Peggy Hageman. Thanks to my agent, Cathryn Summerhayes at Curtis Brown. Thanks to all my amazing foreign publishers. Thanks to Maxine Groves, who definitely gets a mention this time, along with the entire Aspie community. You are all awesome. Thanks to the cool Stroud Spacehoppers coworking gang in the UK for providing me with (literally) the room to write this book. Thanks to my close friends and gorgeous neighbors new and old, to my ace author buddies, especially Gilly MacMillan and Claire Douglas, who I can have a proper vent to—and a belly laugh with. We are all stronger together. Thanks to my RATS drama group—love you guys beyond words. There are others who also need a thank you, because they make my world feel calm—you know who you are. And, of course, thanks to my family and my daughters for all their stellar support. And finally, thanks to you, the reader, for buying and reading my book—I cannot, ironically, put into words what that means to me.